LILITH

Toby Tate

First Edition

DarkFuse
P.O. Box 338
North Webster, IN 46555
www.darkfuse.com

Copy Editor: Steve Souza & Bob Mele

To my mother, the late Donna Conway. I love you and miss you, Mom. I'll see you up there.

Acknowledgements

My heartfelt love and appreciation go first to God and to my family for putting up with my irregular hours and obsession with the written word. I'll make it up to you, I promise!

A lot of research went into this novel and none of it would have been possible without the people I have been blessed to meet along the way.

I owe a debt of gratitude to the crew of the USS Harry S Truman (CVN 75) and her captain, Joseph M. Clarkson, for not only allowing me aboard their ship and answering my questions, but also for putting their lives on the line every day to protect my freedom. Thank you.

The accurate technical details about aircraft carriers and their crews are due entirely to the expertise of Duncan J. Macdonald, LCDR USN (ret), a great guy and a priceless resource, and my brother-in-law, Tod Wills, former (nuke) electrician's mate first class and instructor for the U.S. Navy. Any inaccuracies can be laid squarely at my feet, where I claim sole responsibility (pun intended).

I have to thank my first readers, Professor Steve March, Annie Ross, Andi Hunt and Michelle Brown as well as Donna O'Brien of Crescent Moon Press for her awesome suggestions.

I also want to thank all the agents and publishers along the way who rejected my manuscript, because not only did it encourage me to improve the story, it ultimately led to publication.

I am grateful to Publisher Shane Staley and the staff of Delirium/DarkFuse, and most especially renowned author and editor for DarkFuse, Greg F. Gifune, who took a chance on this unknown author and helped make my dream a reality. Thanks Greg!

Above all, a sincere thank you to the booksellers that keep us in business, as well as all my Facebook and Twitter friends and to all of you who have waited patiently for Lilith to finally see the light of day — your patience has been rewarded!

PROLOGUE

Indianapolis, Indiana
Twenty years ago

Johnny hated babysitting his little sister. It was demeaning, depressing, and just downright wrong. So why did his parents always make him do it? The little witch was...well...a little witch. She never did what he told her to do, and she always got her way. He got blamed for anything that went wrong—a broken dish, a runaway pet— whether it was his fault or not. It just wasn't fair.

But Johnny knew life wasn't fair, so he would deal with it, just like he dealt with everything else.

It was Saturday, and even though he was seventeen and should have been out cruising with his friends, he was stuck taking care of the pest. At seven years old, she seemed like a sweet little girl, until you got to know her and realized that underneath she could be really creepy at times and act like a conniving little monster.

As they made their way toward the Marsh Supermarket, he watched his sister walk ahead of him, her pigtails swinging in the sunlight. The girl loved the supermarket. She bought her candy and her comic books there practically every Saturday, and of course it was Johnny's job to look after her.

He kicked a rock with a dirty sneaker and cursed his bad luck. Why did he have to have a sister, anyway? A brother would have been way cooler.

But somehow he still loved the little brat, though he couldn't understand why. She never brought him anything but trouble.

They turned a corner and began walking down a long alley between two old brick buildings, a shortcut they'd taken many times before, when a large dog came from around a building and began slinking towards them. It looked like a mix between a Shepherd and a Lab, with matted red fur, and as it lacked a collar, Johnny worried it might be feral. He'd heard stories and rumors of coyotes and wild dogs roaming the streets, but had never seen evidence of it before. The dog didn't growl, but didn't look friendly, either.

"Hold up, sis," he said. She stopped just a few feet ahead of him.

They stood watching the dog, wondering whether they should turn back, when another dog appeared behind it. This one was even bigger and looked meaner.

"Come on, let's backtrack and go around to the street," Johnny said. "And don't run."

He said that for himself as much as for his sister, because he definitely felt like running. When he was only four, he'd been bitten by his friend Billy's Mastiff (he'd been trying to ride the dog at the time and probably deserved it), and though he hadn't been badly hurt, he'd been afraid of big dogs ever since.

Johnny waited for his sister to pass him, and as he turned to follow, a third dog appeared at the opposite end of the alley. Before it fully registered, there came a fourth.

His heart jumped in his chest as he and his sister skidded to a stop. Two dogs had taken position in front and the other two were coming up from behind. Johnny scanned the buildings on both sides. No fire escapes...no windows...no doors. Of course not, he thought, that'd be too convenient.

He reached out, grabbed his sister by the shoulders and pulled her close to him. As the dogs closed in on both sides, he realized for the first time just how big they were. Their only hope was that someone might walk by, see what was going on, and call the police.

The dogs moved closer still, as the two kids backed up against the wall of one of the buildings. "Go away, mutts!" Johnny yelled. "Go on! Get the hell out of here!"

The pack stopped less than three feet away and eyed them as if they were a pair of cornered rabbits. The animals smelled like rotten fish.

The Shepherd growled. The others followed suit.

"It's okay," he lied, quiet voice shaking, "It's going to be okay, just stay still."

But his sister did not remain still. Instead, she reached up, removed his hands from her shoulders and walked toward the dogs, reaching a hand out like she planned to pet them.

Johnny wanted to stop her, but was frozen with fear. "What the hell are you doing? Are you crazy?"

Ignoring him, she stood in front of the dogs, both hands raised now, as if preparing to direct a symphony. And then, emanating from somewhere deep inside her, there came a low, guttural, and impossibly horrifying growl.

The dogs immediately fell silent, staring at her in what could only be described as bewilderment. Speechless, Johnny watched as one by one, the dogs became docile and began to whimper. Only seconds before he'd been certain they'd kill her. Now they looked as if they

7

wouldn't hurt a fly.

His sister glanced at the sky, a barely perceptible smile on her face as storm clouds slowly rolled in across what, moments earlier, had been a clear and sunny sky. "Go away, bad doggies," she said evenly. "Go on, run along."

The animals backed away with not only fear in their eyes, but respect.

What the hell was going on?

The dogs turned back in the direction from which they'd come, took off in a trot and disappeared around the buildings.

Just then, the sun broke through the clouds.

Johnny looked down at his sister, his heart racing as he did his best to get his mind around what had just taken place.

"Come on," she said, looking back at him with a wide grin, "let's go get some candy."

CHAPTER 1

River City, North Carolina
Present day

Hunter Singleton was being stalked.

He could hear it, off in the distance—the deep, grunting breaths of a big animal moving almost soundlessly on its feet. Hunting him.

Lights the color of blood illuminated his path, his bootsteps echoing through the empty corridors. Hunter's skin was clammy from the hot, moist air and the walls were too close together, so close it felt claustrophobic, like being squeezed in a vice.

Where was he? Oh yes. On a ship, somewhere in the Atlantic. A carrier. He was here on assignment, a story for his newspaper. He had decided to take a walk about midnight. Most of the crew was asleep and Hunter wanted to wander the passageways, get a feel for the ship, a little time to think.

He had just rounded a corner and was about to climb up a ladder to the next deck when a noise rose from the lower stairwell. It was a rumbling, guttural growl, like one of the polar bears at the zoo in Asheboro. But what the hell would a polar bear be doing aboard a Navy ship in the middle of the sea?

The shadows in the stairwell suddenly seemed to come alive, twisting and distorting into bizarre, unearthly shapes. Hunter knew it was an illusion, but it made the sounds from the darkness below that much more ominous and terrifying. His blood froze as adrenaline shot through his veins. Two opposing forces fought for control—fight or flight. He slowly began backing away from the ladder, through the doorway and out into the main passageway, where he turned and started moving aft. Hunter didn't know where he was going, just anywhere but here.

Behind him the thump of feet, or big paws, bounding up steel steps on their way to the next deck—his deck— echoed down the corridor. Whatever it was, it wanted him. Hunter fought the urge to bolt and steeled himself to turn and look back. Nothing. He kept walking, picking up the pace more with each step.

He realized that he needed to find a room that was occupied, a room with people. That was the only way he was going to save himself.

He was on the third level, where most of the officers' staterooms were. He could hear breathing behind him, feel the stomping of huge paws as each one pounded the steel deck. He couldn't wait any longer. He needed to find someone now, let them know he was being followed.

Hunter grabbed the doorknob on the nearest stateroom and swung it open. Empty. He knew there were often empty staterooms aboard ship, so he moved on to the next one, swung open the door. Also empty.

There had to be somebody on this damn ship.

He moved methodically down the passageway, opening and closing the doors of one empty stateroom after another while he felt the thing behind him gaining ground.

How long until it was close enough to feel its breath on the back of his neck?

Hunter came to a ladder and flew up to the next level, barely touching the steps. Surely there had to be someone in the wardroom, or the XO's stateroom, or the captain's quarters.

But there wasn't. They were all empty.

Behind him Hunter heard the familiar sound of the beast coming up the ladder to the next deck, pursuing him.

What the hell was that thing? And where was everybody? Hunter's brow broke out in a cold sweat and his heart pounded against the wall of his chest.

He found the ladder up to the final deck — the bridge — and climbed it. He felt like he had just climbed the steps to the top floor of a lighthouse. His breathing was ragged, his chest constricted and aching. There *had* to be someone on the bridge. Somebody had to be driving the ship, because they were moving. He could feel it.

He lifted the locking mechanism of the steel door and pushed it open. This time the room wasn't empty. There was someone there, sitting in a swivel chair and facing out the forward window of the bridge. The back of a head with dark brown hair was visible over the top of the chair. Hunter stepped through the doorway and quickly closed it behind him.

"Oh, thank God," he said, moving toward the lone figure. "You won't believe this, but there's something following me, some kind of animal. Why do you guys have animals on board, anyway?"

He put his hand up and swiveled the seat around. Hunter's breath caught in his throat when he suddenly saw his own face staring back at him. But it wasn't exactly him. There was a silvery mass that moved behind the eyes, liquid and alive.

"Sorry, Hunter," he heard his double say. "End of the

line."

The last thing he saw was the flash of a huge blade as it was raised back, ready to plunge into his chest.

*   *   *

Hunter popped up in bed, hyperventilating and nearly swimming in his own sweat. He remembered being chased by something, but couldn't quite recall what it was. An animal, maybe? Whatever it was, it had given him one hell of a jolt.

His racing heartbeat slowly subsided as he sat staring into the darkness of his bedroom. He looked over at his sleeping wife and was grateful that the movement hadn't awakened her. She needed her sleep. Tomorrow would be a big day.

Hunter squinted at the bedside clock—it glowed red with a four and two zeros. He felt his eyelids get heavier and heavier. Unable to sit up any longer, he fell backwards onto the pillow and quickly drifted off to sleep, the dream forgotten.

PART ONE: STORMBRINGER

CHAPTER 2

Naval Station Norfolk, Norfolk, Virginia

Hunter pulled the shoulder straps tight up against his body as he sat inside the fuselage of a C-2 Greyhound, its twin engines thrumming under the wings outside like two immense, angry hornets. Hunter wanted to make a wisecrack to his wife about the lack of in-flight magazines, but he knew Lisa wouldn't hear him with her double hearing protection in place. They both wore cranials—skull-hugging helmets that were as uncomfortable as they sounded—along with goggles and a float coat. The coat was more like a life preserver that hung around his neck and zipped in the front and was supposed to have anything and everything one might need in case of a water landing—except shark repellent.

The inside of the coach smelled like a mix of sweat and jet fuel, and anxiety gnawed at the pit of his stomach. That was rarely a good sign. Hunter hoped it wasn't an omen of things to come, and for the time being, put it out of his mind.

He checked his lap belt, making sure it was tight enough to keep his butt firmly in place against the back of the seat. The seats were pretty comfortable, more so than he had expected. But still, Hunter hated flying, and the thought of landing on an aircraft carrier in the middle of the ocean did not set well with him at all. He prayed that the plane's tail hook wouldn't miss the steel cable that snagged the plane and stopped it from going over the edge of the flight deck, like falling off the edge of the world. But he knew he was just being stupid — these people did this kind of thing every day, right?

Hunter knew he needed to force his mind to focus on something else and looked around the cabin at the equipment stowed in the overhead of the plane. He wasn't sure what any of it was, but he figured it was probably full of inflatable life rafts and other survival gear. At least, he hoped it was. The entire inside of the plane was painted gray, except for the seat covers, which were blue. There were no interior walls in this plane like the ones in a passenger jet. Instead, there were visible wires and hydraulic lines running in every direction. There were also reading lights and air conditioning vents similar to those on a jetliner, but only two seats with windows. The escape hatch was on top of the plane, which would be convenient in case of a crash landing in the water, Hunter thought.

The plane was shaking on the tarmac like a giant, vibrating cell phone and Hunter wondered if the entire flight would be like that. He didn't know if his stomach could take it, and after drinking coffee all morning, knew he was going to have to piss before they got to the ship. He was glad he'd thought to bring a pack of motion sickness pills, but hoped he still had sea legs from his time in the Navy and wouldn't need them. Lisa was practically born in the water and Hunter was sure she wouldn't need them.

He eyed all the Navy and Marine Corps members in

uniform. They were either staring off into space or sleeping. Most were going to their next duty station aboard the USS Gerald R. Ford, their destination. Some were other media members, like him, invited to spend a few days on board a "real" Navy ship and experience life at sea. Hunter thought he had gotten his fill of the Navy when he was enlisted, yet here he was again. At first, there was resistance, for the simple fact that he was afraid to fly, but didn't want to admit it. Then, his photographer had gotten sick at the last minute and Hunter was able to talk his editor into replacing her with Lisa and that had cinched it. Besides, his wife was a great photographer and would take fine pictures, so the old man would be happy.

One of the flight crew suddenly got up from her seat and began closing the bay door. Since all the seats on the plane faced backwards, the light disappeared gradually, like the slowly closing lid of a coffin. Then the crew member turned toward the cabin and asked if everyone could hear her. Everyone said they could and she explained how the seat belts and shoulder straps worked, where the exits were, how to operate their flotation devices and pretty much everything you would expect to hear on a civilian airliner. The only difference was a passenger jet landed on sensible ground and not on some crazy floating airport, and *this* flight would be long, and involve a good deal of white-knuckle flying.

The young lady finished her spiel, and noticing Hunter's apprehension, made her way back to him.

"Everything okay?" she asked, leaning in close to his ear. "You seem a little nervous. Is this your first time?"

The woman was tall, green-eyed, and looked to be about nineteen. Her lips reminded him of Angelina Jolie's.

"Yeah," he yelled. "I'm not a big fan of flying."

"Well, don't worry, this crew has logged plenty of flight time, so you're in good hands."

Hunter nodded and smiled at the young woman when

he felt a pinch on his arm. He turned and saw Lisa staring at him through her goggles. He mouthed the word *what?* at her, then turned back and watched as the sailor made her way back up to her seat.

Hunter reached down and grabbed Lisa's hand, interlacing his fingers in hers. She had nothing to worry about. Lisa was more beautiful to him than any other woman could ever be.

As the plane began to taxi down the runway of Naval Station Norfolk, Hunter found himself suddenly glad they had no window. Soon the plane was airborne. Hunter gritted his teeth like he was about to receive a painful shot in the arm. He gripped Lisa's hand a little too hard and she shook it loose.

Half an hour into the flight, Hunter was surprised that the plane ride was no worse than riding in a bus. While Lisa spent the time sleeping, he spent the bulk of the hour flight staring at the back of the seat in front of him and wishing he'd brought a book along. The heat from the engines and the summer sun did its best to turn the plane into a pressure cooker. The air conditioning on the plane worked well—so well, in fact, that towards the end of the flight, Hunter could see the steam from his own breath wafting out like a tiny cloud.

When they began their descent, Hunter's guts clenched and he began to pray they would survive the landing.

One of the crew made a circular motion above his head, which was the signal for the passengers to cross their arms over their chests in preparation for either landing or crashing. Seconds later, the wheels hit the deck of the Ford and Hunter felt as if a hundred invisible hands were suddenly pushing him into his seat. He found himself wondering what kind of injuries he would sustain if he hadn't been strapped in, a human projectile shooting through the fuselage at the speed of sound.

Toby Tate

As the engines idled down and the Greyhound taxied to its place on the flight deck, Hunter vowed that he would never again leave the ground in anything scarier than an elevator.

CHAPTER 3

The familiar odors of fresh paint, mop water and fuel oil assaulted Hunter's senses as the media group, led by one of the ship's crew, stepped through the first doorway to the ship's interior. Compared to the heat on the flight deck, it was like walking into a giant refrigerator. Hunter noted that the inside of the Ford didn't look much different than the inside of the ships he had served on in the Navy. The passageways were cramped, there were people everywhere and you had to constantly watch your head and footing. Most everything was painted gray according to Navy regulations, and the paint looked fresh.

The public relations officer who was leading them, Lieutenant Michele Delgado, a burly redhead in her mid-thirties, obviously knew her way around the ship, and Hunter, who was right behind her, made sure he paid attention to which door she went through and which ladder she went up. The last thing he wanted to do was make a fool of himself by getting lost. Following Hunter, Lisa and the other eight members of the media team, or "VIPs" as the Navy called them, were making record time, and some were getting winded just trying to keep up.

They finally came to a row of colorful doors all on the same side of the passageway; one yellow, one blue, one red, one green and one black. Hunter didn't know why they were color coded, but knowing the Navy, they probably thought it would help dumb civilians remember which rooms they were in.

"These are your staterooms," Delgado said. "There will be two of you to a room." As she spoke, the lieutenant handed each of the group members a card key.

After handing out the last card, she said, "I'll be back after you've had a chance to drop off your stuff and get situated."

Delgado turned and disappeared in a flash, leaving the group to stand and stare at each other. Hunter noticed to his dismay that there were eight males and two females, meaning he and Lisa would not be sleeping together as planned. She gave Hunter a shrug and a frown, then eyed the other female, Julia Lambert, a gorgeous, petite blonde in tight black jeans and dark sunglasses.

"Well, looks like it's you and me," Lisa said. "I hope you don't snore."

"I don't. In fact, I really don't sleep that much."

Hunter couldn't quite see Julia's eyes through the sunglasses, but he could have sworn she had winked at him. He watched as his wife checked the number on her key then the number on the stateroom door directly in front of her. The door was green, Lisa's favorite color, so Hunter figured at least it had something going for it.

She unlocked the door, turned, smiled at Hunter and waved goodbye. He waved back, feeling like a sad puppy as she disappeared through the door with Julia in tow.

CHAPTER 4

Everyone else in the group stumbled around the passageway with backpacks, camera gear and laptops, eventually pairing up and matching a door to their card key. Hunter ended up with the red door next to Lisa's room and immediately upon entering the stateroom, grabbed the bottom bunk. He knew from experience that the bottom bunk was the place to be during flight ops and during any inclement weather—if you fell out of your rack you weren't too far from the deck.

He piled his gear on the bunk to stake his claim, then checked out the stateroom. He thought about the years he had slept in the crew's berthing areas and how much of an improvement this was. There was a sink and mirror, two gunmetal gray desks attached to the wall with lots of drawers, and plenty of closet space. On another wall was a wide screen TV and next to that was a phone. Overhead were lights, bundles of cables and water pipes with red "direction of flow" arrows painted on them. If it wasn't for the fact they were directly below the flight deck, this would have been ideal.

The door suddenly swung open and there stood a figure with a grin on his face and a bag in each hand. Thick, fiery red hair topped the man's head and his eyes were framed by black Buddy Holly glasses.

The nerd introduced himself as Charles Blakely, though Hunter would have guessed Poindexter. Charles stood in the doorway grinning, waiting to be invited into the room.

"Hi, I'm Hunter. Hunter Singleton." He offered his hand. "Come on in."

"I thought you'd never ask," Blakely said, limply shaking Hunter's hand, then picking up his bags and wading into the stateroom.

Blakely stood looking at the bunk beds, first one, then the other, as if he had never seen such a thing.

"Well, I guess the top one's mine, huh? That's okay. I sleep like a rock. I once slept through a tornado, believe it or not."

The guy had a definite North Carolina accent, Hunter thought, like the people back home in River City.

Charles turned and set a black laptop computer case on a desk chair, then plopped the bigger bag on the floor. He put his hands on his hips and took in the room, like a commanding officer preparing for inspection. Hunter remained silent, watching with a mixture of amusement and bewilderment.

"Well, this is pretty nice. Of course, we're right under the flight deck, so I expect it to be noisy. They should quit around 11 p.m. or so. Like I said, though, I sleep like a rock."

He looked up at the TV on the wall. "I don't suppose we get any good TV out here."

"It's satellite TV. Probably gets over two hundred channels. Something special you want to watch?"

Blakely shook his head. "No, I'm sure we'll all be too busy for any kind of entertainment."

Hunter grunted in agreement, then turned and opened the bag on his bed, pulled out his clothes, shaving kit, shower shoes and several books, and started shoving things into drawers or hanging things in closets.

Blakely began to open up the case on the desk chair and pulled out a laptop. "By the way, you can call me Charlie, just don't call me Chuck."

"Your secret's safe with me."

"You ever been on one of these ships before?" Blakely asked.

"Yeah, I have. Only as a visitor, though. I was in the Navy at one time and had a friend stationed on the Eisenhower."

"I guess you won't get seasick, then."

"Hopefully not. But it has been a while."

"If I start turning green, run and get me a bucket, will you?"

They both laughed as Hunter turned and picked up his laptop bag, opened it up and pulled out a computer.

"Nice MacBook," Blakely said.

"Yeah, I like it. It definitely gets the job done."

Blakely laid his own laptop bag on a desk and opened the bag. Hunter watched with envy as he realized Blakely had one-upped him.

"Is that a MacBook Pro?" Hunter asked.

"Yeah. I'm somewhat of a computer geek and kind of put myself in debt buying this, but it was worth it. You could just about launch a satellite with this thing. I even added a few little extras of my own."

Hunter was intrigued. "Like what?"

"I'll never tell," Blakely said and closed the laptop.

"Where did you say you worked?" Hunter asked.

"I'm with a magazine called 'Military Aircraft.' We're doing a story on the F/A-18 Super Hornets and their pilots. How about you?"

"I'm a newspaper reporter from North Carolina—just

here observing the planes for a story I'm working on. I brought a photographer along, too. Actually, she's my wife."

"Your wife? Too bad you didn't get to share a room. I guess you're a little disappointed at sharing with another guy."

"No, you're okay. It would have been awkward otherwise. Somebody would have had to share a room with Julia."

Blakely snickered like a mischievous school boy. "I would have volunteered for that duty."

Hunter agreed, but said nothing.

"Well, I guess we just need to hook up with our liaison," Hunter said, heading for the door, "and get this party started."

CHAPTER 5

CIA Headquarters, McLean, Virginia

George Saunders stared at a computer monitor, reading an e-mail from one of his operatives in the field. His eyes burned from the strain of long hours and he rubbed them with his knuckles. It was about time he'd gotten some good news—it looked as if the direction of this latest op might finally be starting to go their way. He sure as hell hoped so.

As the retired commander of a U.S. Navy SEAL team, Saunders had seen more combat in two years in the shitholes of Afghanistan and Iraq than most veterans had seen in a career, and had the scars to prove it. Saunders had been shot in the leg once by an ambitious member of Al-Qaeda and almost blown up at least a dozen times. The heat and cold, the insects and blowing sand that got into everything, especially your weapons, and the constant, gnawing anxiety of not knowing exactly what the enemy looked like or where they would strike could really screw with your mind if you let it. You could never drop your guard, never believe that you were out of danger, because the minute that happened, things could literally explode in your face. The commander had killed more than his share of enemy combatants, some with his bare hands. But he had also saved countless lives, pulling civilians out of hostage situations or captured soldiers out of detention cells, getting them back to their families in one piece.

That had made it all worthwhile.

Saunders was a decorated hero with dozens of medals and ribbons, including two Purple Hearts and the Medal of Honor, presented at a ceremony personally by President George W. Bush on the deck of the USS Saipan. But even the recognition didn't make his job any easier and he decided that twenty years was enough. It was time to do something else, to go back home to the farm, to build that house he had always wanted to build and marry his childhood sweetheart. He would start a family and live the dream life he had craved.

It didn't last long. After realizing he hated farming, which is why he joined the Navy in the first place, George applied to the CIA and got himself into the intelligence business. Turned out he was not only good at it, he also loved it. It was challenging, it was interesting and what's more, it paid very well. Saunders had worked his way up from an operative to a team leader and then to the director of the *Special Activities Division,* a team of professionals who performed what the intelligence community liked to call "special operations." As one of his old commanders liked to say, they did the shit no one else wanted to do.

He turned and grabbed the phone from his desk, hit speed dial on the secured line and waited. The man at the other end picked up on the third ring, surprising Saunders, since there was usually no one in the office when he called.

There was irritation in the man's voice. "What is it?"

Saunders took a deep breath and slowly exhaled, wondering if he had called at a bad time. "Sir, I just received an encrypted e-mail from our operative in the field. It looks like he's in place. The operation is a go."

CHAPTER 6

Members of the media group began pouring out of their staterooms and assembling in the passageway, like cattle ready to be herded into a pasture. Lisa was fiddling with her camera equipment when Julia Lambert caught Hunter's attention. Powder-blue eyes focused on him as the ghost of a smile played on her lips. Lieutenant Delgado suddenly made another appearance out of thin air, breaking the contact.

"Well, I hope everyone found the accommodations to your liking," Delgado said. "If you're all ready, we'll go to the media room and you can get together with your individual liaisons. We can come back later and pick up anything you need like cameras or laptops."

Delgado turned and took off like a shot and Hunter mentally cursed under his breath as he ran to keep up, the rest tagging close behind.

*　*　*

Lilith

A virtual floating fortress, the USS Gerald R. Ford, which replaced the decommissioned USS Enterprise, is home ported at the Naval Station Norfolk in Virginia. As long as the Empire State Building is tall, the behemoth stretches two-hundred and fifty-six feet at its widest point and stands twenty stories from the water line to the mast, displacing some one-hundred-thousand tons of water when fully loaded. Known as a supercarrier, and the first of its class, it is the twelfth nuclear-powered aircraft carrier to be commissioned by the U.S. Navy. Its twin nuclear reactors fuel the steam turbines that power electric generators and motors to turn four twenty-one-foot screws, propelling the ship at speeds of over thirty knots. When on deployment, the Ford will carry more than ninety tactical and support aircraft, including the F-35 Lightning, F/A-18 Hornets and Super Hornets and over five thousand crew members. For self-defense, the ship also employs NATO Sea Sparrow missiles, several .50 caliber machine guns and a Phalanx close-in weapons system that reminded Hunter of R2D2 from Star Wars, capable of firing over four thousand rounds per minute.

Hunter was impressed with the Ford and her crew, but by lunchtime he was so dog tired and his legs so sore that he felt like he had just run a marathon.

Hunter sat on the officer's mess deck with Lisa, four people from the media group, and Delgado, while the others sat together at a nearby table. He couldn't help but notice some of the officers looking his way — or Lisa's way. There were some pretty buff looking guys in flight suits that would've made Hunter feel insecure if there were any doubt about Lisa's affections — but there were no doubts. Lisa was fiercely loyal. He felt a little manly pride at the looks he was getting and slyly slipped his hand into hers as they sat side by side. Lisa's kinky black hair, dark, Asian eyes and gymnast's body usually made the male of the species sit up and take notice. But her fourth-degree

Toby Tate

black belt in Kung Fu and "back off" attitude also made quite an impression. She could easily put most of these men in the hospital.

But to Hunter, Lisa was the embodiment of his fantasy woman, the one person he wanted to spend the rest of his life with, sharing countless nights in each other's arms, enjoying each other's bodies, sharing their most intimate secrets. He inhaled the fresh coconut scent of her skin and felt the warmth of her touch course through his body like an electric current.

"I don't know about you, but that meal really hit the spot. How about some dessert?"

Lisa picked up on Hunter's double entendre and silently shook her head as she smiled back at him.

A guy named Hendricks, who was busy wolfing down ice cream covered with caramel, snorted in between bites.

"This food isn't that great," he said without looking up.

Hunter stared at the top of Hendricks's shaved head. It reminded him of a bowling ball.

"Actually, the food on a carrier is pretty good, considering," Hunter said.

Hendricks looked up from his ice cream, a smear of caramel on his lower lip.

"Considering what?"

"Considering how many people they have to feed—about eighteen-thousand a day."

"What are you, like a Navy encyclopedia?"

Hunter smirked. "What are you, like an asshole?"

A collective gasp rose from the women at the table as they turned towards him from whatever they were eating. Hunter imagined executing a well-placed punch to the throat as he saw a flash of rage behind the bald man's eyes that disappeared as quickly as it came.

"Sorry, man. Didn't mean anything." Hendricks looked away and finished his ice cream.

31

Lilith

Lisa turned to Hunter and squeezed his hand, hoping to stifle the exchange of testosterone. Hunter playfully furrowed his brow at her, but he'd already decided he probably wasn't going to like Hendricks.

Delgado cleared her throat. "So, Mr. Singleton..."

"Please, call me Hunter."

"Hunter, what was your job in the Navy?"

"I was an A-Ganger."

Hunter explained that the "A-Gang" spent most of its time fixing any broken-down piece of machinery aboard ship, from air conditioning equipment and washing machines to flight deck elevators and even the CO's lawnmower. Heads at the table turned from one side to the other like spectators in a Ping Pong tournament as the pair went back and forth about their mutual experiences in the Navy.

All conversation ceased when Lisa suddenly stood up, knocking her chair over backwards as she raced from the room holding her stomach. Everyone in the officer's mess watched in stunned silence.

CHAPTER 7

After a trip to sickbay and a check up, the ship's surgeon decided that Lisa was probably suffering from seasickness. She felt as if her entire stomach lining was about to be ejected through her esophagus, and her head spun with vertigo like someone who had just stepped off a speeding merry-go-round. The doctor gave her Dramamine pills and told Lisa to return for a follow-up the next day. Lieutenant Delgado had been kind enough to accompany them through the maze of corridors and even helped Lisa up a few ladders.

Lisa lay on her rack in her stateroom in jeans and a t-shirt, completely drained, Hunter by her side and holding her hand in both of his as if she may die any minute.

"You sure you're feeling okay? Can I get you anything? A glass of water? Another pillow?"

Lisa slowly shook her head and smiled. "Hunter, I'm okay—really. I was just a little seasick, that's all."

"A little?"

"Okay, a lot. But I'm alright now. Stop treating me like an invalid."

Hunter frowned. "Is that what I'm doing? I thought I was treating you like my wife. And you're also my photographer, I might add. Without you, my story is only half told."

"Oh, is that what I am now, your assistant?" Lisa said, propping herself up on her elbows.

"Easy, now, I was kidding. Man, you really are on edge. You're actually taking me seriously." Hunter gently pushed Lisa back down on the pillow. "The doc says you need rest and that's what you're going to get—rest. We've been walking around this ship for hours, up and down ladders, from one deck to the next, so it's bound to take a toll. In fact, I'm pretty tired myself." He stretched, yawned, and looked at his watch. "It's about one o'clock. I think I'll take a little nap before I finish the media tour."

Hunter stood up, pushed the chair aside with his foot and scrunched himself into Lisa's bed, gently pushing her over with his body as he slid in next to her.

"Boy, I hope Julia doesn't come back anytime soon," he said, closing his eyes and letting out a deep sigh.

Lisa let Hunter's body radiate its warmth into hers and she began to relax as sleep quickly overtook her.

CHAPTER 8

Julia Lambert was beginning to get used to the stares from the crewmembers as she cruised around various parts of the ship, her ego inflated by the attention. She was accustomed to men ogling her, anyway, and was aware she made most women uncomfortable and insecure. She was undoubtedly the hottest thing any of them had seen that wasn't on a movie screen or in a magazine. The feeling was euphoric, intoxicating—it made her feel sexy and powerful.

Julia listened to the Commander of Carrier Air Wing Eight, Captain Jimmy Sullivan, drone on and on about the magnificence of his pilots, the amazing technology of their planes and the moral obligations of their mission as she put the back of her hand up to her mouth, trying to stifle a yawn. She imagined herself suddenly slinking up to the commander in the middle of his speech and sliding down underneath his desk while everyone in the room watched in astonishment. She couldn't help smiling to herself.

The whole thing was boring to her—the ship, the Navy, the military in general. She wished she could have been somewhere else, but for now, this was where Julia needed to be. It was necessary.

The monotony of the commander's voice seemed to be slowly lulling her to sleep when something he said suddenly made her mind flash back to her childhood. In her mind Julia saw her old dog Tater, a basset hound she had adored more than her own family. She and Tater, whose potato-shaped head had prompted the name, were inseparable until one day when it all ended with a walk in the park and the sudden appearance of a nervous squirrel.

Julia smiled at the memory. Tater had hated squirrels.

He had taken off like a rocket, ripping the leash out of the ten-year-old-girl's hand, and ran out into a four-lane street full of oncoming traffic. A Navy seaman who was heading back to base that morning after a night out on the town was still reeling from too much bourbon—the dog barely registered on his radar before he finally hit the brakes. There was a blare of horns, a screech of tires and a crescendo of voices as the scene quickly became pandemonium. The Chevy Malibu had rolled right over the top of Julia's dog, leaving tire tread marks across the middle of the animal's back. Julia can still see those tread marks in her dreams and still remembers the piercing scream that issued from her own lungs as she and her horrified father ran toward the dog. Julia could see it was already too late as thick blood oozed from Tater's open mouth onto the black pavement. The smell of burnt rubber permeated the air, nauseating Julia, and she vomited in the middle of the intersection. She had not just lost a dog that day; she had lost a brother, a kindred spirit.

Julia's father, a prominent D.C. lawyer, sued the man for all he was worth, which wasn't much, and made sure he lost his license to drive. The sailor's own lawyer had managed to get him off with six months probation.

Julia had felt more kinship with that dog, and animals in general, than she ever had with the human race. A single tear trickled down her cheek and she wiped it away with the side of her finger, discretely panning her eyes around the room, checking to see if anyone had noticed.

But Julia was here to work, not daydream, and forced herself to pay attention, taking in every word the commander spoke. She was here to learn. Knowledge was power and power was everything. *Environmental Times Magazine* had sent her here expecting a story about the Ford and its crew. But for Julia, this trip was about more than just politics or saving the environment. Indeed…it was about much, much more.

CHAPTER 9

Lisa lay alone on her bunk after a long day of following Hunter around the ship, taking pictures and talking to the ship's crew. They had said their goodbyes, but Hunter was a little reluctant to leave. He began gently kissing her neck, whispering in her ear and soon managed to light a fire in Lisa's belly. As usual, she had to be the strong one and explain to Hunter that they were on a Navy ship in the middle of the Atlantic, not at home in bed. The foreplay would just have to wait. Eventually, after much coaxing, Hunter went back to his stateroom.

Lisa had never taken so many photos in her life. The camera and lenses weren't too heavy, unless she was walking up five decks or more, then they got heavy quickly. Setting up that damn tripod was a pain in the ass, but she managed to get some great shots of the crew with her Nikon. Out on the flight deck, she thought she may get sucked into a jet intake, but the crewmembers who were guiding the media group kept them well out of harm's way.

Lisa had never heard anything as loud as the bone-rattling decibels created by an F/A-18 Super Hornet. She was a little nervous about standing in the middle of the flight deck with planes taking off and landing all around. Crewmembers were ushering the group from one part of the deck to the next while the electromagnetic catapults shot planes into the air like cannonballs from a cannon.

And it was so frigging hot. With the heat from the jet engines blasting away all over the deck and the sun beating relentlessly down from the noonday sky, Lisa thought for sure she just might melt. She wondered how the flight crews could stand it—it was literally like being in Hell. Luckily, Hunter had helped her carry her gear so she was able to move around more freely. She had also been feeling a little woozy and was praying that she didn't lose her lunch in front of the media group. That would have been the ultimate humiliation, a laugh at her expense for years to come.

When 5:30 finally rolled around, Lisa was never so happy to see a bed in her life. Pulling off the combat boots she had bought especially for the trip, she could have sworn there was steam coming out of them. After finally persuading Hunter to leave, Lisa showered and brushed her teeth in the head down the hall, slipped on her favorite night shirt, then lay back down in her bunk and let sleep take her.

It barely registered when Julia finally returned to the room after midnight.

CHAPTER 10

Jessica Blount was a veteran of the war in Iraq and exemplary at her job as an intelligence specialist. She had gathered information about combat operations and made presentations to admirals and even a few defense department officials—and she had yet to reach her twentieth birthday. A raven-haired beauty from the south Bronx, she also had street smarts and she knew better than to allow herself to be in the situation she was now in.

Yet here she was.

Jessica's mother had warned her about military men. "Men in the Navy tend to think with their little head, not with the big one," she had once said after Jessica had announced her decision to join the Navy. And her mother knew what she was talking about—Jessica's father had been a command master chief aboard the USS Nimitz.

How she had been talked into meeting this man in the anchor windlass room was a mystery. The fact that he was her boss was even more unnerving. There was just something about the man that she found irresistible—something she couldn't quite place—his cocky attitude, the musky smell of his aftershave, his impish, disarming smile. Whatever it was, it made her throw caution to the wind.

If they were caught, it would mean court marshals for both of them, and that was something she definitely could not afford. Jessica was a seaman up for third class petty officer soon and she had a very good chance at making it. Her evaluations were perfect and the performance of her job was flawless.

Yet here she was on her knees in a remote part of the Ford performing a different type of job, while Lieutenant Joe Sanchez stroked her dark hair and professed his undying love. Jessica knew he was probably lying, but the fire that burned within her made it not matter. Her only thought was to pleasure this man and then hopefully have the favor returned. She barely felt the pain in her knees as she knelt on the cold steel deck, surrounded by coiled anchor chain with links the size of engine blocks.

For Jessica, the behavior was totally out of character. But tonight, she wasn't herself—she just wasn't herself at all.

Sanchez' breathing suddenly quickened and Jessica knew she was about to get a mouth full. She braced herself for the onslaught as Sanchez' fingers gripped her hair. She imagined the feeling of sweet release that only a good orgasm could bring and knew that it would soon be her turn.

As Sanchez' tremors slowly died down, Jessica waited for the grip on her hair to loosen as she slid his rigid member out of her mouth. But it didn't. Instead, his grip tightened.

She let out a yelp. "Hey, watch the hair. You're about to rip it out by the roots."

Jessica reached up and grabbed a hand, but it was like grabbing a slab of granite. She couldn't even get hold of it, let alone pry it loose.

Lilith

"Hey, what the fuck?" The young sailor tried to stand, but the hand effortlessly held her down on the deck.

A surge of fear, fueled by adrenalin, shot through her as she attempted to grab the only other thing that would force Sanchez to let go, but in anticipation he had already cupped his hand over the slowly dying erection.

Jessica wasn't about to let herself be humiliated like this and her fear turned to fury. "Hey, lieutenant, if you don't let go I'm going to scream my ass off and whoever is on watch is going to come down here. So I'll give you to the count of three."

Jessica never even made it to one when she felt fingers press through the bone of her skull, and before a scream could escape her lips, more fingers passed through the skin of her throat and wrapped themselves around her esophagus, squeezing it shut like a garden hose.

As Jessica slowly asphyxiated, she looked up just in time to see a silvery mass move behind Sanchez' eyes, as if something else were alive inside of them.

Then a complete and overwhelming blackness enveloped her, body and soul.

CHAPTER 11

Aerographer's Mate Second Class Jimmy "Shack" Shackelford stared at the satellite feed of weather radar in the meteorological room of the Ford as it made a sweep, revealing an image of yellow and deep red that seemed to be forming a pattern. Shack didn't like what he was seeing. It could mean grounding aircraft, which would definitely piss off the captain, especially with the media on board.

The thing that troubled him, though, was the speed with which the storm was organizing. He had never seen one pull together so quickly and he had been tracking sub-tropical storms for years. Most took days to go from disorganized storm clouds to sub-tropical storm, but this one was already sub-tropical and it hadn't even been there yesterday. The proximity bothered him, as well. It was only about six-hundred miles out and this looked to be a big son of a bitch, so they would be feeling the outer rain bands in just a few hours.

He took a sip of Starbucks coffee, which he had just gotten from the coffee bar on the mess deck to wake himself up, and thought about how to explain the sudden appearance of the storm. He knew it wasn't the instruments and he was sure he had checked the radar yesterday. He glanced up at the clock and saw it was 0900. He checked the radar before hitting his rack at midnight last night. That means the storm had formed, or at least appeared in their vicinity, in just nine hours. But he had checked the National Weather Service last night, as well, and there were no storms reported in the Atlantic, not even a tropical wave.

Shack figured either somebody had royally screwed up or he was losing his touch. Either way, the old man wasn't going to be happy.

He let out a deep sigh, took another sip of coffee, then picked up the phone and called the bridge.

CHAPTER 12

As a boy with three other siblings, Captain Greg Phillips had been the adventurous one—riding his bike through shoddy obstacle courses on a dare, climbing into the tops of the tallest trees, swimming across the local river with currents powerful enough to drag a horse downstream. Those experiences served as a training ground for the future fighter pilot Phillips would become.

Now captain of the USS Ford, Phillips had graduated from the U.S. Naval Academy at the top of his class with a degree in Aeronautical Engineering, then a master's degree and eventually a professional engineer's license. As a young aviator, Phillips had spent many hours in the cockpits of the F/A-18 Hornet and the Super Hornet, flying sorties into Iraq, Afghanistan, and other hellholes. He had been a squadron commander for the VFC-12 "Fighting Omars" at Oceana Naval Air Station in Norfolk, attached to the USS Eisenhower during his time there. He had last captained the helicopter carrier USS Nassau.

An imposing six-foot-three, and well-muscled with a chiseled jaw, dark brown hair and brown eyes, Phillips possessed the rugged handsomeness of a movie star. As any crewman who had gotten their ass kicked on the hangar deck could attest, he could also hold his own in any kick-boxing match. But the CO had the brains to go with the brawn, as well.

Phillips had just finished talking to the Air Boss in the primary fly tower, or pry fly, where aircraft launch and recovery was coordinated. Everything had gone without a hitch—not even a missed trap, for which the captain was thankful. Catching a wire stretched out across the deck of a carrier with nothing but a tiny tail hook, on a runway that was not only moving at thirty knots, but swaying side to side, could be a nerve-rattling experience. The media group had asked a lot of questions, shot a lot of film and taken up a lot of space, but his crew managed to do their job without even flinching.

The media group had been given the VIP treatment and had interviewed dozens of his crew and several pilots since their arrival yesterday. They were scheduled to leave the ship tomorrow, but now it seemed there would be a change of plans.

The captain studied the radar image, running different scenarios in his mind.

"Well, Shack," Phillips finally said. "You did a good job tracking this storm. It's odd that it came up so quickly, though. You say it wasn't there when you hit your rack last night?"

"No, sir, nothing there but some high, thin clouds. No precipitation whatsoever. I've never seen anything like it. According to my readings, the storm has intensified in just the last few hours."

"Do we know the wind speed?"

"No, sir, the National Weather Service hasn't even had time to send a plane out to investigate, yet."

"Well let me know what they say as soon as you find out anything."

"Yes, sir."

Phillips gave Shack a slap on the back. "Don't worry, Shack, I know it's not your fault. It's just some freak storm. Anyway, check with NOAA when you get a chance and see if they're tracking it."

"Aye, captain."

Before he turned to leave, Phillips could see a look of relief wash over Shack's face and smiled to himself on his way out the door.

CHAPTER 13

Lisa was feeling sick again.

She sat at the desk in her room in jeans and a T-shirt, holding her head between her two hands, trying to keep the room from spinning. It did seem like the ship had been rocking just a little harder than it had been earlier. Or was it just her imagination? It was tough to tell at this point—she only wanted it to stop.

Hunter sat in the other desk chair beside her and Lisa knew that he was wishing there was something he could do to ease his wife's pain. He gently rubbed her tired shoulders and she could feel some of the tension drain out of her. She wanted nothing more than to go home right now, but that wouldn't happen until the following morning. They had the free run of the ship, but Lisa didn't think she would be going anywhere, at least not for a while.

As usual, Julia was somewhere on the ship, interviewing or doing whatever the hell it was she did. Lisa was glad to have the room to herself and her personal masseuse and therapist, Hunter. She let herself relax as his fingers began to send waves of relief all the way down to

Toby Tate

her toes.

"Feel good?" he whispered in her ear.

Lisa moaned in reply.

At that moment, someone knocked on the stateroom door, nearly causing them both to jump out of their skin.

Hunter rose, walked to the door and opened it to find Lieutenant Delgado standing before him.

"Hey, lieutenant. Come on in," Hunter said.

Delgado nodded once in acknowledgement, but remained stoic outside the stateroom. "The captain wants to see the media group on the bridge." She moved to the next door and knocked.

Hunter turned to Lisa. "I don't like the sound of this."

Lisa slowly stood from her chair, testing her sea legs and equilibrium. Hunter moved to help her stand, placing a hand under each arm.

"Hey, you think you can make it?" he said.

Lisa smiled up at him. "If I don't, you can just catch me from behind."

CHAPTER 14

"At about 0900 this morning, AM2 Shackelford discovered a storm just to the east of us," Captain Phillips told the assembled media group in his stateroom. Lisa noticed photos decorating the walls that featured a younger Phillips decked out in full flight gear, looking every bit the hero. Light filtered in through the single portal, but Lisa could definitely feel an increase in the rocking of the ship, indicating the approach of a storm. She turned her attention back to the CO.

"I know that the media group is set to disembark tomorrow morning, but because of the proximity and the size of the storm, we are unfortunately going to have to delay that and try to outrun it," he said. "The storm gives every indication of increasing to hurricane strength within the next few hours, and with the winds already at forty knots, I don't want to take any chances with civilians on the flight deck."

Hendricks raised his hand.

"Excuse me, sir, but since when is a carrier captain afraid to launch a plane in forty-knot winds?" he asked.

"I know you've launched in worse weather than that, and I don't know about anybody else, but I have a lot of other assignments I need to get back to."

Lisa, already feeling irritable, wanted to slap the sneer off Hendricks' face, but gritted her teeth instead. This guy was really starting to annoy her.

The captain seemed unperturbed by the statement, however, and even managed a smile. "I'm sorry, Mr. Hendricks, I know how you feel, but the safety of the crew and the civilians aboard the Ford are my first priority and this storm is acting erratically. It came up extremely quickly and is moving towards us, so if we don't begin steaming right away, we're going to be stuck in the middle of thirty-foot swells or bigger, and I'm sure you don't want that."

Then, Phillips took a deep breath—apparently he wasn't finished.

"Also, because of the size, strength and speed of the storm, I'm afraid we won't be pulling into Norfolk Naval Base." He paused for the inevitable groans that echoed through the room.

"So where are we going?" asked Blakely.

"To be honest with you, I'm not sure yet. We have to monitor the direction of the storm and see where we think it might make landfall, then decide from there."

More groaning.

A young reporter named Jones, who looked like he had just rolled out of bed in his clothes, spoke in a whiny nasal voice that made Lisa want to punch him.

"So in other words, there's no telling when the hell we'll get off this tub," he said.

"We'll make every effort to insure you're all as comfortable as possible. We will provide laundry services so you can wash your clothes and of course you can use the phones and Internet access as long as it works," Phillips said.

And we'll wipe your asses for you, too, Lisa thought to

herself.

Phillips continued. "I want to apologize again for the inconvenience, but sometimes Mother Nature has her own ideas and we just have to make plans accordingly. I'll let you know of any further developments. Any more questions?"

Lisa raised her hand. Hunter turned to her and frowned.

"Yes?" Phillips asked.

"Is there a head nearby? I think I'm going to puke."

CHAPTER 15

Lisa once again sat in her stateroom, where she seemed to be spending a lot of time lately, thinking about her visit to the ship's doctor. Since Hunter was starting to learn his way around the ship, he had gone off to talk to a few more pilots for his story. The media crew was stuck aboard the Ford for an indefinite period, so the CO had decided to give them a little more freedom to move around, as long as they stayed away from the engine rooms and other dangerous areas. Besides, Lisa didn't want Hunter in the sickbay having a coronary thinking that his wife was on the verge of death. She had enough worries of her own without adding his to the mix.

Lisa did like the way Hunter fawned over her though, treating her like a queen while never being over protective. He knew she could take care of herself, but the relationship was still fragile after their separation, and they both knew it.

Lisa picked up the remote from her desk and flicked on the TV, hoping that there was something to watch. *Top Gun* with Tom Cruise blared out of the speakers. She sat down on the bed, trying to put everything out of her mind until Hunter returned. Lisa knew that what she had to tell him would blow his mind and she didn't want to think about it too much or she would go crazy. All she could do was wait.

Lisa sat on the bunk and stared at Tom's image, thinking about how much he had always reminded her of Hunter, right down to the goofy grin. The few short years they had spent together had been both wonderful and turbulent, like an amusement park ride with no end. She had never loved anyone as much as she loved Hunter, and the six-month separation only served to intensify those feelings. She had missed him terribly, and apparently he had missed her, too. Since they had reunited, they couldn't seem to get enough of each other or do enough *for* each other. Sometimes it was like a dream and if it was, Lisa never wanted to wake up.

As soon as she had that last thought, the door to the stateroom burst open and Hunter strode into the room as if seeing her was the only thing that mattered. That realization made Lisa feel like dancing.

"Well, what did the doctor say? Are you going to be okay? Does he know what's making you sick?" Hunter fired the questions off before the stateroom door had even closed, slamming shut with an echo that reverberated down the ship's passageways.

Without even thinking, Lisa blurted out, "Hunter, I'm pregnant!"

Hunter's jaw hit the floor.

CHAPTER 16

Lieutenant Charlie Duncan could not believe his luck. A young enlisted woman he had been eyeing since she had first come to the Ford was now with him in his stateroom. He knew there was a high probability that they would be caught, but for some reason, he didn't care. It was weird, like he had simply lost all inhibition. Yet caution was the last thing on the weapons officer's mind as they sat on his bunk and he kissed her long, shapely neck, then slipped her unbuttoned shirt down and began working on her lovely shoulders. Her skin was warm to the touch and smelled delicious, like fresh cinnamon.

A few more buttons came undone and Duncan glimpsed the tops of her breasts, probably the firmest he had ever seen, and the color of milk chocolate. He'd always loved younger women, and she was no more than nineteen or twenty. Only twenty-five himself, it wasn't like robbing the cradle, but the younger ones had a fire in them and this one was about to burn him to the ground.

Her hands caressed Duncan's face as he worked his way over the left shoulder and down the arm. She moaned softly.

"Oh, lieutenant, you do that so well."

By this time he was ready to explode. He slipped a hand under her bra and felt a nipple, teasing it gently with his fingertip as it became rigid. The girl's right hand crept up Duncan's leg, stopped at his crotch and began to massage it. She found the zipper, pulled it down and then stuck her hand inside to fondle her prize.

It was Duncan's turn to moan.

He reached behind her and undid her bra, letting it fall to the floor, then put a hand on each breast and gently squeezed. He gazed into the young woman's eyes.

"I know you want this as much as I do," he whispered, hoping that he sounded seductive enough to get to the next level.

"You're right," she whispered back.

The woman stood and began to slowly unbutton her blue battle-dress uniform pants, and Duncan thought he had never seen a uniform look so good. She let them drop to her ankles, giving the lieutenant a glimpse of shapely, muscular legs, and he felt his heartbeat quicken. He reached down and caressed a thigh. It was even softer than he had imagined.

"I shaved them today—just for you," she said in a sultry voice that made Duncan shiver.

Duncan smiled and started unbuttoning his shirt. This was going to be the best sex of his young life, and Seaman Jessica Blount was more than happy to oblige.

CHAPTER 17

It was his second day aboard the USS Ford and the CIA operative knew the storm was a bad sign. The fact that it had appeared quickly and was intensifying faster than normal was a classic indicator that the target was making its move. The ability to control weather was still incomprehensible to the human mind. It was like having to learn physics all over again—natural laws just didn't seem to apply in this case. The power this being possessed was almost…godlike. He wondered what the target's next move would be. One thing this case had proven was that he had to keep his eyes and his mind open at all times, because anything was possible.

But the man had definitely seen his share of strange things during his time in the CIA, which was why he was assigned to this case in the first place. Because of his background in parapsychology and physics and his interest in all things strange—ghosts, black holes, time warps, string theory—the CIA operative was offered, and was selected to take on the bizarre cases, the cases that defied rational explanation.

And this case was turning out to be the strangest of them all.

It had taken him almost a year to track down the target after discovering there had been a change of identity that had somehow been undetected. Fooling the CIA was no easy task, yet it had been done and the agency had a hell of a time reacquiring the target. By that time, it was discovered that the target was on the move and had managed to get on board the Ford.

But for what reason?

Headquarters had gotten him on board without a hitch and so far, his cover was working—no one had a clue as to his real identity, or his real purpose. He hoped to keep it that way. The longer he could work undetected, the better chance he had of figuring out exactly what the target was up to, and a plan of action.

But what kind of action could you take against a power that defied all rationality? He figured he would cross that bridge when the time came.

The man took another sip of coffee and stared at the report he had just written on his laptop. Satisfied, he clicked on another program and opened a file, then began to read, hoping to find some kind of pattern, something that would give a clue as to what might be happening and what, if anything, could be done.

Everyone and everything had a weakness, and the operative was determined to find it, because deep in his gut, he knew that before it was all over, the lives of every person on board the Ford could depend on it.

CHAPTER 18

Hunter slowly closed his mouth and blinked his eyes. "You...you're pregnant?"

Lisa wore a wide grin. "You heard right, Daddy. I'm gonna be a baby mama," she said.

Hunter grabbed a chair from the nearby desk and sat down.

"How did it happen? I mean, when...how did you find out?"

Lisa laughed. "I think we already know how it happened, Romeo. I found out when I was in sickbay. The doctor gave me a pregnancy test, and it turned blue. That's why I've been ill—it's morning sickness."

The still-raw memory of their first miscarried child entered unbidden into Hunter's mind and was just as quickly ushered out. He would not let that tragedy rob him of the joy of having another child.

Hunter smiled and held out a hand and Lisa slipped hers into it. "I guess you know how I feel about that," he said.

"Yeah, but why don't you tell me anyway."

"I think it's awesome—the greatest thing that could ever happen to us. And you're the greatest thing that ever happened to me."

Lisa leaned towards Hunter and gave him a deep, long kiss that hit him like a cattle prod. Her tongue tasted good in his mouth and he never wanted to stop.

When they finally did, Hunter was out of breath. Lisa sat back on the bed and they both took in the sight of each other, their eyes communicating what words never could.

That was when the door flew open and Julia Lambert swept into the room, camera dangling from her neck and notepad in her hand.

The trio stared at each other for an awkward moment before Julia finally spoke.

"Oh, am I interrupting something?"

Hunter thought he noted just a hint of sarcasm in her voice, but couldn't be sure. He stood up. "No, I was just leaving. We were talking about Lisa's little bout with sea-sickness," he said, winking at his wife.

A theatrical frown appeared on Julia's lips. "I hope she's okay. I'd hate to lose a roommate."

Lisa remained expressionless, but Hunter could tell that Julia's eyes made her uncomfortable, as if those powder blue orbs were probing down into her soul.

"Actually, I'm okay now. It was just nerves. How were your interviews?"

"Very insightful," the blonde said as she walked between the pair on the way to her rack. Hunter smelled a faint whiff of musk and a sudden animalistic urge nearly took hold of him, but he somehow shook it off.

Julia dropped her camera and notepad on her rack and then glanced at Hunter. "So, this is your husband?"

"My better half," Lisa said.

Hunter found that although he wanted to, he couldn't seem to stop staring at the woman. Her translucent blue eyes mesmerized him, seduced him, and called to him like a voice on a radio inside his head, even as her mouth spoke words he could no longer seem to hear.

Lisa reached up and touched Hunter's arm and the spell was broken. He looked down at her, dazed.

"Are you okay?"

Hunter nodded slowly, laying his hand on top of hers. "Yeah, I'm alright. Just a little hypoglycemic, I guess. Maybe I'd better go eat something."

"Yeah, maybe you'd better," Lisa said.

Hunter leaned down and kissed his wife on the cheek and then turned and nodded at Julia as he left the stateroom. Was his mind playing tricks on him just then? Or had he seen a faint smile slither across Julia's lips?

PART TWO: REVELATIONS

CHAPTER 19

Lieutenant Commander John MacIntyre sat up in his rack, rubbed the back of his neck and let the grogginess slowly drain from his head. This FLEETEX, or fleet exercise cruise, was designed to put the ship and its crew through their paces and prepare them for duty, but it was taking a toll on him, especially with a massive storm on their tail.

The communications officer wondered how far away the hurricane was now. He knew that last night it had been a category three and was continually gaining strength as it moved northwestward. But it still bothered him; it had come up too quickly and was gaining strength too fast for a typical hurricane. It was as if some other *force* was driving it. He hoped that he was wrong, that it was just an anomaly and nothing more.

Mac quickly showered and shaved, ran a brush through his short, blonde mane, donned his khakis and made his way to the officer's wardroom, squeezing past several sailors as they swabbed tile-covered decks near their berthing areas and work centers and prepared for the day's inspections.

That was when he saw her, or at least, thought he saw her. He was hoping it was a case of mistaken identity, because she was the last person Mac wanted to see, especially on board his ship. He only caught a glimpse of blonde hair and a profile, but the resemblance was spooky. He picked up his pace, nearly jumping through each doorway as he made his way through the ship's narrow passageways, trying to catch up to what he hoped was only a ghost.

When he got to the area where he had spotted the woman, there was one ladder leading down and another leading up. She could have taken either one. He was going up anyway and climbed to the next deck, then headed towards the wardroom, following the smell of bacon and eggs. His stomach rumbled in anticipation.

Mac opened the door to the wardroom and there Julia Lambert stood in tight black jeans and a low-cut black shirt, waiting in line with a tray, several eyes ogling her from various parts of the room. She turned to look at him and Mac saw a mix of amusement and disdain in her icy blue eyes. MacIntyre's only emotion at that moment was anger.

"What the hell are you doing here?" he asked a little too loudly, drawing stares from all directions.

"Why, John, I thought you'd be glad to see me."

"How long have you been here? Why haven't I seen you before now?"

"I'm here doing a story for my magazine and I've been eating with the enlisted personnel, doing interviews, that sort of thing. Is that okay with you?"

Mac felt like his head might explode at any second. "No, it's not okay. Since when do you work for a magazine? I thought you were with some environmental group. What happened to that?"

Julia turned back to the line and moved towards the

serving area as the commander stepped in behind her and grabbed his own tray.

"The magazine is just an outgrowth of the group," she said. "I'm doing a story on military machinery like the aircraft carrier and its accompanying air wing and its overall impact on the environment."

"Gee, that sounds very intriguing. It also sounds like bullshit."

Julia suddenly wheeled on her shadow, staring daggers at him. "The slow and steady destruction of the planet is not bullshit. But leave it to you to make a mockery of anything that doesn't fit your political ideology."

As she turned back to the line, Mac rolled his eyes. He stared at Julia's platinum blonde head and wondered what exactly was really going on inside of it and what her real reason was for being on board the Ford.

Whatever it was, he knew it was trouble—*big* trouble.

"I don't suppose you know anything about this hurricane, do you?"

Julia glanced back at him and Mac thought he saw a twinkle in her eyes.

He didn't like the looks of that.

CHAPTER 20

Hunter knocked on the door of the meteorological room and heard a masculine voice say "enter" from the other side. He pushed the gray door open and stepped in, looking around at all the equipment. When Hunter was in the Navy, there had been no such room on his ship, an old tank landing ship that spent most of its time hauling Marines from one place to the next either for training or for combat ops. Several computer stations sat lined up against one wall, while a large, rectangular monitor that was suspended from the ceiling showed the angry looking infra-red graphics of what appeared to be the hurricane that was dogging their heels. There were racks with servers in the middle of the room and a couple of big color laser printers next to them. The temperature in the room was about sixty degrees, probably to keep all the electronics cooled off, Hunter figured. There were a lot of buzzing and whirring sounds and he caught a faint whiff of burning electrical wiring but figured it probably smelled like that naturally or an alarm would have been set off.

An officer in a khaki uniform sitting at a metal desk stood and offered a hand.

"Hi, I'm Lieutenant Anderson. What can I do for you?"

The man had a firm handshake and a pleasant demeanor that immediately put Hunter at ease. The lieutenant was tall and lanky with jet-black hair and seemed easygoing, like he had just returned from vacation. Maybe he had.

Hunter cleared his throat. "I'm Hunter Singleton, a newspaper reporter—part of the media group that's on board—and I was hoping to learn a little bit about how you track hurricanes."

Anderson smiled. "Oh, yeah, I heard about you guys."

The lieutenant turned and glanced back at the giant screen with the swirling mass of reds and blues.

"Well, what do you want to know?" he said. "We've been tracking it for a couple of days. It's officially been named Hurricane Alex and as you can see, it's already a monster, with hurricane force winds reaching over one hundred miles from the eye."

Hunter furrowed his brow. "One hundred miles? That's a pretty long way, isn't it?"

Anderson nodded, then turned and walked over to the screen and pointed to the center of the storm with a pen. "It's got deep convection in the center and the eye wall is very well defined. It's already a cat three…"

"A cat three in only two days?"

Anderson nodded and kept on talking. "It'll soon be a cat four and probably a cat five in the next couple of days. To be honest with you, Mr. Singleton, I've never seen a storm grow this strong this fast. Even with the warm ocean currents in this part of the Atlantic, it takes days for a storm to reach maximum intensity, but this monster's not wasting any time."

"What kind of capabilities do you guys have for tracking storms?"

"We can pretty much do anything the National Weather Service can do — forecast weather in our location as well as at the target location, ingress and egress routes and at all levels from the surface up to the altitudes that the carrier wing's aircraft can fly. We even have our own radiosondes, or what you call weather balloons."

"Impressive. So do we know where Alex is headed right now?"

Anderson frowned. Hunter had a feeling he wasn't going to like the answer.

"Right now, Mr. Singleton, landfall appears to be New York City."

CHAPTER 21

New York City, the Office of the Mayor

City Hall was a blur of activity—TV news camera
crews from every station in the city, the three major net-
works, Fox News, CNN and MSNBC as well as newspaper reporters and photographers were running every
which way and crowding the door of the mayor's office
trying to get somebody, *anybody,* to give them a lead on
what they planned to do in preparation for Hurricane
Alex. This would be the storm of the century and it was
about to hit one of the largest metropolitan areas in the
world. Two stoic New York City detectives stood security
detail outside the mayor's office, effectively discouraging
any would-be party-crashers.

Don Jacobs, the commissioner of the Office of Emergency Management, could hear the cacophony of voices
outside the door and thanked God he didn't have to deal
with it. He knew that Mayor Geoffrey Washington was
determined not to let this thing run over him and be remembered as the mayor who presided over an administra-

tion that didn't have a clue about handling an emergency situation. The trouble was: New York City hadn't been hit by a cyclone of this magnitude since the New England hurricane of 1938 known as the "Long Island Express," a category three that killed sixty people and caused nearly five billion dollars in damages. But Alex was probably going to be much, much worse. The storm surge alone could exceed twenty feet with winds topping one-hundred and fifty miles per hour. Not a good day in the Big Apple. The whole New England region would probably be affected, as well.

"Yes, senator, I have the commissioner in my office right now," the mayor said, speaking into the phone while simultaneously glancing at Jacobs, who was squirming in his seat and resisting the urge to loosen his tie. It was hot in the mayor's office and he was in the hot seat. The combination was causing flop sweat and his heart was racing just a little too fast for his liking. Jacobs looked past the mayor, temporarily blocking out the conversation and staring out the window at City Hall Park, admiring the greenery and imagining how serene it must have been compared to where he was right now.

Representatives of the local police, fire departments and the mayor's staff members sat on couches and chairs and talked quietly among themselves while the mayor finished his phone call. Jacobs preferred to spend the time organizing his thoughts. He had been on the phone since five o'clock that morning, talking to the weather service, his staff, and most of the people that were now in the mayor's office. He was used to stress, but he hadn't seen anything like this since the 9-11 massacre. This could potentially be one of the worst disasters in recorded history. But the commissioner was determined to evacuate and protect as many people as was humanly possible—including his own family—or die trying.

Mayor Washington hung up the phone then sighed

heavily. Perspiration beaded on his dark forehead, and the look on his jowly face indicated he had not enjoyed the previous conversation.

"That was Senator Hinton. I don't think I have to tell anyone that she is extremely concerned over our situation and wants immediate action. So please tell me, Mr. Commissioner, that we have some kind of plan in place to get these people out of the city, or at least to some kind of evacuation center."

Jacobs cleared his throat. "Yes, sir, my office is working with police and emergency services to get as many people as possible out of flood zones and into evac centers or out of the city altogether. We've already begun evacuating Coney Island, Brighton Beach, Manhattan Beach, Sea Gate, Breezy Point, Rockaway Beach, Belle Harbor and several other areas."

The mayor nodded, knitting his brow tightly. "First of all, tell me what we're looking at as far as the storm is concerned. What can we expect?"

Jacobs ran a hand through his silver hair and crossed his left ankle over his right knee, as if preparing for a long interview. God, how he wished he could have a cigarette. He missed the days when he could just light one up anytime or anywhere and not worry about someone bringing a lawsuit.

"Well, Mr. Mayor," Jacobs said, "a category five hurricane basically means devastation. Many of our major bridges, like the George Washington, will experience hurricane force winds long before the rest of the city, so that's going to play havoc with our evacuations. The ferry services will have to be shut down, as well, because of the threat of storm surge, so that's not going to help. The Holland tunnel, Brooklyn-Battery and subway tunnels in lower Manhattan are all probably going to be underwater. The JFK Airport will end being hit by twenty or thirty feet of water, as well. The storm is currently less than a day away and evacuation of the entire city in that amount of time is just not feasible. The jet stream will carry the hurricane up to speeds of sixty miles per hour, which is good in that it will pass through quickly, but also bad, because that gives us so little time to prepare. The best we can do at this point is to get everyone away from the areas most susceptible to flooding and into the center of the boroughs where the evac stations are set up. But no matter how you look at it, there is going to be some loss of life."

The room remained ominously quiet as everyone digested the information. After what seemed like an eternity, the mayor spoke.

"I appreciate your efforts and I know this is not going to be easy," he said as he looked at each person in the room. "It's going to take a hell of a lot of patience and perseverance, but I know you will give it your all because you always do."

The mayor sat back in his leather chair and gazed at the office door. "Alright," he said, "Might as well let the press in."

CHAPTER 22

Jessica Blount sat at the computer terminal in the crypto room of the Ford, searching through classified e-mails for any hint that there may be CIA aboard. So far, she hadn't found a thing. If there was anyone on board, they were well-hidden among either the crew or the media group. But who could it be?

For the last couple of days, Jessica had been feeling strange, as if she wasn't herself, as if there was someone—something—inside her brain, directing her every move. But she had managed to shake the feeling off. And that strange dent in the top of her skull...she couldn't for the life of her think where it could have come from. Had she banged her head coming through a door somewhere? Bits and pieces came to her like the fleeting shadows of a dream, memories of things she thought she may have done, but couldn't quite remember. It was maddening. Jessica prided herself on her excellent memory, but now it was as if her brain was deteriorating, maybe an early onset of Alzheimer's.

Jessica searched through one e-mail after another, like looking for a grain of sand on an endless beach, but there wasn't anything other than typical communications between the Ford and Fleet Forces Command. If she didn't find anything, she may have to have a little "talk" with the ship's NCIS agent.

She stopped typing and just sat, staring at the computer monitor. What the hell was she doing searching through classified files? She looked around at the gray walls of the room — filing cabinets, radio equipment, computers — as if seeing everything for the first time. Jessica could feel the great ship rocking on the waves, side to side, bow to stern, and suddenly began to feel ill. She hadn't been seasick since the first day she had come aboard the Ford, so why now?

The seaman quickly clicked "tools" on the browser and erased her tracks, although she knew if someone searched hard enough they would find out what she had done. She logged out of the computer and stood, running her hands through her hair, trying to think, hoping to jar some kind of memory loose inside the old gray matter.

A flash came into her mind suddenly, like a single frame from a movie, of a man standing over her, caressing her cheek and looking down at her as she…Jessica's eyes bulged and she wanted to retch as the scene hit her full force. She stumbled backwards, nearly falling over the desk chair, but caught herself in time. She had given oral sex to someone, one of her superiors. She remembered it distinctly now. They were in the anchor windlass room of all places. She remembered the sex, but after that it was fuzzy, like there was some kind of interference blocking it out. What the hell was going on?

Jessica pushed the chair out of the way and pulled open the compartment door, making her way to the female head down the passageway. A couple of her shipmates gave her odd looks on the way by, but she didn't care. Seaman Blount simply wanted to make it to a toilet before she blew breakfast all over the floor.

She made it to the female head and stopped at one of the stainless steel sinks to look in the mirror. She leaned over with both hands on the sink and stared into the glass.

She looked like shit. Her eyes had dark circles underneath and her black hair was matted to her head. Had she even showered in the past two days? She couldn't remember. In fact, she couldn't recall much of anything she had done in that time. What was happening to her? Was she going crazy? Was she sick? Jessica was considering going to sickbay when she caught a glimpse of what she thought was perspiration on the side of her face, but it was whitish in color. She leaned in closer to the mirror.

A drop of liquid, which should have been trickling down her face, was instead moving sideways, where it merged with another drop of liquid, then another and another. More drops began oozing from her face as the skin tightened and turned a bright crimson.

She felt something on her arm and looked down. More whitish liquid exuded from her flesh, like she was suddenly perspiring milk, and began to collect at her wrist. Oh, sweet Jesus, what was happening to her?

Jessica shook the wetness from her arm onto the floor and watched dumbfounded as the drops quickly rolled towards one another like magnets with opposite poles, forming a small puddle. She could feel the liquid as it seemed to be coming out of every pore of her body now and she tore off her BDU shirt and pants, tossing them across the room. The seaman looked at her body and saw that it was covered in white sweat, as if all the milk she had consumed in her life was now suddenly leaking out of her.

Then her eyes began to water and burn. She ran to the mirror and stared at herself through a haze of tears. But they weren't tears — it was the white liquid and it was leaking out of her eye sockets.

Then Jessica did something she hadn't done since she was eight years old.

She screamed.

CHAPTER 23

Joey Paducci's grandparents had emigrated from Italy back in the days when America was in its prime during the roaring twenties. His grandfather had started a restaurant in Manhattan that had done quite well, even lasting through the depression. His own father, Joey Sr., had worked in that restaurant as a kid and later took it over when his grandfather had passed away. Joey had expected to be the next in line and in fact, *had* been next in line, to take over the family business—then the seventies happened—recession, inflation, gas shortages, even toilet paper shortages. Joey had never seen anything like it. People just didn't have the money to spend on eating out or doing anything else, for that matter.

Joey Sr. eventually drank himself to death, leaving behind a wife and three kids, including Joey. But as the oldest sibling and the most experienced at running the restaurant, he was determined to keep the business afloat. His brother and sister and even his mother pitched in and worked weekends and nights trying to keep the place going. They started offering food to go and several new menu items, but nothing they did seemed to be enough.

Then, the bank bailouts began and another recession loomed over them like the shadow of death. His brother and sister finally called it quits and got jobs at other restaurants and his mother started collecting social security. It wasn't much, but it kept her going along with the money she made from cleaning rich people's apartments.

Joey eventually declared bankruptcy on the restaurant, nearly in tears as he paid the last of his money to the lawyer that was keeping his creditors at bay. He felt like jumping off the Empire State Building, like a complete failure, having to sell the place to someone else who would start a new restaurant that would probably end up in bankruptcy as well.

Now here he was, sitting in Battery Park, feeling sorry for himself and wondering what his next move would be. He didn't even seem to notice the wind that nearly peeled him out of the park bench as his coat flapped around him and the rain pelted his dark hair and face. What's a little hurricane on top of everything else that's happened, he figured.

Joey knew that he wasn't going to give up. That just wasn't the Paducci way. They were go-getters, and Joey was determined to find another means of support. He was still relatively young and this was America, damn it — land of the free, home of the brave and all that. His grandparents had come here ninety years ago without a cent to their name and he wasn't going to let their life's work go to waste. He would start again; somehow, somewhere, he would start again.

Joey wiped his nose with the back of his hand and decided it was probably time to get off the streets, though he didn't feel much like moving. He was completely drenched from head to foot, but he didn't care. It made him feel alive and that's exactly what he needed right now — to feel alive.

Joey shook the rain out of his hair and looked at his watch. Four p.m., time to hit the road.

He looked up just in time to see a twenty-foot wall of water coming straight at him across Battery Park and Joey felt his heart suddenly begin to hammer against his rib cage. He reflexively grabbed the rosary beads around his neck that his mother always insisted he wear and squeezed them like a drowning man desperately clinging to a lifeline.

"Hail Mary, full of grace," he began, just as the water hit him like a freight train, knocking the breath from him as his world tumbled end over end.

Then everything went black.

CHAPTER 24

Every town between Philadelphia and Bridgeport was being pummeled by Alex's howling, tree-flattening winds, while the thirty-foot storm surge washed away shorelines from Atlantic City to Long Island, even creeping up as far as Broadway in Manhattan, flooding businesses and floating cars down the street like toys in a bathtub. Every evacuation station in New York City, where the brunt of the storm was passing, was overflowing with destitute souls. Though city workers and volunteers did their best to maintain order, trying to care for the needs of nearly five million people was taxing their ability to deal with the crisis while the storm outside roared.

Virtually every business was closed, some permanently. Broken awnings, business signs and metal trash cans flew down the deserted streets like empty soda cans in a wind tunnel. Citizens locked themselves up in their brownstones and high-rises, most without electricity, since the first couple of hours had seen hundreds of power lines in the city toppled. Places with underground power lines managed to keep their lights on, at least for a while. Only radio and TV stations and places with generators and lots of gas were going to weather the storm and maintain any kind of electrical power.

Sleeping would be nearly impossible inside the shelters for the masses huddled there on cots, sleeping bags, blankets or cardboard. People from every walk of life, no matter the race, age or economic status, whether they were from Queens, the Bronx or Brooklyn—they were all equal at an evacuation center. Mothers tried to comfort terrified kids as fathers did their best to be the solid rock of courage, though they were as fearful as most of the children. No one in New York had seen anything like Alex and they prayed that they would never see anything like it again.

CHAPTER 25

Jessica blinked her eyes at the bright lights that greeted her as she awoke, trying to ascertain exactly where she was and what had happened. Was it some kind of nightmare? She slowly raised her head and looked around. A stainless-steel counter with a jar of cotton balls, some posters on the walls with cutaway drawings of the heart and lungs, some scales in the corner, a blood-pressure pump hanging on the wall—she was in sickbay, which meant it hadn't been a nightmare, it had been real. Somebody had found her lying on the floor of the female head and brought her here.

The seaman lay her head back down and stared up at the fluorescent lights, thinking about the last thing she remembered. She was standing in the head looking at her reflection in the mirror, and had noticed something on her face...

"Oh shit!"

Seaman Blount jumped off the bed then stood and looked down at herself for the whitish liquid that had been exuding from every pore in her body. Her uniform was gone and someone had dressed her in a white hospital gown, the kind made of paper. She turned to a mirror and stared blankly at herself. Her dark hair was matted with sweat and her eyes were bloodshot, but otherwise fine.

The curtains on her room were suddenly yanked open by a wide-eyed female corpsman.

"Damn, girl, you scared the shit out of me!" she exclaimed, holding a hand on her heart. "You need to get your ass back in that rack until the doctor gives you the okay. Okay?"

The corpsman, a short, wiry black girl, walked briskly over to Jessica, put a hand on each arm and gently guided her back to the hospital bed.

"You just lie back down and take it easy. We'll see that your work center super knows that you won't be doing any work for a while." She sat Jessica on the bed then pushed her firmly back onto the pillow.

Jessica felt as if she was still in the midst of a dream there was no waking up from. She had to know what had happened, who had found her and what the hell that white liquid was. The corpsman's name badge read *Hunt* and the chevron on her uniform said she was a third-class petty officer.

"Who found me?" Jessica croaked.

Hunt put her hands on her hips. "Wasn't me, that's for sure. It was another girl, somebody from the deck department, I think. She went in to take a whiz and there you was, all spread out on the deck like a rug waitin' to be stepped on."

"Was there anything near me on the floor, some stuff that looked kind of like milk?"

Hunt raised one eyebrow. "Milk? You shittin' me?"

Jessica slowly shook her head.

Hunt cocked her head and looked sideways at seaman Blount like she had just broken out of the nuthouse.

"Wasn't nothin' on the floor that I know of," Hunt said. "Just you, and you was buck naked with your clothes flung all over the place like you was doin' a striptease. That's all I know. But if I find out more, you'll be the first to know. The way you hit the deck, you're lucky you didn't get a concussion." Hunt pointed a thin finger at Jessica. "Now you stay in that bed until the doctor comes back from wherever he is and takes a look at you, understand?"

Jessica nodded and Hunt spun on her heels and left the room, closing the curtains behind her.

The seaman could hear the fluorescent lights buzz overhead, casting their pallid light on the bleak surroundings and she wondered what the hell was happening to her. But throughout the rest of the day, things slowly began coming back, and what she remembered made her begin to doubt her own sanity.

CHAPTER 26

Hunter stood outside the ship on vulture's row, a rail-lined, steel balcony mounted to the superstructure, and took in the panorama of the flight deck against the background of sky and ocean. He marveled at the advanced weaponry displayed there like a high-tech smorgasbord. Jet fighters with wings angled back like glistening, steel boomerangs carried enough firepower to destroy a city under those wings, while huge Sea Hawk helicopters sat like scorpions poised for the kill. Several pilots did continuous "touch and go" take-offs and landings and flight crews busied themselves on deck. The sky was a deep blue, though he could see the clouds of Hurricane Alex off in the distance. It looked docile way out there—almost peaceful, he thought.

The noise from the machinery was deafening. The blast from the jets raised the already hot temperature another ten degrees and the air reeked of jet fuel and burnt rubber. If he thought about it, being here was actually kind of fun. It wasn't everyday you got a free ride on a carrier without being a crewmember and having to say "yes, sir" and "no, sir" all day. Sort of a liberating feeling.

He thought about what Lisa had told him — he was going to be a daddy. Lisa deserved some good news after all he had put her through and Hunter was ready to do a happy dance right there on vulture's row. Hunter thought about his own parents and wondered how they would react when they heard the news. Probably do back flips. They loved babies and he could see them "ooing" and "aawing" and pinching its poor little cheeks red.

Adopted when he was just a baby, Hunter tried to imagine his Cherokee birth mother and white father and wondered if he would ever know them at all, or if they would ever try to find out what had become of their child. Did they know where he lived? Did they know he was married? Were they out there, somewhere, keeping tabs on him? Did they even care?

Hunter quickly banished those thoughts from his mind — this was no time for remorse and regret. Instead, he imagined holding a crying baby in his arms and feeling like a million dollars — their child. His eyes, her nose, his hair, her mouth. Boy or girl? Hunter decided it didn't matter. What if it was twins? He'd probably have to get a second job.

Hunter suddenly felt a presence beside him and turned to see Julia Lambert standing there, leaning over the rail. He couldn't help but be taken in by her beauty — small nose and high cheekbones, icy blue eyes and lips that reminded him of rose petals; long, platinum blonde hair like strands of silk. His eyes wandered down her body. Her ample breasts stretched tight the cotton of her T-shirt to outline areolas the size of two quarters. Her butt was small, firm and round in tight, black jeans, her long legs curvy and well-muscled. Her white Nikes were small and he imagined toes painted blood red.

Hunter's erection pushed against his jeans as sweat

beaded across his brow. He found he couldn't tear his eyes from this woman, and worse yet, didn't want to.

"Like what you see?" she asked, her voice a raspy whisper, barely audible above the noise on deck.

Hunter dragged his gaze up to her face, feeling almost like he was drugged. "Huh?"

"I said, like what you see?" Julia cocked her head toward the flight deck, indicating the buzz of activity taking place there.

Hunter blinked his eyes. What the hell just happened?

"Yeah, it's exciting. At least I think so."

Hunter had to yell to be heard over an F/A-18 coming in for a landing. Its tail hook caught the steel arresting cable and it stopped in less than fifty feet.

Julia flashed a demure smile and winked, long lashes beckoning, body language filled with allure and innuendo.

"Oh, I think there are lots of things that are just as exciting—and much more fun."

Hunter raised an eyebrow, but kept his attention on the flight deck, away from Julia and her devilish blue eyes.

Julia made a subtle move towards Hunter, as if she was about to whisper something in his ear, when a man appeared from the door behind them. Out of the corner of his vision Hunter saw that it was a commander wearing a khaki uniform, no hat on his balding head, a chest full of ribbons and warfare pins. He was a bit shorter than Hunter, about five-foot-six, but Hunter could tell he was all business. Julia seemed to know him, but not in a friendly way. Her eyes were narrowed like a cat that had just spotted the neighborhood Rottweiler.

Julia suddenly turned on her heels and without a word, made her way around the commander and disappeared through the door. The man pushed the door shut behind him and casually stepped up to the rail.

Hunter nodded a greeting then continued watching

the flight deck, wondering who this guy was and why Julia split like the devil himself had just walked through the door.

CHAPTER 27

Manhattan Island, New York City

Don Jacobs walked down the middle of Broadway with Mayor Washington and his entourage. Words could not express his feeling of utter dismay at that moment. It was one thing to imagine it, to theorize about it and to quantify it, but to experience it in person was something else altogether. Jacobs once had a friend whose house had burned down and he had read about it and seen pictures in the paper. But when he had driven there to console his friend and view the smoldering ruins in person, it was devastating. To say Manhattan looked like a war zone was cliché, but it was the truth. It made him feel helpless and small.

They wore rubber boots over their shoes as they trekked through the mud and sand deposited by the swells of seawater that had washed down the street only hours before. The smell reminded Jacobs of a beach full of dead fish. Luckily the water had drained away quickly. The storm had come through like an express train, but now the wind had died down to a breeze, the rain had stopped and the clouds were almost completely gone. The blue skies seemed to mock the depressing scene like laughter in the face of tragedy.

Jacobs was in awe of the power that Mother Nature, or God, could unleash upon the earth.

An old Chrysler lay like a Matchbox car upside down in the middle of the street as the group filtered around it. A Yellow Cab stuck out of a storefront building as if the driver had suddenly lost control in a drunken stupor and the group stepped over dozens of dead, waterlogged pigeons littering the roadway. Glass from building windows far above lay like gravel beneath their feet and Jacobs saw menus from several of the restaurants as well as newspapers and magazines from magazine stands strewn about like debris from a sudden explosion. It was like walking through a landfill. The group remained silent as members of the local and national media hovered around them, snapping pictures of everything and asking inane questions that both he and the mayor were too shell-shocked to answer.

Jacobs knew the city was at a standstill. Thank God he had told his wife to leave before the storm hit. He had enough to worry about without having his family's safety on his mind. He wondered how all the shelters were handling their situations. The evacuation centers in all the boroughs had reported being overfilled with people who had been stuck in traffic while fleeing the city, people whose apartments had broken windows and no electricity and of course there were the homeless. It was a mess of grand proportions and they had yet to visit Queens, the Bronx and everywhere else.

Jacobs was tempted to light up a cigarette right then and there, but he managed to keep his urges under control.

Someone from the media suddenly jammed a microphone in the mayor's face, causing an officer to throw an arm between them and glare at the reporter. Washington stopped walking and held up a hand.

"It's okay, Joe," he told the officer. "I'm ready to talk."

Suddenly, it was pandemonium as everyone began firing off questions at once.

"People, people, one at a time, please," the mayor's press secretary, Donna Walters, said. A diminutive woman with short blonde hair and hazel eyes, Jacobs knew that she could stare down a tank and not flinch. She usually dealt with the press like she would a room full of fourth graders. "Give the mayor a break and raise your hands. Yes, you," she said, pointing to the dark-suited man who had been so quick with the microphone.

"Brian Smith, ABC News," the man said with his best TV anchorman voice. "Mr. Mayor, what is your reaction to the aftermath of Hurricane Alex?"

"It's appalling—it's devastating," the mayor said. "But I want the people of New York to know that we are working diligently to get the power restored and get the city cleaned up as soon as possible. It's going to be a lot of work, but the people of this city have always pulled together when tragedy has struck and I believe they will do no less than that now."

A sea of hands went up as Walters pointed to a woman in the back.

"Andrea James, WNYW," the woman yelled. "Mr. Mayor, is help on the way?"

Washington nodded. "Yes. The USS Gerald R. Ford, the Navy's newest supercarrier, will be pulling in to the piers in Manhattan tomorrow to assist in the aftermath. They'll provide much needed medical assistance and a limited amount of electrical power to the city. They will also be providing temporary housing for the homeless. Emergency rescue teams and volunteers from across the country will be coming in to help, as well. A state of emergency has been declared by the president, which means federal funds will be available to us."

The mayor looked around at the army of media members and directed his attention to a TV camera, focusing on the lens as though he was speaking directly to the viewers.

"All we need now are your prayers," he said.

Jacobs silently agreed, thinking that a miracle would be welcome right about now.

CHAPTER 28

Lisa watched the coverage of Hurricane Alex play out on CNN as scene after scene of devastation flashed across the TV screen. The more she saw the more her heart sank. Cars upside down in the middle of mud-covered streets littered with junk; buildings full of shattered windows; beaches eroded beyond recognition; the trees in Central Park flattened like dead twigs — what's more, several people had lost their lives. It was enough to make her even sicker than she already was.

She prayed that God would have mercy on the city and spare any more loss of life. Lisa had once lost a cousin during Hurricane Isabel, when a fifty-foot pine tree suddenly came crashing down through the roof of her Uncle's house in North Carolina, trapping her cousin Jackie inside. Jackie was thirteen at the time and had been out of school that day when it happened. No one else had been home, luckily. On her way to the hospital, Jackie died from internal injuries. She had been her Aunt and Uncle's only child. Lisa was a few years older than Jackie, but they had been close nonetheless and Lisa took it hard. She understood what it was like to lose someone you loved.

Lisa sighed heavily and reached over to change the TV channel when she noticed Julia's laptop computer. She began thinking about Julia and how utterly strange the woman was. Was she here just to get a story? Or was there something else going on? She spent an inordinate amount of time away from her stateroom. Where the hell did she go?

Lisa noticed that the computer was closed, but not all the way—and the green power light was on. There was also a flash drive plugged into the USB port. She suddenly had a devious idea. Lisa was never one to snoop in people's private affairs, but...

She slid off the bed and stood before the desk, looking down at the laptop, wondering if what she was about to do was right. She turned and looked back at the door, thinking about how she would explain herself if she was caught by Julia's sudden entrance into the stateroom. She figured she could simply say she had accidentally knocked the laptop off the desk while trying to move her suitcase and was checking to make sure she hadn't broken it.

Satisfied with her alibi, Lisa opened up the PC laptop and looked at the wallpaper photo as it popped up—a picture of a ship with "Greenpeace" painted on the side, its bow slicing through the water of some unknown sea, filled the screen. No surprise there, she thought.

She perused the icons on the desktop and saw the usual assortment of word processing programs, security programs, web browsers, e-mail programs and files pertaining to an environmental organization.

But one particular icon caught her eye. It was simply a folder with a "G:\" and a date on it—the same date that the media group had been flown aboard the Gerald R. Ford. It was on the flash drive. Her curiosity piqued, she leaned in closer and clicked the mouse over the icon.

Several Word and PDF documents came up. She clicked on one that said "ENG." On the screen appeared a document listing all the personnel that worked in the engineering department aboard the Ford, from the department head on down. That wasn't unusual, however. Most of those in the media group had done research on the ship and its crew before coming aboard in order to expedite their interviews and make better use of their short time on the Ford.

She closed the file and looked at the abbreviations on the other files. One of them was a PDF file labeled "NR." Lisa clicked on it.

A diagram opened up that made her blood freeze. It was a detailed engineering drawing of the ship's nuclear reactors and instructions on their inner workings. On the next page was another drawing of the steam turbine generators that provided electricity for the motors driving the main propeller shafts. Where would a woman doing stories for an environmental magazine get her hands on obviously classified material like mechanical drawings of the ship's power plant? And why would she need them in the first place?

Something was definitely out of place here, Lisa thought. Was it possible that Julia Lambert was a spy?

With that thought, Lisa clicked off the file and closed it, turned off the laptop and folded it back up. Then, she pulled out the flash drive and stuck it in her pocket. If she got caught, she would say she found it lying on the floor.

Lisa sat back down on the bed and stared dumbly at the blank TV screen, wondering who the hell Julia Lambert was and what exactly she was doing aboard the Gerald R. Ford. She also wondered what else was on that flash drive.

CHAPTER 29

Captain Phillips took a sip of coffee as he opened the door to the Ford's bridge and stepped through.

"Captain on the bridge!" a seaman shouted when he spotted Phillips.

"Carry on," the captain said. He closed the door behind him and walked over to the windows overlooking the forward flight deck, where the officer on deck, Lieutenant Joe Sanchez, stood gazing outside, apparently lost in thought.

The captain tapped him on the shoulder and Sanchez jumped.

"Sir?" he said.

The captain frowned. "Everything alright, Sanchez? You look like you might be coming down with something."

"Yes, sir, everything's fine. Do we have a time for arrival in New York Harbor, yet, captain?"

The CO checked his watch. "Yes, as a matter of fact, I was getting ready to announce that."

Phillips sat his coffee down, crossed the bridge and picked up the mic to the ship's 1MC intercom.

"This is the captain speaking. I'm sure you're all wondering what's going on. We'll be heading into New York Harbor tomorrow morning at zero eight hundred, docking at pier eighty-eight on Manhattan Island. Since Con Ed is still trying to get power up and running to the city, we will provide temporary electricity to a limited area. We will also be providing shelter for the homeless, assisting in rescues and cleanup, and offering medical care as well as creating an operating base for the rescue teams. We will be coordinating with the city's OEM, who will instruct our department heads on what is needed. Enlisted personnel will go wherever they are directed by their various department heads and work center supervisors. Any questions will be addressed to me or the XO. You're likely to see some things that may affect you emotionally, especially those of you with family in the area, but just remember, the citizens of New York are counting on us to help them through this disaster, so try not to let your emotions affect your judgment. I know you'll do an outstanding job because the crew of the G.R. Ford is the best there is. That's why they called us. Thank you and try to get a good night's sleep."

As Phillips hung up the microphone, he didn't notice the smile on Sanchez' lips, or the silvery mass that shifted behind his brown eyes.

PART THREE: LILITH

CHAPTER 30

Something was biting Mac. They were going into New York Harbor and *she* was on board. He didn't know what she was up to, but he knew it was bad. Anywhere she went, there was trouble.

The first indicator of this was the fact that some of the crew seemed to be acting differently, like they had been drugged. Vacant stares, meandering conversation, paranoid eyes darting from one place to the next. He had noticed it in one girl in particular, an intelligence specialist named Jessica Blount. They had been in a meeting with the XO when he asked her about some e-mails pertaining to their stop in New York. She had a blank look on her face, like she hadn't the slightest idea what he was talking about. That definitely wasn't like her, a normally bright, intelligent young woman. When Jessica finally spoke, she sounded at first like she had been taking barbiturates, having a hard time finding the words to say what she wanted to say. Even the captain seemed to notice it.

MacIntyre took a bite of his scrambled eggs, staring across the officer's mess at the TV news, not really seeing it, running a scenario through his mind.

If they pulled into New York Harbor and the infected crewmembers left the ship, he knew they wouldn't be back. They would go out into the city and eventually infect the entire population.

Suddenly Mac understood the plan. The city *had* been hit by the hurricane on purpose, just as he had suspected, in order to create massive chaos and distract the citizens from the real threat. They were vulnerable, an easy target to be assimilated from the inside.

And someone wanted the Ford in New York Harbor. But why? It wasn't just a means of transportation—something else was in store.

Mac laid his fork down on his plate and swallowed hard. He didn't like what he was thinking. The captain would have to be warned, would have to be told about what was going on, and Mac was the only one who could do it. But how? Could he really convince Phillips that his crew was being controlled by a force that most people believed existed only in legend? The captain would have him sized for a straight jacket.

But Mac knew he had to do it. There was no other way.

He looked down at his eggs, pushed the plate away, swigged down the last drop of coffee then headed for the captain's quarters.

CHAPTER 31

Commander Samuel "Sammy" Crane traversed the maze of passageways from vulture's row to the first deck and aft toward sickbay, wondering exactly what it was he expected to find. Something strange had happened to Seaman Jessica Blount and he had a feeling it had to do with *them*. The chaplain knew he probably sounded like a maniac to that reporter, Singleton, but things were coming to a boiling point now. He knew *they* were on the move and were up to something—something that he knew had to do with the Ford. But what? That he didn't know. But he figured the crew would soon find out.

Sammy also realized that the ship would have to be kept from docking in Manhattan. The thought of those things loose in New York City was just too terrifying to imagine. They were on the Ford right now, planning whatever it was they were planning and now was a perfect chance to stop them once and for all. But how many were there? And how much of the crew was under their control? Figuring that out was not going to be easy.

Sammy ducked his head and stepped through the last watertight door, then entered the door into sickbay. He spotted Hunt, the corpsman who had come to his stateroom, putting away some files. She flashed her infectious grin at him.

"Hey, commander, how are you?"

Sammy couldn't bring himself to smile back — dark clouds were beginning to form inside his mind and he knew that was not a good thing.

"I'm fine," he said. "Where's the young lady you said wanted to see me?"

Hunt dropped the file into the drawer and closed it, then walked briskly across the room to a curtain-covered area on the other side.

Hunt pulled the curtain aside. "Seaman Blount, there's someone here to — Oh, my God! Commander, I need your help!"

When he stepped through the curtains he saw Jessica Blount hanging from a water pipe, her bare feet swinging slowly from side to side like a pendulum.

CHAPTER 32

"Mac, I can't just derail our mission because of a gut feeling," Phillips said. "You've got to give me more than this. What exactly do you feel is going to happen if we pull into port?"

"Sir, I know how this sounds, but you have to trust me," he said as he eyed Phillips. "We've served together a long time and you know I'm not given to impulsive behavior. You just have to understand that the ship's crew is in danger and if we pull into port in New York, the whole damn city will be in danger as well."

"Mac, you know I can't run a ship on hunches. You have to give me something concrete and tangible here. Now what the hell are you talking about, 'The ship may be in danger.' In danger from what?"

Mac felt like he was standing inside a pressure cooker, desperately trying to think of a way out before the heat was cranked up. The ship was already inside New York Harbor and was about to begin docking procedures. That left him very little time for a tactful approach—he would have to be blunt. "There's...something...on board the ship. Something that is capable of taking over the minds of crew members and controlling their actions. I believe it began when we brought the VIPs on board. It has probably already affected a lot of our crew."

Phillips furrowed his brow and Mac braced himself.

"Are we talking about some kind of virus here?" Phillips said. "I haven't heard Jeffries say anything about it."

"Commander Jeffries doesn't know about this. It's probably something he's never seen before."

Phillips shook his head. "Mac, look. You're the ship's communications officer, not a doctor. How could you know that the ship is infected with something that the ship's doctor doesn't even know about? That just doesn't make sense. You're going to have to come up with some evidence. Do you know of some infected crew members?"

Mac sighed. "No, sir, I don't."

"Well, then, I guess that ends our discussion, doesn't it?"

The growler on the captain's wall sounded off, causing both men to jump. Phillips grabbed it.

"This is the CO," he said.

Mac couldn't hear the other end of the conversation, but the somber look on Phillips' face said it was probably not good news.

"Hanged? Who was it?" Phillips said to the handset.

More silence.

"Alright, chief. Call the XO and fill him in, then stay on it. I'll be down ASAP."

"What's going on?" Mac asked.

As he hung up the handset, Phillips' countenance was dark. "A young seaman was found hanging from the overhead down in sickbay," he said.

An awkward silence followed.

"Mac, I don't know what the hell is going on aboard my ship, but I'm damn sure going to find out. Let's go."

Toby Tate

Mac followed the CO out of the stateroom and down the cramped passageways of the Ford, towards sickbay.

CHAPTER 33

Hunter made his way to the mess deck and bought a cup of Starbuck's coffee to take back to his own stateroom. He paid for the coffee and continued on across the mess deck, glancing at the few crew members that sat talking or watching TV. He felt as if he was in a daze. Was the chaplain really serious about those creatures? What had he called them? Oh yes — the Lilitu. Could some of the crew be possessed? It was like that sci-fi movie from the 1950s, *Invasion of the Body Snatchers*, where you couldn't tell who was a real human and who wasn't. So how the hell could you tell who you were dealing with if that was true?

It was certainly a sobering and frightening thought, and the commander was so convincing. Damn, Hunter thought, if only he could be sure.

But they would be pulling into port soon in Manhattan and Hunter would be among the first to get a scoop on a great, though tragic, story. He would get a firsthand look at a Navy ship's crew assisting the citizens of one of the biggest cities in the world following a major hurricane. Most reporters at papers the size of the *River City*

Tribune would give their first born to be in on a story like this.

Yet the fact that they would be so close to port with so many weird things going on aboard the Ford left him with a feeling of foreboding. Hunter was not quick to believe in weird, supernatural entities, but he had seen some mind-bending, reality-changing things in his life. Sometimes it was the people that seemed to be the craziest who often turned out to be the ones closest to the truth. He had seen some strange things...no, *felt*...some strange things since he had come aboard the carrier and that little meeting with Julia Lambert and then with Commander Crane just served to validate his feelings. Should he just blow them off?

Hunter reached his stateroom door and opened it. There sat Lisa at his desk, watching some kind of soap opera on the TV. She didn't seem to notice him. Something was wrong.

"Hey, what's going on?" he asked as the door shut behind him.

Lisa sighed and Hunter immediately thought the worst. He knew that sigh very well.

"Is something wrong with the baby?"

Lisa shook her head. "No, nothing's wrong with the baby. I just discovered something and I'm hoping that my conclusions are wrong."

"Honey, I swear, she meant nothing to me," Hunter deadpanned. "I mean, sure, the sex was good, but..."

"Hunter, you are *so* not funny. I am trying to be serious here."

Hunter sat his coffee on the desk and started massaging his wife's shoulders. That always relaxed her, and he could feel the tension begin to drain from her body.

"I think I feel a lot of pent up hostility in this muscle right here," Hunter said as his fingers expertly kneaded her shoulder muscles.

"You are such an ass, but a really nice ass."

"I'll bet you say that to all the asses."

A soft moan escaped Lisa's lips, but Hunter could tell she was about to say something and braced himself.

"Hunter, I think my roommate might be some kind of spy."

Hunter stopped massaging. Lisa looked up at him. "What?" she said. "You think I'm crazy, don't you? But I'm telling you, I saw stuff on her laptop, stuff that nobody without a top secret security clearance should be able to access."

Hunter moved over to the bed and sat directly across from Lisa.

"Okay," he said. "I don't think you're crazy. What kind of stuff did you see?"

"Let me back up a little," she said. "For one thing, Julia hardly ever stays in the stateroom. I mean, you can vouch for that. How many times have you been in my stateroom and never seen her?"

Hunter nodded. "You have a point. I've only seen her in there once."

"Right. So what the hell does she do? Where does she go all that time?"

Hunter shrugged. "The ladies room?"

Lisa slapped him on the leg. "No, not the ladies room. She's out somewhere on the ship, doing God knows what. And the stuff on her laptop. Diagrams of the nuclear reactors and main engines, a list of ship's personnel and their functions aboard the ship — the kind of information a terrorist would have."

"Yeah, or the kind someone would pay money to have."

"Also, I couldn't resist, so I absconded with the evidence." She pulled the flash drive out of her pocket and flashed it in Hunter's face.

Hunter's eyes grew wide. "Holy shit! You'd better

hope she doesn't catch you with that."

"Don't worry, I have an alibi figured out. I'll just say..."

Right then the door opened and Charles Blakely walked in.

CHAPTER 34

A heavy silence fell over the room, as if they had all suddenly forgotten how to speak. Blakely let the door slam behind him and made his way to his desk, which was between the door and Hunter's own desk. The pair felt a little uneasy at Blakely's presence—something seemed to have him perturbed and he was not his usual, jovial self.

He adjusted his ball cap, pulled out his desk chair and sat down facing Hunter and Lisa, casually crossing his legs like a police sergeant preparing to question a suspect. Now he was starting to creep Hunter out.

"Well, you two have been busy, haven't you?" he said.

Hunter and Lisa eyed each other, then Blakely. Hunter realized Lisa was still holding up the flash drive and saw her lower it to stick it in her pocket when Blakely stopped her short.

"I'll take that," he said, holding out his hand. Lisa didn't move.

"What's going on, Charles?" Hunter asked. "Why were you listening outside the door? You're not really with *Military Aircraft Magazine*, are you?"

Blakely shook his head, pulled a wallet out of his back pocket, opened it and flashed a shield at them. "CIA. And I hope I can count on you to keep that to yourself for now."

"Sure, I can keep a secret. But before we hand over the flash drive, I would appreciate it if you could fill me in on what the hell is going on around here."

"What do you mean?"

"I mean is there something to what Lisa was saying? Is that woman a spy?"

"Not a spy. Something worse."

Lisa gasped. "I knew it—that bitch is a terrorist, isn't she? What is she planning? Is she going to blow up the ship or something?"

"To tell you the truth, I'm not sure. But I think the clues may be on that flash drive you're holding. If you let me have it, I can take a look at it on my laptop and figure out things from there."

Hunter glanced at his wife then back at Blakely. "We'll hand it over if you let us help you with the case."

Blakely thought about that and realized this was something he really couldn't do himself. It was too big, there were too many unknowns and he couldn't bring another operative in. He would have to trust somebody.

"Alright, but I call the shots. Understood?"

Lisa slowly reached across the desk and Blakely took the drive from her.

"Thanks," he said. "We've been hoping for some kind of evidence that would give us a clue about what Julia Lambert has been up to. Looks like you found it for us."

Lisa shrugged. "Just lucky, I guess."

*   *   *

Blakely clicked on the flash drive's icon as Hunter and Lisa stood over each shoulder, watching him work on his laptop.

Lilith

"This isn't even encrypted," Blakely said. "She probably didn't bother because she figured if we found out what she was up to we couldn't stop her anyway."

A familiar set of folders popped up and Lisa explained what she had seen in each one. Blakely opened the folder marked "NR" and whistled when the pdf files popped up. "Wow, this is some seriously classified stuff. I might have to kill you two just for looking at it," Blakely said, then turned his head towards Lisa. "Just kidding. But I do have to add that everything we see here doesn't go beyond this room, understood?"

Hunter held up three fingers. "Scout's honor," he said.

Blakely brought up the doc file with a list of ship's personnel and their jobs on board the Ford.

"Now what would she need these files for? It's almost like she's looking to target key personnel aboard the ship—she has certain ones tagged with an asterisk. The operations officer, the weapons officer, engineering personnel, the ship's surgeon..."

"Did you say the ship's surgeon?" Hunter cut in.

"Yeah, why?"

"Maybe it's nothing. It's just that there was this corpsman that said a seaman in sickbay wanted to see Commander Crane, the ship's chaplain, earlier today when we were out on vulture's row."

"The ship's chaplain? Did she say why?"

"She just said the seaman had some kind of traumatic experience. They found her passed out on the deck in the female head."

"Is she still in sickbay?" Blakely asked.

"As far as I know she is."

Blakely suddenly stood up. "Let's go talk to her," he said.

CHAPTER 35

Lieutenant Commander Sylvester "Sly" Johnson was a big, broad-shouldered Mack truck of a man who could intimidate even the most hardened criminal. An agent with the Naval Criminal Investigative Service, Johnson had been in the Navy nearly twenty years and wasn't about to be put out to pasture—he loved the job too much. The nickname of "Sly" wasn't just short for Sylvester. He also had a knack for getting to the bottom of things, and being a child born and raised in Harlem, he was street smart.

After securing the area and questioning what few witnesses there were, Sly stood in sickbay staring down at the young woman who had apparently tried to kill herself. The question was: Why? According to her co-workers and work center supervisor, she was a gregarious and easygoing girl who stayed out of trouble, did her job well and didn't complain. If she was having problems, she kept them to herself. So did she hang herself or did someone else do it?

Johnson turned to the corpsman who had found Blount hanging from the water pipes.

"Petty Officer Hunt, let me ask you this — who was the last person to visit Seaman Blount before you found her?"

Hunt crossed her arms and shook her head. "Nobody, sir. I mean, she was fine when I checked on her first thing this morning at 0700, then the doctor came in and talked to her, then Commander Crane came down and…"

Johnson cut her off. "Wait, you said the doctor? Which one?"

"Commander Jeffries, sir."

"Chief Rodgers, get a hold of Commander Jeffries and bring him down here for questioning," Johnson said over his shoulder.

"Aye, sir."

"Sir, I called the commander right after I found Seaman Blount, but he wasn't in his stateroom," Hunt said.

Before Johnson could answer, Captain Phillips stepped through the door to sickbay, followed by MacIntyre. They nodded at Commander Crane and Johnson. The chief stood in the back of sickbay talking to someone on a growler as Hunt snapped to attention.

"At ease, Hunt," the captain said. "Is that the seaman over there?" He nodded toward the curtained-off area.

"Yes, sir."

Phillips walked toward the curtain, motioning Johnson to come with him, then stopped and eyed the chaplain.

"Sammy, you might as well try to talk to her, since you were the one she called in the first place," Phillips said. "Maybe you can help get something out of her."

All three men filed into the curtained room and stood around the small hospital bed. Blount lay under a sheet and looked as if she had been beaten — both eyes were black and her upper lip was swollen. Her dark hair was matted to her head. Around her neck was a purple bruise made by her own uniform belt. Johnson thought this definitely did not look self-inflicted.

118

Toby Tate

Sly knew Blount was in frail condition, but he also knew the perpetrator was still running around loose on the ship and needed to be apprehended as soon as possible.

Phillips leaned in close to the girl.

"Seaman Blount," he whispered. "Jessica. Can you hear me?"

Her dark brown eyes fluttered open. When she saw the CO, she immediately tried to sit up, but he placed a hand on her shoulder and gently pushed her back down on the bed.

"Don't try to get up," he said. "You've been through hell and you need to take it easy right now."

Blount smiled at the captain and actually looked relieved to see him.

"Yes, sir," she answered.

"Do you feel like you have the strength to talk and tell us what happened?"

Blount nodded.

Johnson pulled out a small digital recorder, switched it on and pointed it at Jessica. She stared up at the overhead, concentrating her memory on the events of that morning. By the time she was done, Johnson felt like he had been punched in the gut.

"Find Jeffries and put him under arrest," Phillips hissed at him. "I don't care if you have to take this whole fucking ship apart."

Johnson switched off his recorder. "Don't worry, sir. We'll find him."

*   *   *

Phillips realized Mac had been right about one thing — they needed to stay away from Manhattan, at least until they could apprehend Jeffries, that crazy S.O.B. He snatched the growler off the wall in sickbay and called the

119

duty officer on the bridge.

"Megowan, how close are we to docking?" Phillips asked.

"The tugs are taking us into the harbor now, sir. We'll be pier side in an hour."

"Tell the tugs to stand down for now, and order the engine room to go All-Stop. Then weigh anchor. Tell the tugs we have an emergency on board and we'll let them know when we're ready to get pier side."

"Aye, sir."

Phillips hung up and glanced at MacIntyre, Crane and Johnson. "Now we just have to find the good doctor and ask him why he hung Seaman Blount from a damned water pipe."

CHAPTER 36

Hunter, Lisa and Blakely sped through the ship's passageways, dodging crew members and ducking through doorframes on their way to sickbay. Hunter had a bad feeling about the story they would hear from the young intelligence specialist and in fact wasn't sure if he was really ready for it. He didn't know what was going on aboard the Ford, but whatever it was it gave him knots in his stomach. His wife was pregnant and now he had just discovered his roommate was a CIA operative keeping tabs on his wife's roommate. What else would he find out? That the ship was being invaded by creatures from outer space? Or worse yet, that there was some kind of mutating virus that could wipe out the entire crew?

He nearly tripped over a doorframe and decided he needed to pay attention to where he was going. Blakely was in the lead, with Lisa in between the two. Hunter wondered what she thought about all this. Lisa was the one that had found that flash drive and seemed a little apprehensive about what it might contain. But so was

Hunter.

He still wasn't sure why Blakely was keeping tabs on Julia in the first place. Was she a spy? She seemed to have some kind of strange effect on Hunter. He had gotten a raging hard-on the last time he had been near her and that was something no one but Lisa had been able to do for the last several years. It was unreal. The woman was definitely hot, though, no doubt about that.

Hunter found himself thinking about her again and had to consciously force her out of his mind. That was just something he didn't need right now.

Blakely stopped abruptly in front of a sailor that was posted in front of sickbay in BDUs and wearing a sidearm. The operative reached into his back pocket, pulled out a shield and flashed it at the man.

"I need to get into sickbay. Will you let the CO know that I'm out here?"

The man, well over six feet tall with a neck like a bull, simply nodded and disappeared inside. Probably a master at arms, Hunter thought.

After a few seconds, the CO stepped out with bull-neck in tow.

"Nobody told me there was CIA on board," Phillips said in a flat voice. He sounded pissed. "Can you tell me why you're here and why no one decided to let me in on it?"

Blakely didn't flinch. "Can we step inside?"

Phillips seemed like he was going to object, but instead moved inside and held open the door. He was about to close it on Hunter and Lisa when Blakely spoke up.

"They're with me," he said. "They have some information that could be pertinent to our problem."

"Our problem?" Phillips asked as Hunter and Lisa entered the room. "Do we have a problem, Mr. Blakely? Or is that even your real name?"

Blakely faced the CO. "Captain Phillips, I know my

presence here might be a little disconcerting, but there are things going on aboard the Ford that may not be all they appear."

Hunter marveled at the change from Blakely's goofy personality into this all-business, take-charge undercover operative and wasn't sure if he liked it. He glanced over at Sammy, who was quiet and seemed to be surprised at this latest turn of events. Beside him stood the young corpsman he had seen earlier, who looked a bit nervous, and another man, an officer that Hunter didn't recognize. They all were watching the exchange between Blakely and Phillips.

"What the hell do you mean, 'May not be as they appear?'" Phillips shot back. "What exactly is going on aboard my ship, Blakely? Is there some kind of virus or something that I don't know about?"

Blakely shook his head. "No, captain, it's not a virus. But it could be something infinitely more dangerous."

Phillips looked like he was about to launch into a retort when the door to sickbay opened and three men entered.

"Captain," a huge black man in a khaki uniform said, "We found Commander Jeffries."

Another man, apparently the ship's surgeon, stood sheepishly between the black man and another man in khakis, a chief petty officer. Hunter figured he was probably the chief master at arms and the black man the ship's NCIS officer. The surgeon's hands were cuffed behind his back. It was starting to get a little crowded in sickbay, Hunter thought.

"We, uh, found him in a rather compromising position, sir," the NCIS agent continued.

Phillips frowned. "What do you mean, *compromising?*"

The big man cleared his throat. "Well, sir, a seaman told us he had seen the commander go into a stateroom with a female crew member. When we knocked on the door, we heard noises inside, but no one answered. We kept on knocking, but still nothing. We finally had to unlock the door and we found the doctor and one of the engineering officers having sexual intercourse. Sir."

Phillips' jaw looked like it might come unhinged.

"You're shitting me," he said.

The black man shook his head in reply.

The next thing Hunter saw was the ship's chaplain suddenly lunge across the room and plunge a hypodermic needle into Commander Jeffries' neck.

CHAPTER 37

Sickbay was in chaos. Hunter was having a hard time trying to discern who was yelling at whom as he, Phillips, Johnson, Mac and Blakely stepped in and began prying the doctor and the chaplain apart. Sammy was as stocky as a pro wrestler and it took several seconds before the group managed to get him off of Commander Jeffries, who had fallen to the deck, taking out a cart full of surgical instruments on the way down.

Hunter saw that Seaman Blount, still looking somewhat weak, had dragged herself out of her bed and through the curtains to see the spectacle of high-ranking officers and civilians scuffling on the sickbay floor.

"Damn it, Sammy, what the hell's wrong with you?" Captain Phillips was yelling as Sly and Mac hoisted the chaplain off the floor and Hunter, Blakely and Lisa tended to the doctor.

Once the chaplain had been pulled away, Seaman Hunt ran to the doctor and grabbed the hypo sticking out of his neck. But the plunger was empty. Sammy was hyperventilating like he had just run the New York marathon. MacIntyre and Johnson each held an arm as he kept his focus on the prostrate Jeffries.

"Sammy, what was in that vial?" Phillips asked.

"Captain, if you'll wait about five minutes, I believe you'll get your answer. If I'm wrong, you can lock me in the brig and throw away the key."

But they didn't have to wait five minutes. Even as Sammy finished his sentence, the doctor, who appeared comatose, began sweating large drops of white liquid out of his forehead. Hunter and Lisa, who were crouched next to Jeffries, stood abruptly and Hunt threw a hand over her mouth to stifle a scream.

"Oh shit," Seaman Blount said. "He's got that stuff inside of him. Just like I did."

"What's happening to him?" Phillips asked. No one answered.

The liquid soon covered Jeffries' face, oozing out of his eyes and nose like rivers of white blood. It ran down the side of his face and onto the deck, gathering itself together as if running downhill. The rush of fluid abruptly stopped like the faucet had been turned off and it stood on the floor in a perfectly round puddle. The puddle began to move and undulate like a living organism in its death throes. It suddenly stood up on the deck, a solid mass shifting and mutating from one bizarre shape to the next like some living abstract art exhibit, wet tentacles reaching out, probing the air around it, a parasite looking for a host. Finding none, it slowly melted back into a puddle.

Then, the liquid evaporated into nothing.

Several seconds of dead silence filled the room.

"Well, one thing is for sure," Sammy finally said. "The serum works."

*   *   *

Hunter, Blakely, Lisa and Mac helped put Doctor Jeffries, who was still out cold, onto a gurney and wheel him into the room that had been occupied by Jessica Blount. The ship's senior medical officer, Captain Dunhill, and the general medical officer got the bizarre details of the day's events from Petty Officer Hunt. Neither of them had any idea what had happened to Commander Jeffries and decided it might be best to fly him to the nearest medical facility in New York City.

But they still had not discovered what was in the syringe that Sammy had jabbed him with. Sammy stood between the big NCIS agent and Commander MacIntyre, his hands in flexi-cuffs behind his back, waiting to be thrown in the brig.

Phillips, who had known Crane from their time aboard the USS Eisenhower several years ago, was worried that his friend might be losing his mind.

"Sammy, this isn't like you," he said. "You just don't go around jabbing people with needles. Do you have any kind of explanation at all for your actions?"

But instead of Crane, it was Blakely who answered.

"Captain, I think it's time we all went and had a little chat in your stateroom," he said.

Phillips raked a hand across his thick, graying hair and nodded at Blakely.

"Yeah, I think we'd better do that," he said.

CHAPTER 38

Phillips sat behind the oak desk in his stateroom with hands folded in front of him. Hunter stood with his arm around Lisa. After the day's events, it was an attempt to comfort her, and perhaps himself as well. He could feel the tension in his body rising, seeping into his brain like a slow leak. He was growing ever more concerned for the welfare of his wife, and the affect it might have on her pregnancy. If only he could get her the hell out of all this right then and there.

"Alright, Blakely, enlighten me," Phillips said. "What exactly is going on aboard my ship?"

The CIA operative uncrossed his arms, drew a deep breath and exhaled slowly. "Captain, I know you're going to find all this a bit unbelievable, but hear me out before you pass judgment."

Phillips' expression remained stoic. "I'll do my best, Blakely. Just don't tell me we're being invaded by aliens or some bullshit."

A few chuckles echoed through the room.

"We've been monitoring someone for the past several years that is a member of what we consider to be an eco-terrorist group. They call themselves the Ecological Victims of Evolution."

Phillips raised his eyebrows. "EVE? You've got to be kidding me."

"No sir. The acronym is probably an attempt to make the organization seem more benign. Believe me, they're anything but. It also alludes to their 'Earth first' ideology."

Phillips sat back in his leather chair and it squeaked from the weight shift. "So what does that mean to us? Are you saying those people are onboard my ship?"

"We believe there is only one onboard. The leader of the organization, who we think came aboard as part of the media group."

Phillips sat up in his chair. "Part of the media group? Who is it?"

"It's a woman that goes by the name of Julia Lambert. But that's not her real name."

"What is her real name?"

"Lilith MacIntyre."

Every eye in the room fell on Mac. He frowned and nodded slowly.

"Yep." he said. "She's my sister."

CHAPTER 39

"So there's a terrorist onboard my ship—your sister, no less—and you didn't warn me?"

Mac sighed. "I wasn't sure exactly why she was here. But that's what I came to tell you about. There's much more to Lilith than meets the eye. She's dangerous. I don't know what she's planning, but I know it can't be good. Not only that, she hates me. Ever since I left home to join the Navy she's hated me. She feels like I've betrayed her somehow and now she wants revenge."

The CO sat back in his chair. "You said there was some kind of virus taking over the crew. You never said anything about your sister."

"That's the thing, sir. I believe she's the one behind the takeover."

Phillips raised a brow. "How could one person take over the entire crew of a U.S. Navy supercarrier?"

"Believe me captain; you don't know what she's capable of. You saw Commander Jeffries. That stuff that came out of his body is like a parasite, a living organism that controls the will. And she controls the parasite. Once a person is infected, it can be passed on, usually through sexual intercourse. I remind you that the same thing also happened to Seaman Blount."

Jessica squirmed in her chair. "I can tell you, sir, it's not a pleasant experience. I did things that I never would have done otherwise. I'm sure I did a lot of things I don't even remember."

"So you're saying these infected people can only pass on their...*infection*...through sex?" Phillips asked MacIntyre.

Mac shook his head. "No sir, it doesn't have to be through sex, only bodily fluids. A kiss or even sweat would do it. But sex makes the victim more open to the transfer and more vulnerable because they're completely relaxed and have their guard down. But mainly, well... for her, sex is addictive, like a drug. That's just the way she prefers to make the transfer. But without a host, the parasite dies quickly."

Phillips glanced at Jessica. "So how was Seaman Blount here able to get the parasite out of her system?"

"Extremely strong-willed people are harder to control," Mac continued. "At some point, she must have realized what was happening to her and when she did that, the parasite was automatically cut off from its source — her brain."

Awkward silence.

Mac shifted in his seat. "Sir, maybe I need to give you a little history."

"I wish you would."

"Have you ever heard the legend of the Lilitu?"

Hunter, Blakely and Sammy all perked up at the sound of that word.

"What do you know about the Lilitu?" Sammy asked.

"More than I care to. When we were young, our father used to tell us stories about demons that would come in the night and steal away little human babies, leaving de-

Lilith

mon babies in their place. I thought they were just make-believe, just scary stories to tell little kids. My father died from a stroke when he was only fifty and my sister, my mother and I inherited his estate. Part of that estate included a diary that my father kept and which my sister and I read. He wrote in that diary that he had uncovered ancient church documents while researching our ancestry in Scotland which proved that he, Lilith and I were descendents of a race of beings called Lilitu. We thought he was crazy, believing his own fairy tales. But my sister decided our father wasn't crazy, that the stories were true, and she set out to prove it. She began researching the legend and discovered that she was able to tap into something, some supernatural power that had survived in her—in our—chromosomes down through the centuries. Our father knew that it had survived, but only needed to be reawakened. He even named my sister after the very first Lilitu, the one that legend says was the first wife of Adam, before Eve came along.

"Jewish folklore says that Lilith, Adam's first wife, was created at the same time as Adam, but she refused to obey him and left the garden. She was supposedly cursed by God. But according to the Sumerian and Babylonian mythology, which predates the Jewish legend, she was the mother of demons—a succubus. According to myth, female Lilitu have sexual relations with men while they sleep and steel their semen so they can give birth to their demon children. God sent three angels to go and try to bring Lilith back, but she refused. The angels retaliated by killing a hundred of her children every day until she returned, but instead of giving in, she continued to give birth to even more demons."

Mac gazed around at all the eyes staring back at him. Hunter thought he looked like a prisoner on trial.

"When we were children we lived in Indianapolis. One day, when I was seventeen and Lilith was seven, we had gone for a walk to the grocery store. We took a shortcut down an alley that we had taken a hundred times before, but this time a pack of wild dogs cornered us between the buildings. There was no way to escape and even though I was scared shitless, I was determined to protect my little sister.

"In less than thirty seconds, Lilith had those dogs cowering like little puppies and running away with their tails between their legs. Then she acted like nothing had even happened."

Hunter could sense that the man was telling the truth. At least *he* believed he was.

"As we grew up, I saw her do incredible things. There's another name for the Lilitu: storm or wind demons. I once saw her create a storm that spawned a tornado in the middle of a cornfield. A huge, black cloud billowed up out of nowhere while she stood there staring at the sky. A wall cloud came down and formed a funnel cloud so quickly I thought we were both dead. When the tornado got too close, she waved it away and the whole thing just disappeared like a drawing erased from a chalkboard.

"I tried to tell my parents about it, but Mom thought I was crazy and Dad actually encouraged Lilith. None of my friends believed me. I even started to doubt my own sanity for a while. Lilith told me stories about the different powers she had discovered, all the things she could do. She tried to persuade me to join her, to help her, but I was afraid of what that power was doing to her mind and I didn't want any part of it. I wanted to be human, not superhuman.

"When I graduated high school, I got into the Naval Academy and Lilith ended up at Indiana University in Bloomington as a biology major. She stayed on as a research assistant for a while and began studying her own cells on her off time. What she discovered was amazing.

"Human cells contain a certain number of chromosomes: forty-six to be exact. A female has twenty-two pairs of autosomes, plus two X chromosomes. But Lilith discovered she actually had a forty-seventh chromosome. Not a copy, but a new chromosome unlike any of the others. She named it the Lilith Chromosome. She believed it gave her power—supernatural power.

"Then she started that...organization. She became more and more prone to violent behavior. I believe she may have even contacted other Lilitu. Eventually, I went to the FBI with it and they took it to the CIA. I guess that's one reason she hates me, considers me a traitor.

"After the hurricane appeared, I saw her here on the ship and I just got a bad feeling. I couldn't prove anything, but somehow I knew Lilith was involved."

"What got her into this anti-military thing?" Phillips asked.

"When she was ten, a drunken sailor hit our dog with his car and killed it. She was never the same after that. She had always loved animals, anyway. Lilith once told me that if she had the choice between saving a baby or a puppy from a burning building, she would save the puppy. That's just the way she is."

The room fell silent and Hunter could hear the hum of the ship's generators from the engine room far below.

"There are a few other things you need to know about Lilith, captain."

Phillips arched his brows. "Like what?"

"For one thing, she's strong. Incredibly so. I've seen her lift up the front end of my stepfather's Mercedes."

"Mac, I gotta tell you I'm having a hard time buying all this," Phillips said.

"I understand, captain. But you have to believe me."

"What about Alex?" Hunter asked. "Why hit the city with a category five hurricane?"

"To help create confusion and chaos. Also to get the Ford to go where she wants it, which is right here. I be-

134

lieve that she intends to leave the ship at some point and go into the city. Right now it's vulnerable, which means the people there will be easy prey."

"I have a way to put a stop to this once and for all, captain," Sammy said, his hands still cuffed behind his back.

"You mean with that little potion of yours? First, I need to know exactly what that stuff is and where it comes from before I let you go sticking needles into my crew members."

Blakely cleared his throat. "Um, actually captain, the CIA created that potion," he said.

CHAPTER 40

Julia Lambert/Lilith MacIntyre was enraged. No matter how hard she searched the stateroom, she could not find her flash drive. Shredded pillow down floated in the air and the contents of both her locker and Lisa's locker littered the floor. She punched the side of the steel rack and dented the frame, leaving her knuckles bloody. But the pain helped her focus.

The only explanations were that she had either misplaced the flash drive or it had been stolen. Lilith doubted seriously that she would have lost it. The contents were much too sensitive to be so careless. Yet she had been careless enough to let it get stolen. The most likely suspect was that bitch roommate of hers, Lisa.

On top of that, two of her "slaves," the young seaman and the doctor, may have been freed from her control somehow. Things were not going according to plan. She would have to accelerate events somewhat. Lilith took a deep breath and thought about what she had to do. The ship wasn't sitting pier side as she had hoped, but it was inside New York Harbor, so her plan could still work. There were many crew members on board passing the parasite from host to host. Even if the senior officers had figured out what was happening, it was too late to do anything about it. The sex had been fun, enthralling, exhilarating…but soon, she would own them all.

And then there was her darling big brother John—the asshole. Joining the Navy and being sent to this carrier was probably his lifelong dream. But it was the perfect setup for her. She could kill two birds with one stone. In fact, she could kill many, many birds.

But the first thing she needed to do was to appease the hunger inside of her that had grown since she had boarded the ship. It was almost to a crescendo now, crying out with an insatiable appetite that demanded to be fed. This was something that she hadn't understood before, but now that she was here, she knew what had to be done. It was time to begin the change, to facilitate the metamorphosis.

And to do that, she would have to go deep into the bowels of the G.R. Ford.

CHAPTER 41

"What do you mean the CIA created it? Are you telling me that my chaplain is in cahoots with the CIA?" Phillips asked, sitting up in his chair and nearly shouting at Blakely now. Hunter couldn't believe what he was hearing.

"He's been working with us, yes. We pulled a few strings and got Commander Crane transferred to the Ford when we realized what Lilith MacIntyre was up to. We were monitoring her Internet usage as well as her personal laptop computer, phone calls, text messages and other things."

Blakely surveyed the room.

"Sir, a lot of what I'm about to say is highly classified. Maybe we should discuss this in private," he said.

Phillips leaned closer to Blakely, folding his hands on his desk.

"Mr. Blakely, everyone in here has top secret clearance. I really don't think you have anything to worry about except for the two civilians you brought along with you." He nodded toward Hunter and Lisa.

"Captain, I brought them along because Ms. Single-ton has uncovered some information that may have given us the upper hand in this case."

"What kind of information?"

Blakely reached into his shirt pocket and produced the flash drive that Lisa had given him.

"This contains files with lists of the ship's crew, their jobs on board the ship, diagrams of the engine room and the power plant, including details of the reactors and prob-ably many other interesting things. I haven't had time to go through it all yet, but I'm sure we could find out a lot more about what she's up to by taking a look at it."

Lisa piped in with her observations about Lilith. "She keeps very irregular hours. I've only seen her in the state-room two or three times and I spend a lot of time there. Nobody takes that long to do interviews."

Blakely nodded. "We were monitoring Lilith's orga-nization for some time when she dropped out of sight. Then, by the time we figured out she was using an alias, she had already gotten her way on board the Ford."

"And how did she manage to do all that without the CIA picking up on it?" Phillips asked.

"We haven't exactly figured that out, yet. But one thing we can do is hack into EVE's mainframe computer. That would probably give us a lot of information."

"Can you do that from here?"

Blakely grinned. "Captain, we're the CIA."

CHAPTER 42

Captain Phillips had Sammy released under his own recognizance and sent Johnson off to find Lilith and bring her to his stateroom for questioning. Blakely passed the agent on his way through the door into the captain's quarters, carrying his MacBook Pro. Hunter sat with Lisa on the vinyl couch and watched as Blakely stopped in the middle of the room and inspected the captain's dining table with its red vinyl table cloth.

"Mind if I borrow your fine dining area?"

Phillips shrugged. "Be my guest."

Blakely plugged the AC adapter into the nearest receptacle and set the laptop up on the table, then plopped into a chair as the others in the room gathered around to watch the proceedings.

"I'm obliged to remind everyone that everything that happens in this room stays in this room," Blakely said. "Understood?"

"What happens in the Navy stays in the Navy," Hunter quipped and Lisa lightly elbowed him in the gut.

Blakely plugged the wireless adapter into the USB port and the light flickered to life. Not surprisingly, after entering his password, the first thing to pop up on the operative's screen was a giant blue CIA logo with its eagle profile and shield. In front of that, several icons began to materialize with names and acronyms that Hunter had never seen.

Blakely clicked on an innocuous looking icon that opened into a blue screen with several open fields like a search engine and typed in something that looked like another password, all in asterisks. The screen went blank again and opened into a screen with more open fields across the top and several buttons down the side filled with acronyms. Blakely began typing in words in each of the fields and after several minutes the screen blipped into yet another screen, this one with a realistic painting of a raccoon wearing a shirt and tie, a possum wearing a blazer and several other animals dressed as humans and standing around a steel cage filled with tiny, naked humans. The humans had their hands on the bars and were looking forlornly out from between them. Above the drawing were the words "Ecological Victims of Evolution."

"Looks like we're through the firewall," Blakely said.

Seeing the picture on Blakely's screen, Hunter said, "Reminds me of Planet of the Apes, but with little furry animals instead of big monkeys."

"Monkeys aren't apes," Lisa said. "Monkeys have tails."

"Whatever."

"Couldn't you just access the site through the Internet without using a hack?" Mac asked.

"No, I need to access files through their mainframe that will probably be encrypted, so that won't work. We just need to hope that they don't have another program that can detect us. If they do, they'll shut down the system and we're screwed."

Blakely used various tools to gain access to encrypted files, zipping through them as if it was second nature.

"Did you learn this at hacking school?" Phillips asked.

"I shouldn't even be letting any of you see this," Blakely said.

Hunter was mesmerized by the man's skill. "Can you guys really access people's computers that easily? Makes me a little nervous about all that porn I have on my PC."

Lisa elbowed him again, a little harder this time.

Blakely said, "Let's check out a few of her e-mails and see if there's anything interesting in there."

A Microsoft Mail window popped up followed by a string of e-mails.

"Geez, she doesn't clean out her inbox very often," he muttered.

He moved the mouse around and began clicking on various e-mails, read the contents and closed them after finding them of no interest. He opened an e-mail file marked "keepers" and did the same. Blakely continued this for over an hour, opening and closing e-mail files while most of the others in the room finally got bored and began watching TV or going for coffee on the mess deck.

When all the e-mail files had been searched, Hunter saw Blakely pull Lilith's flash drive out of his pocket and plug it into the USB port on his laptop, then click on the "F" drive of his Mac.

"I'm looking at the dates these files were last modified," Blakely said. "All the dates on the files are within the last few days, meaning they were last modified, or received, since she has been on board the ship."

Blakely sat back in his chair and sighed.

"Captain, I can only draw one conclusion from the fact that Ms. MacIntyre hasn't received communications from anyone with access to secret or confidential information. It means she probably got it after she arrived on the Ford. It could have come from Jessica Blount or any number of people. There's no way to know. But I do know one thing."

"What's that?" Phillips asked.

"We need to stop her now before she can use this information against us."

CHAPTER 43

Lilith figured the Ford's chief engineer knew that he probably shouldn't be doing what he was doing but just didn't care. She had power over him that made everything else in his world fade away like a weak radio signal and did things to him that no other women had ever done, or could ever do. Lilith knew she owned him.

He had made sure that all those on this particular watch shift were "slaves" who would allow them access to the ship's reactor compartment, where they now stood. The CHENG and Lilith stood regarding the lead reactor shield. Though she felt no discomfort, the temperature in the compartment was well over one hundred-twenty degrees, caused by the heavy machinery that screamed all around them. She could feel the harnessed power of the reactor radiating through the shielding, shining like a beacon in her mind, reaching out and beckoning her forward. Lilith didn't know if she would live or die once she performed her task, but somehow she felt she wouldn't be harmed. Once she was in touch with the source of radiation, it would make her strong and cause a physiological change that would bring about miraculous results.

The beginning of a new race.

She thought about her brother John and their childhood, the way he had turned his back on her and then turned her in to the FBI. All the miracles he had witnessed and yet he still never became a true believer. Lilith had developed almost godlike powers and what she was about to do would make her even more godlike. Who was he to think he could ever stand in her way, to stand in the path of divine providence? Mankind was nothing more than a blight on the earth and Lilith was a prototype for the new, improved humanity, one that would reign throughout the eons. John and the other weaklings aboard this ship would be the first to pay and after that, the entire population of New York City. Only then could the change come.

Lilith focused on the reactor door, grabbed the handle, pulled it open and stepped into the fire of God's creation.

CHAPTER 44

Captain Phillips held the phone up to his ear, listening to the admiral and trying his best to keep his anger in check.

"Yes, sir, I understand sir," Phillips said for the fifteenth time. He had debriefed the admiral on the situation and was now sitting in the sleeping quarters of his stateroom listening to a pep talk that he really didn't have the time or patience for. Out in his main quarters Blakely was hacking into the files of the Ecological Victims of Evolution, trying to get something, anything, that could tell them what MacIntyre's sister, Lilith, was up to. It was beginning to look like Mac himself may even be involved. Somehow, though, Phillips just didn't believe that. Mac was a patriot and gung-ho Navy all the way. Someone else was involved — someone higher up in the chain than Mac, or Phillips or even the admiral. But who?

It made his head hurt to think about it.

"Greg, I know you're doing all you can and I understand all this is unprecedented," the admiral said. Phillips couldn't help but let out a barking laugh.

"You can say that again," he said.

"I want you to continue working with Blakely. He's got a handle on this and you need to do your best to see that he has whatever he needs to get his job done."

The problem is, Phillips thought, I'm not exactly sure what his job is.

" And Greg..."

"Yes, admiral?"

"Don't let this thing get you down. You'll get through it."

Phillips sighed. "Yes, sir."

As soon as he hung up the phone, there was a knock on the door of his sleeping quarters.

"Come," he said.

Blakely cracked the door and peeked through before opening it all the way.

"Captain, you should take a look at this. I think we've figured out what our lady might be up to. And it doesn't look good."

*　　*　　*

Phillips, Hunter, Lisa, Jessica, Crane and MacIntyre all stood around Blakely as the operative scrolled through several windows on his way to the one he was looking for. It was a Word document with underlined internet links and several footnotes and photos of different types of atomic mutations—a black cat with two heads, a sheep with six legs, a human infant with no arms and legs that resembled the flippers of a seal. There were also several photos of burned and scarred survivors of Hiroshima and Nagasaki that made Hunter's skin crawl. He wondered to himself how humans could bring themselves do such abominable things to each other, even if the other guy did shoot first.

Next to Blakely on the table sat several empty coffee

cups, marking the passage of time since he had started his search.

"Right here. I found a file containing some notes taken from various studies on uranium toxicity and the effects of uranium on the human body. It seems that Ms. MacIntyre was doing research on how enriched uranium interacts with certain biological life forms."

Hunter didn't like the sound of that.

"She apparently had this idea that some types of radiation like alpha or gamma rays would somehow mutate her chromosomes and cause a physiological change, one that could actually be beneficial to her."

"Beneficial in what way?" Hunter asked.

"It would mutate her genes and cause her cells to do something quite extraordinary...spontaneous reproduction."

A hush fell over the room as Hunter pondered the thought of hundreds of thousands of Liliths overrunning Manhattan, the United States and eventually the entire planet.

"But she would have to ingest enriched uranium to get exposed to that kind of radiation. Where would she be able to find that much enriched...?" Phillips' words trailed off and he suddenly bounded across the room and grabbed the mic for the ship's intercom. "Captain Geralds, call the CO's stateroom ASAP. Captain Geralds, call the CO's stateroom ASAP."

Five seconds later, the growler on the bulkhead howled and Phillips grabbed the handset.

"Lance, have you located Ms. Lamber... I mean MacIntyre yet?" he asked.

Judging by the CO's face, Hunter figured the answer was no.

"I think she may be in one of the reactor compartments. Find out which one and bring her into custody. Use force if necessary. Got that?"

Phillips hung up and glanced at the CIA operative.

"Well, Blakely, do you have any more frightening revelations you care to enlighten us with?"

Blakely shook his head. "No, but I shudder to think about what she's going to do next."

CHAPTER 45

After receiving a call from the executive officer, Johnson hung up the phone, then picked it back up and called Chief Rodgers, who was still monitoring the ship's surgeon in sickbay.

"How's the doc doing?" Johnson asked.

"He's still out, sir. Probably will be for a while. Lieutenant Mason was concerned that the commander may be harmful to himself if he wakes up so they gave him a sedative."

Sly simply grunted a response. How could he be sure Mason wasn't infected with the parasite and under Lilith's control? For that matter, how could he be sure of anyone?

But at the moment, the first order of business was finding that woman.

"I need you to do something. Arm yourself and go down to the number two reactor compartment and see if you can find Julia Lambert, AKA Lilith MacIntyre. The CO wants her brought to his stateroom for questioning. If she gives you any hassle, use force if necessary. Be careful, though. She could be dangerous."

Toby Tate

"Aye, sir."

Sly hung up the phone and headed out the door of the operations department office.

*   *   *

Lilith stood inside the shielding, bathing in the radio-active sun that was the core of a nuclear reactor. She gazed directly at it through the containment structure and the metal cladding, seeing the block of enriched uranium as it emitted alpha particles and gamma rays that would kill most humans, searing their flesh and mutating them in monstrous ways. With intense concentration, Lilith tentatively felt the lead casing, then passed her hand directly through it and the cooling water and into the uranium fuel. She felt no pain, only warmth; the warmth of life. It was smooth and solid to her, changing from one element to another through the process of nuclear fission. She could see the huge hafnium fuel rods as they moved down, controlling the rate of reaction. The amount of free energy that was contained in this process was almost limitless and radiation bombarded her hand, invaded her bloodstream and began changing her atomic structure even as she stood there. It was like finding the key that unlocked the secrets of life.

Lilith could feel the beginning of something else, something growing inside of her, moving with a life of its own. She thought of the Immaculate Conception, a child born of God, and smiled. It would be like a miracle, the beginning of a new race — the chosen race.

Lilith sighed deeply with a euphoric sense of power, then finally pulled her arm and her hand free of the fuel and the lead casing.

She glanced at the door that she had come through to get into the compartment, then slowly turned to the six-inch-thick shielding that surrounded her, focused every bit of energy on it and walked forward. The sensation was like stepping into a giant ball of putty—it required concentration and forward momentum against the resistance to keep from being trapped and becoming a permanent part of the shielding. She forced her way through, inch by inch, glimpsing the molecular structure of the lead as she passed through each layer. Lilith realized that the interaction with the uranium had not only made her powerful, it had also enhanced her eyesight.

Inside the room, the CHENG waited with mouth agape as Lilith's form poured out of the lead wall, materializing from solid mass as easily as walking through a door.

"What's the matter, never seen anyone walk through walls before?" she asked.

CHAPTER 46

The Command Information Center, or CIC, is the nerve center of any ship. From that point, radar and weapons systems could be utilized to acquire and obliterate a target within hundreds of miles with nearly pinpoint accuracy. The Ford carried enough firepower to wipe out a fleet of ships — or an entire city. Counting the air wing, the Ford could devastate several cities.

But for now, Lieutenant Charlie Duncan was only concerned with the surface-to-air Evolved Sea Sparrow Missile he was about to launch. With the latest missile guidance technology, the ESSM could literally take out a fighter plane or even another missile in mid-air. But he would be using it for quite another purpose.

He and his partner, a first class gunner's mate with arms like telephone poles, had already incapacitated the lieutenant that had been standing watch inside CIC and duct-taped her to her chair. The big gunner's mate stood at the door with an M16 rifle and kept a lookout, just in case anyone tried to interfere with their mission.

Lilith

Duncan knew what he was doing was probably wrong, but the whole thing was like a dream, as if his body was being controlled by another person and he was just along for the ride. That girl, the operations specialist that had given him the wildest sex of his life, had mesmerized and hypnotized him somehow and he would do anything for her. She was achingly beautiful and he longed to have her again. But his job now was to do whatever the woman named Lilith wanted him to do.

The weapons officer looked down at the radar console and plugged in the coordinates as instructed then he pulled his cell phone out of his pocket, took a seat in the chair and waited.

*   *   *

Lilith and the chief engineer made their way out of the reactor compartment and into the engineering space where the giant steam turbines pulsated with enough energy to power a small city.

The crewmen that manned the space seemed to regard Lilith differently than they had when she had entered the first time — not with lust, but with animal fear. They saw that she had changed, knew that she could snap her fingers and end their miserable lives. And she would — soon enough.

Their feet clunked against the steel deck plates as they walked past the crewmen in their blue coveralls and hearing protection and Lilith realized she could see right down to their bones, like X-ray vision. She turned to one of the turbines and saw the intricate blades inside the steel casing rotating at incredible speeds, driving the massive electrical motors that powered the ship. But she knew they were still at anchor and would be so for a while. In fact, she thought, they would soon be there forever, a permanent fixture at the bottom of New York Harbor.

They came to the end of the engineering compartment and climbed the ladder to the next level, then up again until they reached the watertight door on the fourth deck. She undogged the door and pulled it open.

In front of her stood Chief Master at Arms Dan Rodgers with a nine-millimeter pistol pointed at her chest.

"I'm afraid I need you to accompany me to the captain's stateroom," he said.

CHAPTER 47

Lilith stared at Chief Master at Arms Rodgers with a mix of surprise and amusement. It looked as if they had figured out what she was up to, so she had to give them credit for that. She had obviously underestimated the captain and his crew. Lilith wouldn't make that mistake again.

"So, the captain requests my presence, does he?" she said. "What if I refuse? Are you going to shoot me?"

"If I have to," Rodgers said.

"What if I take your gun away? What will you do then?" She gave a playful, mischievous smile.

"I wouldn't try it."

In the blink of an eye, the gun was in Lilith's hand and pointed back at him. Rogers' stomach clenched in sudden fear.

"How the hell did you…" he began as Lilith squeezed off a round and put a hole in the chief's forehead. The pop of the pistol inside the narrow passageway was deafening but Lilith didn't notice. A trickle of blood oozed down the man's face and his eyes went blank as he fell back on the deck like an uprooted tree.

Lilith inspected the polished, hot metal of the Beretta M9 semiautomatic as she turned it over in her hand. "I never did like guns," she said, "but this could come in handy." She stuck the pistol in the waistband of her jeans and stepped over the chief's body. The CHENG followed close behind, stopping to glance at his dead comrade.

* * *

Everyone in the captain's stateroom snapped their eyes toward the growler on the wall as it squealed for attention. The CO picked it up and Hunter watched as the muscles in Phillips' face went slack. Someone on the other end was relaying what was obviously more bad news.

"Get a security team down there ASAP and seal off the area. And find Lilith MacIntyre; I don't care if you have to tear the ship apart. Is that understood?"

Phillips slammed the phone down and glared at MacIntyre.

"Well, Mac, she managed to disarm my chief master at arms and put a hole in his head. Some crewmen said she was heading forward down the passageway with the CHENG. I want to know what she was doing in engineering and I want to know now!"

Phillips' face was crimson as he spoke and Hunter thought he could almost see steam coming out of the CO's ears.

"Captain, believe me, I don't know. The only thing I can think of is that she somehow got into the reactor core and came in contact with the uranium. If that's true, then only God knows what it might have done to her. But I swear to you, I had nothing to do with this."

The two men engaged in a staring contest, testing each other to see whose will would bend first. Phillips' demeanor eventually softened.

"I believe you, Mac. But my chief master at arms is dead and now his killer is loose on the ship. We need to find Lilith and we need to do it soon. You've got to try and think. She's your sister. Where would she go? What would she do next?"

Mac considered this as he sat down in the nearest chair and rubbed his temples. "I'm not sure. She's not acting rationally, and she certainly never killed anyone — that I know of."

"Well, I know what I would do if I were her," Hunter said.

All eyes swiveled in his direction and Lisa raised an eyebrow.

"I would be trying to get myself off this ship. Lilith has obviously accomplished whatever she came here to do and knows she can't stay here now that she's killed someone."

Phillips slowly began to nod. "That's a good point. It's as if she's burning bridges she doesn't intend to cross again."

"So if you were trying to get off the ship, how would you do it?"

"There are really only two ways, three if you count swimming, and I seriously doubt she'll do that," Phillips said. "She's either got to fly or take a boat."

"I think we can rule out flying. What about a boat?"

"The Ford has several life boats, but they're not powered. There is the admiral's barge, but it has to be lowered into the water with the crane."

"Where is the barge?"

Before Phillips could answer, the growler squealed frantically and everyone jumped at the sound. The captain grabbed the handset off the wall.

"This is Phillips."

Phillips ground his teeth together, his jaw muscles

tensing as he listened to the voice on the other end of the phone. After several long seconds, he slowly placed it back in the cradle.

"Looks like you were right, Mr. Singleton. Lilith wants us all up on the flight deck near the admiral's barge."

CHAPTER 48

Phillips pushed open the door to the flight deck and broke into a trot around the back of the ship's island and between two C-2 Greyhounds, their wingtips folded up as if standing at parade rest. All seven people followed behind Phillips as they crossed the flight deck out under the sky's deepening twilight and ran aft toward the port side. When they reached the edge, the mobile crash crane had already been moved into place and several deck hands stood awaiting orders—not from the captain, but from Lilith. When Phillips arrived, the crewmen didn't even glance at him.

Lilith and the CHENG stood watching as the group assembled in front of them. Lilith had the nine-millimeter pointed at the CHENG's head while the officer stared straight ahead impassively, like he was ready to give his life for the cause—whatever that was.

The first thing Hunter noticed was Lilith's eyes, glistening silver like two pools of mercury, a sharp contrast to her platinum blonde hair. He figured Phillips probably didn't even notice—he was too pissed off to do anything besides get her into custody, or die trying.

"Put the gun down, Ms. MacIntyre. There's no way you can get away with this, nowhere you can run."

Lilith smiled. "Ah, so my dear brother has finally told you about me. I'm so glad. He always was such a good boy, playing by the rules, staying out of trouble."

"Lilith, this is crazy," Mac said. "Why are you doing this? Don't you know they'll kill you?"

"Let them try, big brother, let them try. But first, let's see exactly what one of these magnificent machines can do. Let's have a little demonstration. What do you say, captain?" Lilith had her eyes trained on Phillips like she was waiting for some kind of reaction. The CO stood his ground.

With her free hand, Lilith opened up her cell phone and hit autodial. While she did that, a dozen members of the ship's self-defense force, led by Captain Geralds and Lieutenant Commander Johnson, arrived wearing camouflage uniforms and carrying M16 assault rifles. Lilith didn't flinch, but only waited.

At first, nothing happened. Suddenly there was a rumbling sound that came from beneath the flight deck. Hunter knew exactly what that sound meant and his heart lurched into his throat.

Everyone turned toward the starboard side of the ship in time to see a huge, billowing cloud of smoke fill the air, followed by the white-hot exhaust flames and deafening roar of a launching Sea Sparrow missile.

CHAPTER 49

Terrell Jackson loved to shoot hoops. In fact, he was so good he had won a scholarship to play for the University of Georgia Bulldogs after a scout from the school had seen him and his team play against a Georgia high school—Terrell had racked up some forty points in that game. Not bad for a kid from the Bronx, he thought as he laid another one up, his seven-foot frame doing "hang time" in mid-air for what seemed like eternity as the ball made a *shoop* sound on its way through the net.

Terrell had just finished a game with some friends from school at playground 174 in the West Farms neighborhood. The court had been built in the early 1950s, but still held up pretty well after the hurricane. He had managed to clear enough leaves and trash off the court to make a space to play in. It was close to his house and he would stop by the Audry Mini Market and grab a sandwich on the way home—if it was open. For some reason, he had always loved their sandwiches. Maybe check out a few of the Latino girls. He liked them, too. Terrell smiled at himself as he laid up another shot from twenty feet away, his size twelve Reeboks squealing on the blacktop. If he had been playing an actual game, he would have scored about thirty points by now, he thought.

Terrell had spent the weekend helping with the Bronx River Project, a massive cleanup effort that had pulled tons of garbage and old tires from the water in an effort to make the dirty waterway what it once was—a beautiful river. The hurricane had managed to dump even more garbage and debris in there and along the streets where he lived. But he loved his city, in spite of its flaws, and he would miss it when he was in Georgia.

Terrell hoped that his little brother would eventually follow in his footsteps. That boy loved his video games, though, Terrell thought. His mother and father, still together after nearly twenty years, were supportive of Terrell's dream to play college ball and hopefully professional ball. He was thankful for that. He had many friends with dysfunctional families and knew that it caused some major heartache for them. He just hoped he could make the grades in school that he needed to stay on the team. So far, though, his grades had been steady As and Bs, so he didn't think there would be much problem there. Still, it would be a challenge. He hadn't even thought about a major yet.

Terrell's mind was distracted when he began to hear what he first thought was a jet plane. He noticed a few people across the street looking up in the sky behind him and he turned to see what they were staring at.

It looked like an airplane with a trail behind it, but it was too skinny for a jet. It was some kind of rocket...or missile. The scary thing was that it seemed to be getting closer and it was headed in a downward direction.

Terrell held the basketball against his hip with one hand and stood mesmerized by the sight. Flames were shooting out the back—he could just make them out in the early-evening sky—followed by a trail of white smoke.

Lilith

The longer he stood there, the more he realized the missile was indeed headed straight for them, and there was no chance of hiding from it. He couldn't imagine why on earth this might be happening, unless it was a terrorist attack.

Terrell's stomach tied itself in knots as the missile nosed its way toward the ground. He had faced gang-bangers and hoods with guns, but never anything like this. His senses were heightened from the rush of adrenaline that shot through his body and his first instinct was to run, but he had never been afraid of anything in his life. He wasn't going to start being afraid now—not even of death. He could hear the voices of the people that were left in the neighborhood scream out in fear and astonishment. Terrell hoped it would be quick—he said a silent prayer for himself, for his neighbors and a silent goodbye to his family and to his dreams. He prayed that his parents would either be unharmed...or die quickly.

As it closed to within a few hundred yards of where he was standing, the missile was louder than anything Terrell had ever heard in his life. He let the basketball fall to the ground as he covered both ears and shut his eyes tight. When it hit, blistering heat and searing pain struck him like a burning tidal wave, but only for a fraction of a second.

Then...oblivion.

CHAPTER 50

A collective gasp went up from the onlookers that stood on the aft deck of the Gerald R. Ford, watching in helpless terror until the missile was finally lost from sight over Manhattan Island. Hunter felt a mix of horror and awe as the smoke trail lingered like a long, white finger of death until that, too, began to fade.

The sky over the Bronx glowed bright white for a split second, followed by a thunderclap. Soon black smoke began rising into the sky like a cloud of locusts.

Phillips turned to his XO and whispered, "Get down to CIC and find out who the hell just launched that missile. Use force if you have to, but make sure they don't fire another one."

Lilith slowly shook her head at the XO, Captain Geralds. "I wouldn't, captain, or your chief engineer could get splattered all over the flight deck."

Hunter knew that Phillips had probably never wanted to kill someone as much as he did at that moment. He watched as the CO glared at Lilith, who still had the M9 pointed at the CHENG's head. She smiled playfully, as if the whole thing was nothing more than a game.

But Hunter knew Phillips couldn't afford to anger the woman, so he had to keep his own emotions in check. Hunter was having a hard time doing that, himself.

Through clenched teeth, Phillips said, "Tell us what it is you want."

"That was only a foretaste, Captain. If my demands are not met, and I fail to dial a certain number on my cell phone, there will be another missile, this one aimed directly at City Hall on Manhattan Island. Now, you wouldn't want to see the mayor and his staff incinerated would you?"

Phillips shook his head, saying nothing.

"Good. Now, I want the admiral's barge lowered into the water with myself and one other person on board," she said.

Phillips look puzzled. "One other person?"

Lilith looked directly at Hunter and smiled. "I would like Mr. Singleton to accompany me on my journey."

Hunter felt as if the breath had just been sucked out of his body. "Me? Why me?"

"I think you would make an excellent father for our children, and in time, you'll learn to love me and forget about...*her.*"

Hunter glanced at his wife and saw rage creep over Lisa's face like a dark storm cloud ready to cut loose with unbridled fury. She took a step toward Lilith, but Hunter moved into her path.

"Lisa, no!" He grabbed her shoulders in both hands. "Don't. She'll kill you—and the baby. Don't worry about it. It's going to be alright—I'm going to be alright. It may not seem like it now, but it will be, I promise."

Hunter had never felt so utterly helpless, like a cornered rabbit with nowhere to run. But he had to be positive for Lisa's sake.

"She's too strong for us to fight now, but when the time and place are right, we'll know it," he said. "She has to have a weakness, we just need to find it. And we will."

Lilith laughed. "Yes, Lisa, there has to be a weakness, and your weakness is my survival — mine and my child's. I guess that makes me the same as you. The only difference is, my child will live and yours will die."

"Where do you plan to go? No one is going to harbor a fugitive with a hostage," Sammy said. "Are there more of you out there that we don't know about?"

"Commander Crane, you surprise me. I thought you knew everything about us. You've already killed one of us, you and your CIA friends. Is that where you got the blood to test for your serum? Well, there won't be enough serum in the world to stop me once I get into New York City. And my friend here is going to help me make more babies, aren't you sweetie?"

"I thought you didn't need men for that anymore," Hunter said.

"True, but that would take the fun out of it, now wouldn't it?"

Lilith winked at Hunter with these last words and Hunter had to work to restrain Lisa from charging the woman and tearing her head off.

The crane motor started up and made everyone on deck jump as deck hands under Lilith's control hopped down to the boat davit and the steel cable and its hook began to pay out.

"Now, if you'll send Mr. Singleton over my way, I'll send the chief engineer yours," Lilith said.

Hunter stared hard into Lisa's eyes. "Honey, it's going to work out, I promise," he whispered. "There's nothing she could do to make me stop loving you. I'll figure out a way to escape and I'll come back to you. Just don't give up hope."

Tears streamed down Lisa's face as Hunter spoke, and

he knew that frustration was gnawing away at her insides like a hungry parasite. Hunter reached down and grabbed her hand, then gently placed it on her belly.

"You've got to stay here and take care of junior while I'm gone," he said. "Tell him his daddy is out saving the universe."

Lisa couldn't help but crack a smile. "Junior? How do you know it's a boy?"

"I just have a feeling, that's all." Then he leaned down and kissed her tenderly, holding her in his arms as if he would never let go.

"Come on, lover boy, it's time to start a brave, new world," Lilith said.

Hunter reluctantly let Lisa slide from his arms as he slowly backed away to the side of the deck, then turned and jumped down to the boat davit and climbed the ladder up the side of the boat. Lilith switched her aim from the CHENG to Hunter and followed Hunter up the ladder and into the barge as Phillips and the others on deck watched helplessly.

Hunter saw Jessica Blount walked over to where Lisa stood and put an arm around her shoulder. Lisa crossed her arms, hugging herself tightly.

The crane roared to life and began taking up slack, lifting the barge by its steel eyebolt out of its perch and then over the water. Hunter stood looking over the rail of the twenty-foot green and black barge, determined to watch his wife, taking in every last detail, until he could see her no more. The boat slowly began descending into the harbor and Hunter thought of the mythical boat on the river Styx that carried its passengers to the gates of Hell. He prayed that he wasn't headed somewhere worse.

As soon as the boat hit the water, Hunter fired up the diesel engine and black smoke poured out of the exhaust port. Lilith walked over to the eyebolt, disconnected the big hook, and swung it away from the boat.

Hunter glanced up at Lisa one last time and mouthed the words, "I love you," and she did the same. He turned and hit the boat's throttle, kicking up a rooster tail of water and praying that Lilith would fall overboard as they plowed their way farther into the darkness of the harbor and towards Manhattan.

CHAPTER 51

Before the barge was even out of sight, Phillips motioned Sammy over.

"How much of that serum do you have? Enough for the entire crew?"

"Yeah, more than enough," Crane said. "I made sure of that before I brought it on board."

Phillips was hesitant to use it, but he could see no other way. "Alright, go down to your stateroom and grab a couple of syringes full of that stuff and meet me at CIC. And make it fast."

Sammy answered "Aye captain," as he jogged off toward the ship's island.

Phillips glanced at Lisa and felt a twinge of guilt for her situation. Because of his inaction and disbelief, her husband was now at the mercy of a psychotic killer. But he couldn't afford to take the time to berate himself or more people were likely to die.

"Ms. Singleton, we're going to do everything we can to get your husband back, I promise you that." he said.

Lisa nodded and smiled weakly.

"Seaman Blount, take Ms. Singleton to her quarters and stay with her, alright?"

Jessica put an arm around Lisa and gently led her off toward the ship's island.

"Captain, I don't believe Lilith took her laptop with her," Blakely said. "If I can get into her hard drive, I may be able to find something we can use."

Phillips nodded slowly, wondering how much more the CIA operative knew that he wasn't telling.

"Alright, Blakely, go for it. But keep me updated."

The captain turned to his XO, Johnson and his security detail.

"Commander Johnson, take the chief engineer down to the brig and lock him up, then meet us at CIC. I want the rest of you to remember that whoever has taken over CIC is a fellow crewmember. There are probably one or more of them guarding the door and they may even have the room booby trapped, so don't open the door until I give the command. When it's open, I'm going to have Sammy jab the first person he comes to with that hypo. Once we do that, I want one of you to get inside the room and disarm whoever else is in there, understood? I don't want any shooting. The first person to shoot for any reason other than self-defense will be seeing me at captain's mast, is that understood?"

The group said "aye, sir" in unison—except for MacIntyre, who seemed to be lost in his own world. Phillips knew he was probably hurting.

"Mac, I know what you're thinking," Phillips said, "but you can't blame yourself. There's no way any of this could have been predicted. In fact, you tried to warn me and I didn't listen, so if anyone is to blame, it's me."

"No captain, if anyone is to blame, it's Lilith."

Phillips couldn't argue with Mac's logic. He was right—Lilith had come unhinged and was determined to right whatever perceived wrong was done against her at the expense of the people of the USS Ford, Manhattan Island and maybe even all of humanity.

"Well, the first thing we have to do is get our ship back," Phillips said. "Let's start with CIC."

With one last glance toward the harbor and the admiral's barge that was now long gone, Phillips took off in a trot toward CIC, waving a hand over his shoulder for the others to follow.

CHAPTER 52

Seawater sprayed over the side of the small boat and Hunter could feel the salt pummel his skin like it was being sandblasted. He shouted over the roar of the diesel as Lilith stared from beside him into the darkness of the harbor ahead.

"So tell me, your bitchiness, what do you hope to accomplish by taking me hostage?"

She turned her silver eyes on him. In the dark, Hunter thought they looked liked empty sockets and he cringed.

"You are an impetuous man, aren't you Hunter? Defying the odds to the last."

"I don't care how powerful you are—you can't force someone to love you. It doesn't work that way."

Lilith moved closer to Hunter, until she was only inches away. He could feel her warm, wet breath in his ear and it sent a shiver up his spine.

"Who said anything about force? Once you've tasted the sweet nectar of the Lilitu, nothing else matters. You should know that."

Hunter shifted his head slightly to the left, away from Lilith's breathy whispers.

"Where are we going, anyway?" he asked.

"To the 79th Street Boat Basin on the Hudson. There will be someone there waiting for us."

Hunter raised a brow. "Someone? You mean more of you?"

"Not exactly like me, just followers. They have witnessed my powers and have devoted themselves to serving me."

"I get it. Kind of like the Manson Family, right?"

Lilith shook her head. "That's what I like about you, Hunter, always laughing in the face of danger."

"Aren't you supposed to send a signal to your...minion...on the ship to stop that missile launch? Or were you just bluffing?"

Lilith reached into her pocket and pulled out the cell phone, smiled, then tossed it over the side of the speeding boat.

Hunter looked behind the boat where the phone fell, then back at Lilith.

"You really are psychotic, aren't you?"

"Hunter, Hunter, such harsh words. The CIA can easily trace the signals of a cell phone, so there's no sense in keeping it. As a matter of fact, why don't you hand yours over." Lilith held out her hand.

Hunter hesitated at giving Lilith the only means of communication with his wife, but changed his mind when the barrel of the Beretta was pushed firmly into his ribs. He fished it out of his pocket and handed it to her, then watched as that, too, was flung over the side of the barge.

"That thing costs me forty dollars a month," he murmured.

The lights of the boat basin soon began to come into view and Hunter wondered what awaited him there and whether he would ever see Lisa again, or see his baby born. But that thought gave him even more determination to stop Lilith, whatever the cost.

CHAPTER 53

Phillips slid down the ladder from one deck to the next on the handrails without touching a step, then rounded the corner of the passageway to CIC. The ship's self-defense force, led by the XO, followed close behind, doing their best to keep up. Phillips had no way of knowing whether any of the crewmembers on the force were controlled by Lilith, but that was something he would have to sort out later.

He arrived at CIC and saw that the watertight door was dogged down. Whoever was inside likely had it blocked with a pipe wrench on the door handle. Phillips thought for a moment. If they tried to undog the door and arrest everyone, the person controlling the console would probably fire the missile in response. The same scenario would apply if they tried cutting a hole through the door. There was simply no other way into the room and no way to override the controls from outside the room. He had to stop it here.

Then Phillips had an idea. As the XO and his team rounded the corner, Phillips held up a hand and put a finger to his lips, indicating silence. The XO stopped in his tracks and raised a hand for his team to do the same. The heavily armed crewmembers watched Phillips expectantly, wondering what his plan was.

Phillips motioned for his XO and the NCIS agent, who had just joined them, and they quietly moved to where he stood.

"I have an idea," he whispered to the two men. "Johnson, go down to Lisa Singleton's stateroom and have Seaman Blount come up here on the double."

"Yes, sir," Johnson said, making tracks down the passageway.

Geralds smiled at the CO. "Going to try to bluff him out of there? How do you know who it is?"

"I don't, but I have a pretty good idea."

Within minutes, Phillips could see Johnson's bulk moving down the passageway with Jessica Blount in tow.

"Seaman Blount...Jessica," he said, placing his hands on the young woman's shoulders. "I wouldn't ask you to do this, but it could be a matter of life or death. I believe the person inside that room controlling those missiles is probably our weapons officer, Lieutenant Duncan. Do you remember being with him while you were infected with the parasite?"

Jessica furrowed her brow, as if trying to repress a painful memory, then looked the CO in the eyes.

"Yes sir. I think so, but I don't know for sure. The memories from that time are like a dream that fades in and out."

The CO nodded. "I understand. But Duncan doesn't know that you're no longer infected. For all he knows, you're still under Lilith's influence, right?"

"Yes, sir."

"Good. What I want you to do is talk him out of that room. Tell him that Lilith's cell phone was damaged by a bullet or that she dropped it in the water and she can't send the message. Promise him anything. Lay it on thick if you have to, but get him out of that room. Understand?"

"Yes sir. I'll try."

"I know you can do it, Jessica. And when this is over, I'll see that you make third class petty officer. I promise."

Jessica turned to the door of CIC and Phillips motioned for the rest of the group to back off farther down the passageway to give her some privacy.

As Phillips was ushering them down the hall, Sammy appeared from behind the group, holding up two syringes of yellow liquid for the captain to see. Phillips waved him up to the front.

"Good job, Sammy," he whispered. "Seaman Blount is going to try to talk whoever is in CIC out of there. When they open that door, be ready to load somebody up with that stuff ASAP."

"Who do you think is in there, captain?"

"I'm pretty sure it's Lieutenant Duncan."

Crane's eyes grew wide. "The WEPS officer?"

"Yeah, afraid so."

Sammy shook his head as he eyed Blount down the hall. "Let's hope she's good at bluffing," he said.

It was at that moment the alarms went off.

CHAPTER 54

The sun had just gone down as Hunter and Lilith pulled up to the 79th Street Boat Basin. The famous restaurant with its row of dramatic stone arches stood dark and empty because of the storm and the few boats that were still there looked beat up and half sunk. Several pylons were bent at different angles and most of the boards were missing from the piers. Hunter was surprised there was anything left at all. The restaurant itself looked to be intact, though most of the surrounding trees in Riverside Park had been flattened, roots sticking up in the air like mud-caked branches, many lying across the boardwalk between the river and the restaurant. The lights were still out since power to the city had yet to be restored. He could see two figures standing on the rickety pier as he throttled down, then reversed the engine to slow the barge.

As Hunter maneuvered the boat pier side, Lilith tossed the mooring line to one of the people and Hunter could see that they were both men. He wondered if it would be possible to make a run for it once he got off the boat. New York City was a huge place, literally a jungle.

There were so many places to hide, he could easily get lost until he had a chance to make a call to the ship and find his way back to Lisa. He would just have to wait for the opportunity.

Hunter managed to get the boat next to the pier and mentally prepared himself to make a break for it. If he waited until they got wherever they were going, he might never have another chance. At least it was dark and there was the park and the fallen trees to take cover in. The debris from the hurricane that covered the streets would also make it difficult for them to give chase once he was on the run.

The two dark figures tied up the boat as Hunter stood at the wheel, waiting to step off the barge. He mentally pictured himself punching one man in the stomach while simultaneously kicking the other one of the face. Anyone that chased him would get a well-placed throat punch and maybe a kick in the knee. Hunter had been keeping in practice with his Kung Fu since Lisa had returned, and she had always been his best sparring partner.

Hunter felt the Beretta in his back as Lilith came up behind him.

"Alright, lover-boy, let's get moving," she said.

Hunter stepped over the side of the barge and onto the rickety pier, eyeing the men that stood on either side. Up on the boardwalk, he spied four other people waiting. He would take care of them when the time came.

As one man tried to take his arm, Hunter pulled it away, grabbed the man's wrist and brought his knee up at the same time, knocking the breath out of him. With a grunt, the man fell over the side of the boat and into Lilith. Before anyone could react, Hunter turned a 180 and aimed a well-placed blow to the second man's throat. The man grabbed himself in pain, struggling to breathe through a partially-crushed larynx.

Hunter was ready to make a dash down the pier when

the plank he was standing on cracked and he fell through into the water with a splash. He considered swimming under the pier and out into the river, then realized he was stuck between the slats on either side of the one that broke. He couldn't move.

"Fuck."

The other four people that had been on the board-walk were now running toward the pier and looked to be armed with handguns. Hunter craned his neck and saw Lilith stepping onto the pier, the M9 pointed in his direction.

Lilith looked like a feline eyeing her prey. "Hunter, you are just full of surprises aren't you? Do you really think you could escape that easily?"

"What do you expect me to do, just wait around while you take over New York City and destroy the Ford?"

Lilith walked toward him slowly, with the grace of a model on a catwalk. She stopped inches from Hunter then knelt on the deck beside him and stared into his face, her eyes boring into his.

Hunter flinched, expecting her to strike. But instead, she leaned in closer, laid the Beretta down and grabbed the back of his head. "Perhaps you just need a little...per-suasion," she whispered.

She pressed her lips onto his and Hunter could feel her wet tongue slip into his mouth. He grabbed her arm and tried to pull it away, but she was incredibly strong—it didn't budge. He wanted to punch her, but he had never hit a woman and couldn't bring himself to do it, even now.

Then something else invaded his throat. Something wet and cold, something that was definitely not flesh and blood. Hunter forgot his chivalry and brought a fist down into Lilith's ear. It didn't faze her. He grabbed a handful of hair and yanked it out by the roots. She showed no sign of pain as she kept her mouth over his, giving access to what Hunter realized was the parasite. He flailed about, trying to gain some kind of leverage to get himself out of the hole he was stuck in, but couldn't move. Suddenly it became hard to breathe and as he tried to close his mouth he found it impossible. Gelatinous, slimy ooze slid down his esophagus and into his belly and it was as if his whole body was getting numb. He felt like going to sleep, like someone had just given him a sedative.

The last thing Hunter remembered thinking as he slipped off into unconsciousness was how much he loved his wife and unborn baby and how much he would give to see Lisa just one more time.

CHAPTER 55

An alarm trilled like a European police siren throughout the ship, signaling trouble with the ship's power plant. Phillips felt his stomach clench as he prepared for the worst. What the hell had Lilith—or someone—done to the power plant?

Or to the reactor core.

He could hear crewmembers yelling and running through the passageways and up and down steel ladders as they made their ways to their assigned duty stations for this latest crisis.

Jessica stared at the CO, as if wondering what to do next. The door to CIC remained closed. Whoever was inside probably knew what was going on in engineering, but Phillips didn't have time to interrogate them right now—he had to get down there.

"Seaman Blount, stay here with the XO and try to get them to open that door," Phillips said, then said to the XO, "You and Johnson keep the self-defense team here and be ready when that door opens, then get control of CIC ASAP. Sammy, be ready with that syringe and pop whoever comes out of that door first, got it?"

"Aye, captain. You can count on it," Sammy said.

"Mac, you come with me down to the number two engine room. That's where Lilith came from so I'm sure that's where the problem is."

Phillips and MacIntyre took off down the passageway to the nearest ladder and began their descent to the engineering deck far below.

*   *   *

The alarm finally stopped its shrill wailing and Jessica waited for the go-ahead from the XO to coax whoever was in CIC, out of CIC. He nodded to her, mouthing the words, "good luck."

She cleared her throat and tried to think of what she would say if she were still under Lilith's control. Then inspiration came.

"Lieutenant Sanchez," she said, hoping that was really who was in the room. "Open up."

No response.

Jessica rapped her knuckles on the steel door. "Lieutenant Sanchez...Joe, let me in. I have to talk to you."

A faint male voice came from the other side. "What do you want?" it said.

"Joe, Lilith doesn't have the phone. She dropped the phone in the water and told me to tell you to stand down as she was leaving in the admiral's barge."

Slight pause, then another voice, different from Sanchez. "How do we know you're not lying, Blount?"

"Why would I be lying? Lilith left the ship and doesn't want missiles hitting New York while she's there, that's all. The missile you launched did the trick and she was able to leave the ship."

A long pause of silence, then Jessica had another idea.

"Come on out, guys, and I'll do both of you. We'll

have a great time."

After a few seconds, Jessica could hear movement inside the room. Then, the door slowly began to unlock.

CHAPTER 56

Phillips and MacIntyre stood before the control panel in the maneuvering room of number two engine room, watching the neutron detector gauges going haywire as lights flashed and the siren continued to wail. A trickle of sweat dripped down Phillips' forehead but he ignored it.

"Jacobs, shut off the alarm," he yelled to a nearby watch stander. Seconds later, the siren wail ceased and only the sound of the steam turbines filled the room outside, muffled by the soundproof walls of the room.

Phillips eyed the gauges on the wall, his eyebrows knit with apprehension. He picked up the phone and called the watch stander at the reactor control panel. First class machinist mate Simpson picked up.

"What the hell's happening? It looks like the control rods are being pulled out," Phillips said. "Are we pulling them?"

"We're not pulling them, sir," Simpson said.

"What do we show—do we show them moving or not? Check the circuitry," Phillips said, unsure of whether the men in the engine room were under the influence of Lilith. He hated not being able to trust his own crew.

A few seconds later, Simpson said, "The circuitry indicates the rods are not moving, sir."

"They're moving!" Phillips spat. He realized he was beginning to lose his temper, and took several deep breaths as he considered the consequences of damaged control rods — nuclear meltdown. But he was determined that wasn't going to happen — not on his watch.

"Scram the reactor," he said to Jacobs.

The petty officer flipped several switches that would allow the control rods to descend to the bottom of the core, absorbing the alpha and gamma particles and stopping the nuclear reaction.

Phillips and MacIntyre watched the gauges, but the rate of reaction continued to increase.

"Shit," Phillips said.

"What's going on?" MacIntyre asked.

"The reactor core is overheating. Without the control rods, the reactor will run away and cause a meltdown of the nuclear fuel."

"What happens then?"

"It will probably overheat to the point that it catches the ship on fire, then you'll have a radioactive cloud hovering over New York Harbor and probably over the city, as well."

"Can't we move the ship?"

"There's no time — we only have minutes before it overheats."

"Surely there's something we can do."

Phillips shook his head slowly. "Not unless we replace those rods, but each rod is over ten feet long and weighs a half ton. My question is when the hell did Lilith do this? The alarms would have gone off almost immediately and she left the ship an hour ago."

"Captain, you have to let me go in there," MacIntyre

said.

Phillips eyed the commander warily. "Let you go in where? The reactor core? You'd be killed from the radiation, and besides, you'd need a chain hoist to lift those hafnium fuel rods."

"I wasn't being completely honest with you, captain, when I said I didn't have the same powers as my sister."

"What do you mean?"

"Remember when I told you I watched Lilith pick up the front end of a car once?"

Phillips nodded.

"Well, just to one-up her, I lifted the front end of an old school bus about three feet off the ground—with one hand."

Phillips stood silent, momentarily stunned. It was a little disconcerting to suddenly discover that your communications officer was Superman.

"You're shitting me, right?"

Mac was lying. He had no idea whether he could pick up any more weight than the barbells he lifted at the gym. But he had to try. If it was possible he was a Lilitu, then it was also possible he had the same powers as Lilith.

"What about the radiation?"

"I doubt that it will even affect me. It didn't seem to faze Lilith at all."

After all the crazy things Phillips had seen in the last few days, he figured letting Mac try to reinsert gigantic control rods into a runaway reactor core was a no-brainer. If he could prevent a meltdown, it would be worth whatever risk was incurred.

"Sure, what the hell. Go for it. You just have to guide them into the top of the core and they should fall all the way in. That will stop the reaction—that is, if we're not already too late."

Without a word, Mac opened the door to the engine room and ran out toward the reactor room, steel deck plates clanging under his feet. Phillips watched him go, praying that the man knew what the hell he was doing.

CHAPTER 57

After Jessica left Lisa's stateroom, Lisa felt as if she might go crazy thinking about Hunter and where he might be — or whether he was even alive. She needed a distraction and ended up next door in Blakely's stateroom, watching as he pored over the files in Lilith's laptop.

Blakely sat at his desk, his shock of red hair sticking out in all directions like a lawn that hadn't been mowed in months as he sipped his coffee and scrolled through page after page of files. Lisa sat next to him, trying her best to concentrate on the operative's actions instead of the morbid thoughts that raced through her own mind.

Blakely sighed. "There's a lot of stuff on here," he said. "It looks like she had a blog that she posted about the ecological balance between man and nature and so forth, plus articles for various magazines and websites. She's pretty prolific."

"I'm not impressed," Lisa said flatly.

The alarm that suddenly went off caused them both to jump.

"What the hell is that?" Lisa asked.

"I think that's the power plant casualty alarm. That probably doesn't bode well."

Lisa massaged her temples. "God, what else can go wrong around this place?"

"Lilith probably did something to the reactor. Let's hope they can contain whatever it is."

"Or what?"

Blakely frowned. "Or it's Chernobyl all over again."

Lisa felt like she was coming to the end of her rope. Being pregnant and then having your husband kidnapped by a crazy woman was bad enough, but now she was on board a floating bomb. Maybe it was time to start doing some serious praying, she thought.

*   *   *

George Saunders scrolled through the phone numbers listed on Lilith MacIntyre's cell phone and the bill from her work phone, looking for familiar numbers of incoming or outgoing calls and some clue as to what she might have been up to before she boarded the Ford. Most were the numbers of other magazines, staff members of her own organization and magazine, and the numbers of several political organizations.

But one number in particular interested Saunders. It was not suspicious in and of itself since it was a number that she would be expected to call quite regularly—her own stepfather. The troubling thing was, Lilith's stepfather was quite well connected in the Washington establishment and could easily acquire any documents he needed to get her on board the Ford. What's more, he also had access to lots of classified information concerning the mechanical workings of Navy ships and their personnel, something that would come in very handy for Lilith.

But Lilith's stepfather was also a patriot, or so it seemed. He had served in the military and had an exemplary record. It looked as if the two had shared a large number of phone calls over the last few months — more than usual. Of course, it could have been a family emergency or just a daughter wanting to talk to her father.

Saunders didn't like where this line of reasoning was leading. In fact, he hoped and prayed that what he was thinking was wrong, but decided to follow up on it anyway, just in case.

CHAPTER 58

As Jessica watched the handle on the door to CIC slowly move upward, Captain Geralds, Commander Johnson, Sammy and armed members of the ship's self-defense force crept silently forward, ready to spring into action the minute the door opened. Sammy held the syringes up, his thumbs on the plungers, ready to inject whoever exited the room.

The first person to look out the door, however, wasn't Lieutenant Duncan or a master at arms, but a huge first class gunner's mate named Dave Hodges. Before anyone could make a move, Hodges spotted the team in the passageway and slammed the door shut, then dogged it back down as Geralds and Johnson ran forward, grabbed the handle and tried to raise it back up.

*　　*　　*

Inside CIC, Sanchez watched Hodges use his considerable muscle to keep the door handle down, but it was a losing battle. Sanchez knew now that Jessica had been lying—Lilith had never spoken to her. It was a trap. That was too bad, because Sanchez was really hoping to have some more sex with her. Maybe he still would, he thought as he turned to push a button and fire the second missile.

*   *   *

Lieutenant Shelly Glasser, who had been on watch in CIC when Sanchez and Hodges had stormed in and duct taped her to the chair, craned her neck around to see behind her. Over the course of the last hour she had managed to loosen the tape on her legs and was now able to move them somewhat. She still couldn't move her hands, though, but she couldn't wait for that. Sanchez was about to fire another missile and she had to stop him. She was angry and frightened and had a good bit of adrenaline going—enough to help her do what she had to do.

Glasser placed her feet firmly on the deck and with every ounce of energy she could muster, launched herself backwards into Lieutenant Sanchez, hitting him squarely on the back of the knees and sending him banging face-first into the control panel, then sprawling to the floor.

Glasser was lying on her back and seeing stars, but from what she could surmise, Sanchez wasn't moving. Across the room, she saw Hodges finally lose his grip on the door handle, which caught him squarely under the chin on the way up and knocked him to the deck. She thought he probably lost a couple of teeth in the process. In seconds the room was full of officers and members of the self-defense force running toward them. Glasser recognized Seaman Blount, who darted over and cut off the rest of her bonds with a pocketknife.

The ship's chaplain quickly emptied one syringe of yellow serum into Hodges and another one into Sanchez. Immediately, the two men began convulsing and white liquid poured from their bodies.

Glasser thought she was going to be sick as she struggled to get off the floor and away from Sanchez. "What the hell?" she said.

"Don't worry, ma'am, it's just a parasite," Jessica said. "We've been killing those fuckers all day."

CHAPTER 59

MacIntyre stood before the watertight door of the reactor room. Its yellow and black sign resembled the hub of a wheel with DANGER, RADIATION HAZARD written in block letters beneath it. He was sure the radiation wouldn't harm him—at least, he was mostly sure. It hadn't harmed his sister that he knew of. But if the ship caught fire and contaminated the entire city of New York, whether he was irradiated or not wouldn't matter. It had to be stopped and he was the one to do it.

Mac said a silent prayer and undogged the door, releasing the watertight seal. He moved inside quickly and sealed the door shut behind him. It was hot as hell in there, like standing fully clothed in a sauna. He surveyed the room—there were pumps and valves everywhere and Mac was not trained in nuclear physics, so he had no idea what most of it was for. It looked just like any other engineering space on the ship, everything painted the usual deck gray and the pipes stenciled with arrows to show the liquid's direction of flow. The only noise in the space was from the water flow, which he knew was useless since the rods had been pulled. He could see the top of the huge pressure vessel that held the reactor core and noticed a ladder leading up the side. He ran to it and scrambled up as quickly as he could.

Immediately, Mac counted four rods lying horizontally on top of the pressure vessel. They were huge, about ten feet long and maybe four feet across. They looked like the columns that were sometimes used to reinforce the roofs of buildings. Did he actually believe he could pick those things up? Yet he had to—or people would die. Lots of people.

They didn't seem to be cracked, which was a major plus. They had a multi-colored layer of film covering them, like they were coated with some kind of oil. He hoped it wasn't oil, because that would make them slippery. He inhaled deeply, letting his mind and body relax, and concentrated all his focus on the task at hand. He leaned over to pick one up and was pulverized by a bone-crunching blow to the face. He fell backwards off the vessel, landing on the floor below with enough force to knock the wind out of him. He realized that somebody had kicked him in the face.

MacIntyre lay on his back trying to catch his breath when a pair of biker boots thudded hard on the steel deck in front of him—someone had leapt from the top of the pressure vessel. When he saw who it was, his jaw fell open. He had seen the man before, many years ago, with Lilith before she had started her organization. She said he was just a friend, though Mac had suspected much more. But he hadn't suspected this. The radiation had turned the man's eyes as silver as Lilith's had been—he was a Lilitu.

"Larry Hendricks," Mac said, still gasping for breath. "How the hell did you get onboard the ship?"

Hendricks sneered at him. "I prefer Lawrence," he said. "I got onboard the same way Lilith did—as part of the media group. You could have been one of us, John. But your love for the humans has made you weak, now you're just as impure as they are. I can't let you stop us, John. We've come too far. The radiation will make us strong and kill the humans that infest Manhattan. We will be the dominant life forms, repopulating the island and eventually the Earth."

"Sounds like you have high aspirations. But tell me, Lawrence, exactly who is Lilith going to be doing this repopulating with?"

Hendricks raised his brows and grinned. "Why, haven't you heard? Me, of course—who else?"

It was MacIntyre's turn to be impudent. "I hate to tell you this, Lawrence, but Lilith has already chosen a partner. You've been double-crossed."

Hendricks' eyes burned like lasers. "You're lying. What do you mean?"

"Before she left the ship, Lilith made them put Hunter Singleton into the admiral's barge with her. Apparently, she plans to make him the father of her new master race."

Mac thought Hendricks looked as if his head might explode. "That bitch!" Hendricks screamed. "I'll kill her— I swear I'll kill her."

Now totally oblivious to Mac, Hendricks walked past him to the door, opened it and raced out toward the engine room. Mac figured he would probably get off the ship and make his way to wherever Lilith was hiding in New York. He only hoped Hendricks could stop Lilith without killing her or harming Hunter.

Mac turned his attention to the task at hand—preventing a nuclear meltdown. He knew that confrontation with Hendricks had cost him precious seconds; seconds he didn't have. He peeled himself up off the floor and began climbing the ladder back to the top of the pressure vessel, praying that he wouldn't be too late.

CHAPTER 60

Sly Johnson undogged the blue, watertight door to the ship's brig and led the large group inside. Several of the sailors on the ship's self-defense force carried the limp forms of Hodges and Sanchez, who were still recovering from their ordeal with the parasites. They managed to wedge the men through the doorframe, where Johnson unlocked a steel mesh door leading down to the third deck and yet another watertight door that led into the actual brig.

They stood in an office with a large metal desk covered with papers weighed down by an old black rotary dial telephone. Sammy Crane, having never been inside the brig of the Ford, noticed a short passageway leading to several jail cells. Towards the back was a larger cell obviously meant for a general population. A colorful nautical mural painted on the starboard side bulkhead depicted the Ford at sea. A fire extinguisher and a water fountain occupied a corner and a couple of lockers stood next to them. There were charts along one wall with drawings of the cells where the master at arms could use a grease pencil to keep track of who was in which cell—on one of the cells was written the acronym CHENG. Sammy figured they must have sedated the poor bastard. A 1MC communications device was mounted directly below the chart.

The sailors carrying the two men whisked past Sammy and down the passageway to the general population area and carefully laid the two slumbering figures on a couple of the metal racks. The sailors made sure the two men were comfortable, turned and filed out of the cell, closing and locking the barred metal door behind them.

Once the men were secured in the cell, the XO crossed his arms and studied Crane.

"Sammy, I want to know what the hell is in that concoction of yours. It isn't toxic, is it?"

Sammy frowned. "Toxic? Of course not. I wouldn't give something toxic to my own crew. To tell you the truth, I don't know all the ingredients because the CIA won't tell me, but I do know that it's mostly garlic vinegar."

The XO raised one eyebrow. "Garlic vinegar? You're kidding me. I thought garlic was for vampires."

Sammy shook his head. "Once we figured out they were parasitic in nature, we started trying different drugs like Vermox and Mintezol, but they had a lot of side effects and believe it or not, the garlic vinegar seemed to work the best—they hate that stuff. And when they leave the host, as you saw, they evaporate almost immediately, like a volatile liquid."

There were a few moments of silence as the gears seemed to turn inside the XO's head. He suddenly grabbed the 1MC and called Captain Phillips in the number two engine room. After about a minute of conversation, he hung up the phone and turned back to the chaplain.

"Sammy, I want you to go to your stateroom and bring every last ounce of that stuff here to the brig," Geralds said. "If you have any unused hypos, bring those, too."

Geralds turned to one of the enlisted sailors. "Bennett,

go to sickbay and tell them we're going to need all the corpsmen they can spare down here in the brig. Tell them to bring every damn hypo they have."

*   *   *

Boxes with thousands of hypodermic needles were brought and stacked in the brig's main office. Every person in the brig besides the three men in the cells was inoculated with Sammy's concoction. They tried to come up with a name for the yellowish liquid and since it was a mix of garlic and vinegar, decided to call it "Gin," which Sammy found quite amusing — Gin and Tonic was one of his favorite drinks.

The toughest part was assembling the entire crew, except for watch standers, on the hangar deck of the Ford under the pretense of inoculating them against a rampant and dangerous flu virus. Once on the hangar deck, the self-defense force, along with the master at arms staff, armed themselves with Berettas and M16s and surrounded the crew at evenly spaced intervals just in case someone decided they wanted to make a break for it. The crew eyed them warily. Once everything was in place, the corpsmen, doctors and even the chaplain's staff began the monumental task of inoculating several thousand people, going division by division, row by row. To the dismay of their fellow sailors, a number of the crew crumpled to the deck when the Gin hit their bloodstream and the white, milky liquid poured out of their bodies, slowly evaporating into thin air. It was all the guards could do to keep the sailors from bolting in all directions when they saw the parasites for the first time.

CHAPTER 61

Sweat poured off of Mac like raindrops as he wrapped his arms around the first huge control rod. There had to be no doubt in his mind that he could lift the hafnium rods. There was no choice. But was he already too late? Mac was no expert in nuclear fission and he didn't know how long the fuel would continue to heat until it reached the point of no return. He only prayed that the rods would work and stop the reaction before a total meltdown could occur.

Mac hefted the half-ton rod as if he was lifting a heavy bag of groceries. At first, he thought he was going to get a hernia. Then the rod started to move. With every ounce of focus, he willed himself to lift the rod and drag it across the top of the pressure vessel, inching it over to one of the holes. He hoped that all the holes and rods were the same size and that each hole wasn't made for a specific rod. He moved to the last hole in the row and stood over the opening, edging his way around other rods and straining to keep the huge rod from slipping out of his grasp, then gently released pressure until it slid down into the hole next to the oversized electromagnetic control motor. The rod went nearly all the way to the bottom of the pressure vessel, which he hoped was a good sign.

Mac continued the procedure with each rod, dropping them one by one into the vessel until the last one was finally in place. From his perch he checked out the room for anything that seemed out of place. Hendricks probably figured no one would be able to replace the rods so he didn't bother doing any other damage. Thank God he hadn't ripped out one of the cooling water pipes — they probably wouldn't have been able to fix that, though they could have still used the control rods to scram the reactor, Mac thought.

He remembered that he was soaking up a ton of radiation, then walked to the edge of the vessel and climbed down. Mac made one last sweep of the room before opening the watertight door and heading out to the engine room to see whether the reactor was stable or if they were soon going to die.

*   *   *

The CO saw the reactor core temperature climb to fifty-one hundred degrees as his stomach bunched up into knots. Another one hundred degrees and he and the rest of the crew and probably most of Manhattan Island could kiss their asses goodbye. Just then he noticed someone, a man he recognized from the media crew, whiz by the control room. What the hell was that about? Was that guy one of *them*? That would explain how the reactor got screwed up. Phillips decided he would have to worry about that later and hoped Mac was making some kind of progress.

He raised an arm and wiped it across his brow, transferring some, but not all of the sweat. He desperately wanted to run to the hangar deck and see how things were going, but he dared not leave the engineering space. Phillips wondered exactly how much stress a human body could take, because he figured he had just about reached the breaking point by now.

When he was an ensign, Phillips had once seen the chief engineer escorted off the ship after having a nervous breakdown. Someone in the crew who had no desire to experience a six-month Mediterranean cruise had sneaked into the engine room and dropped a large bolt into the reduction gear casing, which the CHENG had inadvertently left open. When the main shaft had been engaged for a test, the reduction gear, a half-million dollar piece of equipment, was damaged beyond repair. The next day, the CHENG was gone.

As Phillips watched the gauges, the temperature suddenly leveled off and began moving in the opposite direction—fifty-one hundred, five thousand, four-thousand fifty, four thousand degrees. Relief washed over the captain as he realized MacIntyre had been successful in replacing the rods. As he had that thought, he saw Mac making his way through the engine room toward the watch stander's station.

Phillips opened the door and Mac, who was completely drenched in sweat, stepped into the soundproof room. The commander went directly to an air conditioning vent where the cool forced air blasted the heat from his body. Phillips stared at him slack-jawed.

"Well, is the temp going down? How are we doing?" Mac said.

Phillips replied after several seconds. "Yeah, great job. The temperature is steadily decreasing."

The staring continued.

"Something wrong?" Mac asked.

"Mac, your eyes. They're silver, just like Lilith's."

CHAPTER 62

Lisa lay in the rack in her stateroom, tears staining her pillow.

Every time she closed her eyes she saw Hunter's face, his goofy smile, felt his hot breath on her cheek, tasted his sweet kisses. It was almost unbearable to think of him with that monster that called herself a woman. Lisa had never felt so much like killing in her life, but right now she knew she could do it easily. She wanted to crush the life out of Lilith with her bare hands. Lisa knew it probably wasn't the Christian way to feel, but she figured if God had righteous anger, then so could she. She just wanted her husband back and would do anything to make that happen.

Was he in danger? Was he locked up somewhere like a slave? Was he even alive? There was no way to answer any of those questions and Lisa had never felt as hopeless as she did right then.

She laid a hand on her belly, thinking about the life that now grew inside of her. Hunter's baby. She hoped it would have his eyes—Lisa loved Hunter's eyes and warmed at the thought of them, sparkling and golden in the sunlight. She could almost hear his voice whispering in her ear, feel his fingers massaging her shoulders, caressing her cheek. But now, he was gone, somewhere out there in the darkness of Manhattan. Was he thinking of her? She hoped so.

Intense emotion coursed through Lisa's heart like a river of flame that threatened to burn the life from her. The tears fell like a rainstorm to quench the fire and fell long and hard until her pillow was soaked and Lisa finally drifted off to sleep.

PART FOUR: METAMORPHOSIS

CHAPTER 63

The days ran together in a blur. Hunter watched people come and go, remembered voices, but not words. He was aware of his own thoughts, but it was as if another person was inside his head thinking them, like someone had taken control and he was only along for the ride. He reeked of body odor and his head throbbed with pain, but he didn't care.

When he had awakened after arriving at the apartment, he couldn't remember who he was, where he had come from or much of anything about his past life. His clothes were soaked, but it hadn't been raining. Had he fallen in the water? Hunter only knew one thing—he had to please Lilith. She was all that mattered now. The thought of her was intoxicating, like a powerful drug that constantly needed to be resupplied. Yet there were fleeting shadows, vague recollections of another life. It was like trying to remember a dream.

He had spent his time doing things for Lilith, but he didn't remember what. The city outside was like a wasteland. Something had happened there—a storm, maybe? It had been nearly destroyed. There was trash in all the streets, many of the storefront windows were shattered and buildings flooded, vehicles were smashed, dead birds and other animals lay strewn about. The city was strangely void of people. It was like the aftermath of an apocalypse.

The apartment where they stayed was spacious, a brownstone somewhere in Manhattan, well-decorated with a huge rain-forest mural on one wall, a big, well-used kitchen and art deco-style furniture. It was *her* apartment, though she shared it with several others. Hunter was actually hoping those others would eventually leave so he and Lilith could be alone.

A sudden primal scream from a room down the hall pierced the silence, invading his daydream and sending a chill through Hunter's spine. It sounded like some kind of large animal. Then he remembered—something was happening to Lilith. She was changing, mutating. At least, that was what the others had said. Lilith had become unhinged, enraged about an event that should have occurred aboard the USS Ford, a Navy carrier that sat just inside New York Harbor. Something about a meltdown. She said that someone had prevented it and vowed to crush the life out of them, whoever it was. She launched into a tirade, throwing a lamp at the TV and smashing the screen, then punching her fist through the wall of the apartment.

That was when Lilith noticed the bumps on her arms. They were dry and patchy, like the scales of a reptile. At first, they began to appear on her legs, then on her face and in a matter of hours covered her entire body. She was growing a second skin. Lilith was frantic, locking herself in her room and refusing to come out.

Then the screams began. That was when the others started to leave, one by one, until no one was left but Hunter.

Whatever she was becoming, he didn't care. He only wanted to serve her. Didn't he?

But something wasn't quite right. There were memories of a past life, subconscious thoughts that he just couldn't quite reach though he tried to dig as far down as he could, desperate to bring them to the surface. He sat on a couch in the living room, staring at the smashed TV, thoughts running rampant through his confused mind. A golden shaft of morning sun filtered through the windows, illuminating the clouds of dust that swirled in the stale air. Had he eaten? He couldn't remember. He didn't seem to have much appetite.

A face suddenly rose unbidden in his mind's eye—a woman's face—olive skin with amazing, curly black hair that fell about slender shoulders; a smell, like the sweetest honeysuckle; a beautiful face, tender and mesmerizing. It was saying his name as tears streaked down her lovely cheeks. Hunter could almost remember…almost…

Then the front door crashed open.

*   *   *

"So, there you are," the stranger said, looking Hunter over as he sat on the couch. The man was short, about Hunter's size, sporting blue jeans, biker boots and a black *Rancid* T-shirt. His head was shaved. He had no facial hair and wore a scowl that seemed to be permanent judging by the lines in his face. He was thin but wiry and he looked pissed.

But the most striking thing was his silver eyes.

"Giving any more lessons in naval history, asshole?" the man asked.

Hunter had no idea what he was talking about.

"Who are you, again?"

The man nodded in understanding.

"Lilith has you under her control, doesn't she? Well, the name is Hendricks and I'm your worst nightmare."

Before Hunter could react, Hendricks reached down, grabbed Hunter by the shirt collar and tossed him across

211

the room like a piece of crumpled up paper. Hunter hit two of the kitchen chairs, slamming them into the oak table and knocking it on its side. He lay on the floor in a daze, wondering who the hell this guy was and what he was angry about. Hunter's back would probably be bruised from where he had hit the chairs, and it hurt like hell.

Hendricks advanced toward him. Hunter sprang from the floor in one fluid movement and stood head-on with his knees slightly flexed and fists up in a Kung Fu stance, ready for another assault. When it came, Hunter was ready. Hendricks took a swing and Hunter deflected it with a sweep of his arm, using his free hand to land a lightning-quick blow to the man's solar plexus, effectively leaving him breathless and bent forward. Hunter kneed him in the face, sending him flying backwards, blood from his broken nose spraying the room like a geyser.

Hunter felt like he was watching the whole scene from another perspective, like a mind-out-of-body experience.

"Where the hell did I learn that?" he murmured.

But Hendricks didn't fall. He had maintained his footing and now was angrier than ever. He charged ahead at Hunter like a raging rhino. Hunter had no doubt that he would be pulverized, but he wouldn't be taken down easily. He braced for the impact of Hendricks' body crashing into his.

The collision never came. A white blur flew violently across the room, landing directly on Hendricks and taking him to the floor like a deflated balloon. The thing howled in rage, a sound that was unnaturally loud and inhuman. Bits of cloth mixed with flesh and blood sprayed up around the two figures like a hail of gruesome confetti. Even with his great strength, Hendricks had no chance against this beast.

Hunter felt a wave of nausea wash over him and then he realized who the monster was—Lilith. She was naked and the scales had disappeared, leaving in their place skin covered with pale, white fur. From behind he could see that her once lustrous blonde hair now hung in only a few strands. Her feet had elongated into the hind legs of a quadruped, the toes ending in curved claws. Lilith had also gotten much, much larger and more powerful, a lethal combination of animal, human and demon. He could hear a low, guttural growl, like a wolf enjoying a fresh kill.

He was glad that she was facing away and so he couldn't see her face.

As Hunter stood mesmerized by the scene, someone touched his shoulder and he spun around. It was a woman, one that had been part of the group that had brought Hunter to the apartment. Her name was Gabrielle Lincoln, or "Gabe" as everyone called her, and she was quite easy on the eyes—a tall, thin brunette with long legs and a red dragon tattoo on her left shoulder. She seemed to favor wearing tight-fitting jeans and T-shirts, which was okay with Hunter. But her deep brown eyes were conveying a message, a message of urgency.

"We need to get out of here while she's busy," Gabe whispered in her Australian accent. Hunter found it quite alluring and in fact had thought about talking to Gabe, if only he could get the image of that other woman out of his head.

"Why would we want to get out of here?" Hunter asked. "This is where we belong, isn't it?"

The woman glanced at the back of the temporarily-occupied creature crouching over the broken and bloody lump of flesh that was Hendricks and Hunter thought he saw a flash of fear in her eyes.

Then he felt the cold barrel of a gun against his ribs.

"Move," Gabe said.

Hunter looked down at the pistol and back up at Gabe. Left with no other choice, he walked toward the door of the apartment and away from Lilith.

CHAPTER 64

The USS Ford had finally pulled into port and now sat moored at pier eighty-eight on Manhattan Island, twin electrical cables as big around as a human thigh running across her deck and down to the pier where they connected to a temporary power station. With her now-functioning reactors and generators, the ship was supplying about two hundred megawatts of power to ConEd and the city. The Ford also provided the use of her satellite-based communications, as well as temporary air traffic control assistance for LaGuardia Airport, which had been severely damaged during the hurricane.

The Red Cross, several teams of medical experts and scores of volunteers were provided room and board in either spare staterooms or tents that had been set up on the hangar deck. The medical facilities on board the ship were practically full. Many who had lost their homes in the storm or who had already been homeless were brought aboard the Ford until they could be provided more permanent shelter in New York. The flight deck, the hangar deck and pretty much everywhere else on the ship was a flurry of activity.

Mac stood on the flight deck, peering over at the USS Intrepid Sea, Air and Space Museum and beyond that, the Lincoln Tunnel. The Intrepid, an old aircraft carrier, was huge, Mac realized, though not as big as the Ford. Several old jet planes and turboprops and a white domed building sat on its flight deck. Buildings lined the pier next to the ship and he could see that several had been severely damaged, mostly with their roofs torn off from the high winds. He wondered how the ship had survived the hurricane and figured its sheer size probably kept it from being demolished. He was surprised to see that the pier didn't seem to have sustained much damage.

Toward 49th Street and across the Hudson Greenway Mac saw more broken buildings and washed-out cars. He wondered where Lilith was. She could be practically anywhere and may even have left the city, but he doubted it. In fact he was sure she hadn't. She wanted to start her new master race right here in one of the biggest cities in the world. That would make much more of a statement—civilization brought to ruination by Lilith. But her plans to overload the reactor had failed and he knew that had made her furious. She would be out for blood.

He wondered if Hunter was still hanging on and how many other people she had brought under her power since leaving the Ford. Perhaps she now had a whole army.

After hacking into her laptop, Blakely had found an address for a brownstone apartment that Lilith had rented under the name Julia Lambert. Mac knew that was probably where she was—holed up there and working on her plans of domination and destruction. But Mac knew that if she wasn't stopped soon, she and her kind—*his* kind—would repopulate the city. Once that happened, the fate of the human race would be sealed.

Blakely said the area for miles around the brownstone

had been quarantined by the DOD. No one would be allowed in or out until Lilith was either captured or terminated.

Terminated, like squashing a bug or killing a rodent. But it was his sister and in spite of what she had become he still had some feelings for her. They had a history together, had lived together as children. He had watched her grow up, tried to be a good big brother, always watching out for her even though she probably didn't care.

But he should have done more. When their dog Tater had died, he should have been more understanding, helped her find her moral compass. Then Daddy had passed away and she became another person, someone he didn't even know. Mac felt like he had let her down and now it had come to this. It wasn't fair. And it wasn't right.

"Dammit, Lilith, why?" he muttered to himself, then headed off to a meeting with the CO.

CHAPTER 65

Lilith leaned over the dead and bloody form of Hendricks. She felt nothing in killing him. He was a Lilitu, but would never have evolved as she had. He was inferior. Over the last few days she had…changed. The growth was painful, almost more than she could endure, but she did endure it.

Now she felt strong, alive, as if she could do anything.

Nearly all traces of her humanity had disappeared. Lilith was no longer ruled by her emotions, but only by intellect and by animal instinct. Her senses had been heightened beyond human limits—she could hear the squeaking of rats and the crawling legs of a cockroach inside the walls of her apartment; she was able to discern one person from another from the smell of their sweat; Lilith could not only see in the dark like a cat, but she could see through walls and through skin, down to the bones like an X-ray machine.

Lilith found she no longer needed clothes. Her fur-covered hide was tougher than leather, yet resilient and flexible. Her claws were retractable and as sharp as razor blades, yet her fingers were still nimble enough to manipulate the smallest things. She also found that she was fast, as fast as a cheetah, and ten times as powerful. There was nothing on earth that could stop her.

Lilith surveyed the apartment. Hunter was gone and now she would have to find him. Hunter was her prize and she wasn't about to let him go this easily. She would track him down with her heightened senses and make him her permanent slave.

She laid a clawed hand on the warm flesh of her belly and thought about the life that now grew there. Not just one baby, but dozens, maybe hundreds, and she would soon give birth to them. But not here.

She turned her enormous head and looked over at the door of the apartment. Hunter had gone out there only moments before. Lilith sniffed the air. He wasn't alone. He was also with someone else...Gabrielle.

So, Gabe had betrayed her. Lilith had never trusted the woman. Lilith raised a claw and marveled at it like a piece of grotesque art, turned it over, inspected it. An extremely efficient weapon, she thought. She would use it to kill Gabe — very, very slowly. She smiled, baring rows of razor-sharp teeth that glistened like ivory in the sunlight.

Lilith stepped over the wet, oozing mass of flesh that had been her former lover, then made her way to the door and out into the streets of Manhattan.

CHAPTER 66

Hunter walked ahead of Gabe as she held her gun at his back. She hated having to take him this way, but he had left her no choice. He obviously wasn't going to go willingly. Now it was up to her to get Hunter to a secure location and administer the antidote for the parasites she knew now infected him. Once that was done, she would have to wait until he recovered, which could take up to twenty-four hours. Since the area around Broadway had been quarantined, she figured their best bet would be to follow Park Terrace all the way to Isham Park. She could sleep on a park bench and just wait for Hunter to return to his old self. Not the most desirable way to spend the night, but the most practical under the circumstances.

They walked along Park Terrace East, passing the apartments and businesses that lined the road, mostly five- or six-story red brick buildings with fire escapes at each level and a tree here or there. Virtually every tree had been toppled by the hurricane, smashing windows where they had landed on the buildings, busting down fences or caving in the tops of cars. Most of the power and telephone lines were buried underground since there wasn't much room in Manhattan for utility poles. It was strange not to hear traffic noise, except for the occasional siren, or see any people in one of the biggest cities in the world.

They followed the sidewalk as it curved around into a cul-de-sac with an island of trees and bushes in the center, past several red NO STANDING signs and eventually came to the entrance of the park, bracketed by two short concrete pillars. They passed through and continued walking, Gabe about two paces behind Hunter. They hadn't spoken most of the way there and Hunter apparently had decided it was time.

"So, do you always use a gun on your first date?" he quipped.

"I'm glad you at least retained a sense of humor. Do you remember anything about the last few days?"

"Not really. I know my name is Hunter, but something happened to the rest of my memory, like it's been wiped clean. I guess I'm lucky I still remember how to speak."

"Well, Hunter, we're going to fix that very soon."

"Who are you with, anyway? You're not really with Lilith, are you? You're some kind of law enforcement, right?"

"CIA."

As they went deeper into the park, Gabe saw there was quite an abundance of green open space and decided to forego the park bench and instead camp out under a tree. That would provide shelter and the grass was probably more comfortable than a wooden park bench, anyway.

"Come on, let's go this way," she said, indicating an open area with a tree in the center. "We'll rest here temporarily."

"What are we resting for? Are we going somewhere?"

Gabe decided it would be futile to try explaining things to Hunter in his present condition.

"I'll tell you later," she said.

They approached a large dogwood tree with flowers

sprouting up from the branches in tiny white explosions.

"Take a seat in the grass," she said.

Gabe reached inside her back pocket and pulled out a small canvas case with a zipper around it. She tossed it down to Hunter as he got comfortable with his back to the tree.

"Open it," she said.

Hunter picked up the case, unzipped it and pulled out a small glass vial of yellow liquid.

"Open the lid and drink it. All of it," Gabe said.

Hunter opened the lid and inspected the contents. He took a sniff, made a sour face and glanced at Gabe.

"All of it?" he asked.

Gabe simply nodded her head, the barrel of her gun still pointing at him.

Hunter shrugged his shoulders and downed the liquid in one gulp. He threw the vial in the grass and screwed his face into a grimace.

"Holy shit, that's worse than cod liver oil," he said, and tried to spit the taste out of his mouth.

But then something happened. The white liquid began appearing on his brow almost immediately. He wiped his hand across it and stared at his fingers.

"What the hell did you do to me?" he said.

Hunter began oozing more of the liquid from all the pores of his body and stood up in the grass looking down at himself. He stripped off his shirt as the liquid continued secreting from his dark skin, like all the white blood cells suddenly decided to leave his body. This was the first parasite Gabe had seen and she found herself backing away as Hunter stumbled around in the grass.

The liquid trickled from his nose and ears and finally came up his throat. He fell down on his hands and knees and began vomiting rivers of white, and Gabe could hear him choking and trying to suck in a breath between each wave.

When his eyes started to tear up, Hunter screamed that he couldn't see, flailing his hands around like a blind man. After a few minutes, the parasite had released its grip on Hunter and he fell over on the grass, looking completely exhausted and in shock.

Gabe watched the parasite as it formed a puddle, every drop coming together like tiny balls of white mercury being sucked into a black hole. The puddle undulated and rippled, then stood up on end like a groundhog searching for its shadow. Gabe took a few cautious steps back and the white shape slowly melted back into a puddle, then became smaller and smaller as it evaporated.

Once she was sure the creature was gone, Gabe stuck the pistol back into her waist band, walked over to Hunter and gently rolled him onto his side. His dark hair was matted with sweat and his eyes moved under the lids like a dreamer in REM sleep. He groaned and Gabe could hear him softly whisper a name.

"Lisa," he said.

Gabe knew that Lisa was Hunter's wife, who was back at the Ford waiting for him.

"Don't worry, Hunter, you'll be back with her soon, I guarantee it," she whispered.

She picked up the shirt Hunter had taken off and covered him with it, sat down on the grass, edged her back against the tree and stared up at the quickly darkening sky.

It was going to be a long night, she thought. She reached into her pocket and pulled out her cell phone, punched autodial and waited while the phone rang. Someone picked up.

"I've got him," Gabe said. "We're in Isham Park."

"Good," George Saunders said. "Now all we have to do is wait."

CHAPTER 67

Lisa knew that something was about to happen because her gut was in knots.

They had finally pulled into New York Harbor and tied up at the pier. Soon hundreds of people had begun coming aboard looking forlorn and destitute. She imagined that they had probably lost everything. Her heart ached for them. Earlier she had seen a small boy and a girl with no shoes walking across the hangar deck, their clothes ragged and dirty, reminding her of children from a third-world country. They looked tired and worn out, like they had been through hell. Their parents looked even worse, the father carrying all they had in the world in a tattered backpack flung over his shoulder. The little girl saw Lisa and smiled shyly. Lisa smiled back.

But in spite of their misery and Lisa's empathy for them, her first priority was finding her husband. She hoped he was still out there and she knew they would be searching for him and for Lilith and her accomplices.

As she stepped out from between the planes and helicopters, she saw MacIntyre walking across the flight deck and hurried over to catch him.

Mac looked surprised to see her and stopped.

"Ms. Singleton, how are you?" he asked.

She was jolted by his silver eyes, but tried not to show it.

"You can just call me Lisa," she said.

"And you can call me Mac."

"Well, Mac, I was wondering if there is going to be a search party going ashore to look for my husband."

"That was the plan."

"That's great, because I want to go."

She could tell Mac was stunned. Women just didn't go into combat in the Navy.

"Look, Lisa, I know you want your husband back, but this is a dangerous mission. We're going after a killer. And there's no telling what she may do. It's just not safe."

Lisa knew they would probably balk at her request and she was ready.

"I understand your concern, Mac, but I'm a trained law-enforcement officer and believe me when I say I've been in situations just as dangerous. You've got to let me help. Besides, I'm in way over my head and I have a personal stake in this case."

There was a long pause as Mac seemed to study her.

* * *

Lisa, Phillips, the XO, Johnson and MacIntyre stood around the desk in the CO's stateroom.

"I'm not really comfortable with this," Phillips said, eyeing Lisa. "You're not part of my crew and I can't take responsibility for a civilian..."

"I'm not a civilian," Lisa interrupted. "I'm a park ranger and I am trained to use weapons in dangerous situations. If it makes any difference, I'm also a fourth-degree black belt in Kung Fu."

If Phillips was impressed, he didn't let on. "I simply

can't take responsibility for your safety."

Lisa sighed, exasperated by hard-headed men. "Look, captain, if you don't let me go with the team then I'll go on my own."

"If you try it, I'll be forced to confine you to your quarters, Lisa, and I really don't want to do that."

"Dammit, captain, that's my husband out there. How would you feel if your daughter or your wife was being held hostage by that monster? Would you just stand by and do nothing?"

Phillips shook his head. "No, I wouldn't."

Lisa took a deep breath and calmed herself. "Captain, all I'm asking is for you to let me do my job as a trained law enforcement officer. Try to look past the fact that I'm a woman."

"Your gender has nothing to do with it."

"Then what does?"

Seconds ticked by. Phillips crossed his arms and seemed as if he was determined not to give in. But he did.

"You will take orders from the Special Ops commander, is that clear? We don't want any more casualties. And you will use your weapon only when told to do so. Have you ever used a Beretta?"

Lisa nodded. "I carry a Beretta myself. Standard issue."

Phillips glanced at Johnson. "Issue Ms. Singleton a weapon, a holster and some ammo."

"Yes sir."

"Sly—you, Mac, Sammy, Ms. Singleton, Blakely and I will be joining a team that the CIA is sending. I don't know much about them, except that they're Special Ops and they're going to be in charge. We're going to be there to assist them since we have first-hand knowledge about Lilith and everything that's been going on. Just do whatever they ask us to do. We'll meet with them in the Fighting 31 Squadron ready room at 0700 to go over the details."

Phillips leaned toward Lisa and placed both hands on his desk.

"I don't think I have to tell you, Lisa, that Lilith is not going to be happy to see you, especially since Hunter is your husband. She is going to want to eliminate the competition."

"Don't worry, captain," she said. "I'm ready for anything that bitch can dish out."

CHAPTER 68

The light that filtered through his closed eyelids felt to Hunter like someone was banging on his forehead with a sledgehammer. He scrunched his eyes closed more tightly, then slowly let them loosen up until they finally fluttered open.

He lay sideways on the grass in what looked like someone's front yard or maybe a park. He felt like he had been hit by a truck. He lowered his right arm, put his hand flat on the ground and slowly pushed himself up. The blood drained out of his head and caused some dizziness, filling his vision with little dancing white and blue lights. He sat up on the grass and looked around.

A few yards away were a sidewalk and a park bench, so he was definitely in a park, but where? The last thing he remembered was falling through a rickety pier at the 79th Street Boat Basin and Lilith kissing him while he dangled helplessly in the water. He had to be somewhere in New York, probably still in Manhattan. The park didn't look big enough to be Central Park unless he was near the outer edge somewhere.

He swiveled around to look behind him and saw a dogwood tree and leaning against it was a beautiful, raven-haired woman in dark sunglasses.

"Hey. I see you're awake," the woman said.

Hunter was speechless for nearly a minute as the gears turned in his head, trying to dredge up a name. There was nothing. The woman laughed.

"Don't worry about trying to remember who I am, Hunter," she said. "You've been through quite an ordeal. You're lucky—most people don't usually come out of it this quickly."

Whoever she was, she had an Australian accent. Hunter repositioned himself in the grass until he was facing her. She wore a lavender short-sleeved shirt and on her upper right arm was a long, red, Chinese dragon tattoo.

"So, you know who I am," he said. "But I still don't know who you are, or where I am, or how I got here, or…"

The woman cut Hunter off before he could ask another question.

"Whoa, one question at a time, mate," she said. "First of all, the name is Gabrielle Lincoln, but everyone calls me Gabe. You're in northern Manhattan, in a place called Isham Park and you walked here. With a little coercion on my part, I might add."

Hunter blinked at her. "How long was I out?"

"I wouldn't say you were out, exactly, just under the influence of one of Lilith's parasites. It's been about two days since you first came to us."

Hunter grimaced. "That's what I was afraid of. What exactly did I do in that time? Or do I want to know?"

"Not much, really. The group mainly spent time gathering supplies and just biding our time. Nobody was really sure what was going to happen next. My group wasn't infected with parasites. We were supposedly her loyal followers." Gabe made quote marks in the air with her fingers at the word "loyal."

"A lot of them worked with her at the magazine and had gone to some of her protests. But when she tore the place up and then started to mutate, the others were afraid she would kill them and they left. I can't blame them. She was already psychotic and now she's not even human. She killed Hendricks and he was a Lilitu, like her. Apparently that's not enough."

"So you're not one of them?"

"CIA," she said and told Hunter the story of how she had infiltrated the organization. Hunter was impressed with her skills and felt glad that she was on his side.

"Where did all this happen?" he asked.

"We rented an apartment a few blocks from here. But believe me, nobody in the group knew about her overloading the reactor except for Hendricks. Even the crazy ones in the group thought that was over the top. That was one of the reasons they left. She would have fried us along with everyone else in the city."

"So what happens now?"

Gabe shrugged. "Now, we head back to the ship and let Special Ops handle it from here. They're probably already in the city."

"What will they do when they find her?"

"What do you think? They'll blow her to shit, of course."

"I don't think she'll wait that long."

"What do you mean?"

Hunter's mind was racing a mile a minute with scenarios he really didn't want to consider.

"I mean, she's not going to just let me walk away. She's going to come after me. Wherever I go, she's going to follow. If I go back to the ship, she's going to follow me there. Lilith isn't one who just gives up what she believes is hers."

"That's a good point. I think I should call in and see what they want us to do."

"I already know what they're going to say—'get the civilian out of harm's way and let the Special Ops team handle it.' But the problem with that is she doesn't care about Special Ops teams. She'll rip through them like a polar bear in a herd of caribou."

"I'm open to suggestions," Gabe said.

"I'm working on it."

CHAPTER 69

After a hot shower and breakfast in the officer's mess, Lisa was feeling better. She had gotten over her morning sickness for the time being and even though she was still worried, a lot of praying had boosted her faith that they would find Hunter and bring him back alive. She knew it would take more than firepower to win against Lilith, no matter how many men or weapons they had. But the weight of a nine-millimeter Beretta would still feel good against her torso, like a lucky rabbit's foot. She hoped she wouldn't have to use it, but sometimes things didn't always work out the way you hoped. Lisa had never shot anyone and she certainly didn't want to start now. But if she had to end up shooting Lilith, she could probably live with that.

Lisa smiled at the thought as she transited down the narrow ship's passageway on her way aft to the ready room, stepping through doorways and around ogling sailors.

Ready rooms were normally reserved for pilots and their squadron commanders to go over the day's routine and for pilots to relax and await their turn to launch. But Captain Phillips decided that although this wasn't an airborne mission, it was still a mission and he needed a good place to meet with the CIA ops team.

Lisa finally arrived at the door with its giant yellow logo featuring Felix the Cat smiling and carrying a bomb in his paws. Along the bottom of the logo in block letters it read, FIGHTING 31. She knocked on the door.

"Come," a voice said.

Lisa pushed the door open and saw that the room was filled with men she knew and men she didn't know. It was wall-to-wall testosterone. She sighed and stepped across the threshold. All eyes were on her, a few looking more like leers than stares.

She passed a coffee bar with a popcorn maker where a couple of men in dark civilian clothes watched her walk by. The seats in the ready room were set up like the chairs of a movie theater. Several men craned their necks, quickly assessing her without trying to be too obvious. In front of the room was a dry-erase board and next to that a big-screen TV showing the currently inactive flight deck. Against one wall was a bar with barstools where the pilots could drink and every once in a while maybe get a beer if any was on board.

"Ms. Singleton, glad you could make it," Phillips said.

The familiar faces of MacIntyre, Blakely, Johnson, Captain Geralds, Sammy and a few others peppered the room. The ones in civilian garb she figured were the Special Ops guys the captain had mentioned the previous night.

Lisa walked to where she saw Mac sitting and took a seat next to him.

"Did you sleep okay?" he whispered.

"Not really," she whispered back.

* * *

Toby Tate

The Special Activities Division of the CIA, an outgrowth of the World War II-era Office of Strategic Services, was one of the legacies of the global war on terror. Created to perform the most difficult operations imaginable, its members have traveled to every corner of the globe, from the Middle East to South America, rescuing hostages, rooting out insurgents, destroying enemy strongholds, disseminating propaganda and even overthrowing governments. The elite of the elite, SAD handpicks its candidates from U.S. Special Forces units like the Navy SEALS and Delta Force, sending them through months of rigorous training and making them experts in everything from espionage and intelligence to small arms and ordinance.

The paramilitary arm of SAD, called the Special Operations Group, answers directly to the president and the National Security Council. Unattached to any arm of the military, the covert actions of SOG officers can be disavowed by the president.

But Lisa figured that this particular operation was new even for the SOG. They had probably never dealt with anyone...or anything...like Lilith.

In the front of the ready room, Phillips stood by a younger man dressed in a black vest, T-shirt and jeans with a close-cropped haircut and a dark goatee. He had a neck as big around as his head and a chiseled face that held a serene confidence. A small scar ran across the bridge of a nose that looked as if it had been broken at least once. Lisa could see by his well-defined biceps that he obviously worked out and trained consistently. She could see a hardness in his eyes, cool and calculating—the eyes of a trained killer. Yet his demeanor communicated a sense of humanity.

Behind the two men was a diagram on the white board that looked like plans for a football game strategy.

There were several people talking amongst themselves when Phillips raised his hands over his head indi-

233

cating quiet.

"Alright, listen up," he said. "This is Jason Fredrichs of the CIA's Special Operations Group and he will be in command of this operation. You take orders from him and act only when he says. We will be assisting, so you are to take no action of your own unless authorized." Phillips swept a hand toward his left. "Mr. Fredrichs?"

As Phillips walked away, Fredrichs stepped into his place and stood with hands behind his back.

"First off, just call me Jason—this Mr. Fredrichs shit ain't gonna get it. I'm not an old man yet," he said, eliciting chuckles throughout the room.

"There are a lot of misconceptions about the CIA that I would like to straighten out before we get too heavy into the mechanics of the mission. Yes, we are all former Special Forces and yes, we are sometimes called in to do things that make the public a little uncomfortable. But put whatever you've seen on TV or in the movies out of your mind. I want you all to be confident in our abilities but at the same time, don't ascribe supernatural powers to us. You watch our backs and we'll watch yours. We are all trained in small arms, hand to hand combat, ordinance, intelligence, communications and some of us have more specialized training."

Jason pointed a big hand at the back of the room.

"Slater over there is an expert tracker, for instance, while Anderson could probably build any kind of bomb known to man. Chin knows almost everything there is to know about biomechanics and has a master's degree from Stanford. Samson could hack into Bill Gates' personal computer and Harrison here has a degree in nuclear physics from MIT."

Harrison interrupted. "And Jason has a BS degree in B.S.," he said, setting the room off in laughter.

Jason ignored the remark and continued his speech. "Add all that to the fact that we're highly trained soldiers,

I think you can be confident that we have a better-than-average chance of success. Now, besides Blakely here, we have another operative in the field that has managed to infiltrate Lilith's organization and win her trust. So far we know that all the other members have fled, though we don't know exactly why or where, yet, but we think it's because Lilith has mutated."

"Mutated?" someone asked.

"Yes, mutated. According to our operative, so far her body mass has increased by at least two hundred percent, she has grown claws and large canine-type teeth and has the strength of several men. She also has enhanced senses. For instance, she can smell and hear as well as a canine and our operative has seen evidence that Lilith may be able to see through solid objects, almost like an X-ray machine."

Lisa raised her hand.

"Yes, Ms. Singleton," Jason said.

It unnerved Lisa a little that the man knew her name, but she continued.

"Have you heard anything about Hunter?"

"Yes, Ms. Singleton, your husband is in good hands and free of the virus, thanks to our operative. They have fled the area where he was being held and are now awaiting our arrival in a park not far from here."

Lisa felt relief replace the tension that had held her captive for the last forty-eight hours, but Hunter still wasn't in the clear, yet. "Why not just bring him back to the ship or airlift him out?"

"Because Lilith may be following him," Jason said. "But rest assured that he is in the best hands."

Lisa did not feel reassured.

Fredrichs turned around, walked back to the dry-erase board and stood beside it. He pulled a small laser pointer out of his pocket and shined it up on a rectangle that was drawn there.

Lilith

"This is where Lilith and her group were last located. It's an apartment building near Broadway on Park Terrace. We believe Lilith may have vacated the building, but it's where we'll start to look for clues. From there, we'll attempt to track her and take her alive if at all possible."

Lisa raised her hand again. "What if it's not possible?" she asked.

"Well, that's what carbines and rocket launchers are for, aren't they?"

PART FIVE: RESCUE

CHAPTER 70

"Good news, Hunter. The SOG team is meeting us here and your wife is with them," Gabe said, as if that bit of information might cheer Hunter up. But it didn't.

"They're bringing Lisa here? What the hell for?"

Gabe shrugged. "I thought you'd be happy. Anyway, I was told that she pretty much demanded they bring her along."

"That figures. She never could resist putting herself in dangerous situations. Why didn't they just tell her no?"

"Please. You ever try telling a woman no?"

Hunter thought about Lisa's pregnancy and the fact that if something happened to her, it would also happen to the baby. He would not just be losing one, but two.

Gabe and Hunter had been in the park since yesterday and it was now around nine a.m. Hunter had awakened nearly two hours ago and had eaten a breakfast of freeze-dried rations and coffee that Gabe had brought in her backpack. It reminded him of the rations he had eaten in the Navy when the food on board the ship sometimes left a little to be desired. He was dying for a shower and in fact wasn't sure if he had even taken one in the last several days. He rubbed a hand across his stubbly face and realized he could probably use a shave, as well.

Hunter stood up in the grass, walked over to one of the surrounding bushes and undid his fly.

"Hope you don't mind, but I really have to take a whiz," he said over his shoulder.

"Doesn't bother me, mate. Long as you don't mind whipping out your donger in public."

Hunter scanned the surrounding park.

"What public?" he murmured.

*   *   *

Lisa was amazed at the firepower that filled the ship's armory. As the group filed into the compartment to be issued their weapons, a long metal table was loaded with an array of things from shotguns to semi-automatic rifles, carbines and pistols. The room stank of machine oil and gunpowder. There were a few weapons that Lisa knew were not standard Navy issue and she didn't recognize many of them. They were all flat black in color.

The group stopped at the end of the table sporting the vast display of firepower as Anderson, a black-haired, dark-skinned man that reminded Lisa of Hunter, stepped to one side and grabbed what looked like a carbine with a short barrel and a scope on top. He turned it over in his hands and grinned like a boy with a new video game.

"This is a modified M4A1 with a close quarters battle receiver, making it ideal for the type of mission we are about to undertake. It has a ten-point-three-inch barrel and fires a thirty-round magazine of seventy-seven grain, mark two cartridges at twenty-six hundred feet per second. Like all the rifles and shotguns, it's equipped with an ATN ThOR 3 thermal optical rifle scope that can see in the dark better than a cat." He held the gun up in front of his face. "It only weighs about nine pounds fully loaded, but it will definitely do some damage."

Anderson laid the carbine down and grabbed one of the shotguns.

"Mossberg M500 twelve-gauge pump-action shotgun. These particular guns have a shorter fourteen-inch barrel and fire five to eight rounds with an effective range of about forty meters. Just aim it in the general vicinity and chances are you'll hit something. But be careful—they do have a kick, so you may get some bruises."

The next one Anderson picked up looked like two guns in one.

"This is an M16 SCAR-H combat assault rifle fitted with an MK13 Mod 0 forty-millimeter grenade launcher. The MK16 has a thirteen-inch barrel that fires six-hundred- and twenty-five rounds per minute, a muzzle velocity of twenty-three hundred and forty feet per second and an effective range of three hundred and thirty yards. The MK13 has an effective range of over six-hundred yards and fires five to seven rounds per minute. It can also be operated either right- or left-handed. It will blow a hole in anything you shoot and create a lot of shrapnel, so make sure you're not in the immediate vicinity of whatever you're firing at."

Anderson laid the M16 down and picked up a Beretta.

"I think everyone knows what this is. The nine-millimeter Beretta is standard issue for most of the services except the Coast Guard and is a workhorse. Drop it in the sand, drop it in the water, pick it up and it still fires. Great little weapon with an eighteen-round magazine."

Anderson turned the gun around and offered it butt-first to Lisa.

"I believe this will be your weapon," he said. "You might want to pick up a shoulder-holster, too."

Lisa nodded and grabbed the pistol. "Thanks. I'll do that."

241

Jason appeared and picked up a box off the floor, set it on the table, then reached in and pulled out what looked like a smartphone and a Bluetooth wireless earpiece.

"This is the Android phone used by Army Special Forces," he said. "It runs the new Tactical Situational Awareness Application Suite, or TactSA, works in low connectivity areas and utilizes an encrypted peer-to-peer network. This phone does a hell of a lot more than we're going to use it for, so don't worry about figuring out all the goodies for now. Just make sure it's turned on and ready to go."

Fredrichs handed everyone a phone and waited as the group looked their gadgets over.

"I'd prefer my own men to carry the modified M16, but the rest of you can choose whichever weapon you think you're most comfortable with—preferably one that you've used before, since we don't really have time for any training. Once you have your weapons and ammo, meet me outside the armory so I can put you with your group leaders."

CHAPTER 71

The assault/rescue team stood outside the armory, armed to the hilt and anxious to get the operation underway. Lisa had three magazines of eighteen rounds each for her Beretta, confident that would be more than enough. At least, she hoped it would be. Her kinky hair was wrapped up in a bun and tucked under a black ball cap and she wore jeans, sneakers and a T-shirt. It was hot and she felt nervous, but otherwise okay. She was thankful the morning sickness had subsided.

Lisa noticed that the other team members had either gone for the M4A1 or the Mossberg. Though it would be nice to have the extra firepower, Lisa was glad not to have to haul around a heavy carbine or shotgun. She had pretty good aim and could pull the pistol from her holster about as quickly as she could raise a shotgun.

Jason and two of his men carried the modified MK16 with grenade launcher while the other three carried the M4A1. All six SOG members carried Berettas in case they ran out of ammo or lost their primary weapon. Lisa was pretty sure they also carried knives and knew how to use them. Besides the Android phones, everyone on the team wore Dragon Skin ballistic vests and had backpacks loaded with food, water, extra ammo and gas masks in case they had to use tear gas. Each of the SOG team members wore special MTM Pro Ops Navigator Tracking watches equipped with GPS tracking, latitude and longitude display and practically everything but invisibility cloaks. The entire team was in civilian clothes and, except for the artillery, looked like they might be a group of Goth tourists.

Jason faced the team in the passageway, eyeing each of them in turn as he spoke.

"I'll be the first to admit this is a weird assignment," he said. "I've never done anything like this and I'm sure none of my men have either. We're used to hunting humans, not monsters, so there are bound to be some unknown variables that will arise. I just want everyone to be alert and aware. Also keep in mind that although her 'minions' or whatever you want to call them appear to have run off, be alert. They may still be around."

The passageway was silent.

"Alright, Chin, I want you to pair off with Ms. Singleton and when we meet up with Hunter and our other operative, I want them to join you, as well. Slater, you and Commander Crane will pair off. Harrison, you go with Commander MacIntyre. Anderson, pair off with the captain. Samson goes with Johnson and Blakely, you'll be with me. Remember, this is a CIA operation, so SOG personnel are in charge — you will take orders from them and they will take orders from me. Whoever finds Lilith or one of her accomplices will contact me and the rest of the team and apprise us of your situation. Make sure to keep at least ten feet from the other team members at all times. Everyone got that?"

Grunts in the affirmative and a couple of "ooh-ras" erupted from the group.

"Our first objective will be the apartment on Park Terrace. Alright. Let's hit it," Fredrichs said, then turned and headed toward the bow and into the fray.

CHAPTER 72

The rotor from the Sikorsky SH-60 Sea Hawk helicopter that awaited the team on the Ford's flight deck created a mini-hurricane that threatened to push Lisa over backward, but she managed to make her way across the deck sandwiched between the line of men without losing her footing. Though they were wearing hearing protection and goggles, Lisa was thankful they didn't have to wear the float coats, which would add considerable bulk to her already bulging backpack and sidearm.

The team would be dropped some distance away from the objective, in the middle of Columbia University's Baker Field in North Manhattan. From there, it would be a short walk to 50 Park Terrace East, where Lilith's hideout was located. Lisa doubted very much that they would find anyone there, but the team agreed that was the best place to start, just to find clues if nothing else.

Across the harbor Lisa saw the white fiberglass hull of a half-sunken yacht sticking up out of the water. The pier next to the Ford, where the USS Intrepid was moored, looked like it had been bombed. The buildings that stood there were nothing more than shacks without roofs and several cars were huddled up at one end as if huge waves had pushed them there.

The skies were clear and the weather mild, but the temperature was already close to ninety, making her back sweat where the backpack lay up against it. Being from North Carolina, Lisa was used to hot, humid weather, but she still didn't like it.

She looked out over the city and saw helicopters in the distance patrolling around the perimeter that had been marked off-limits for this mission. The CIA had it locked-down tight — tight enough, she hoped. Beyond that, far over the northeast horizon she saw a column of black smoke that she knew was the result of the missile that had come from the Ford. She wondered how many people had been killed. Locals were still filtering back into their neighborhoods, so with any luck there were either low casualties or none at all.

Lisa couldn't fathom how another human being could be so cold and ruthless as to send a guided missile into the middle of a highly populated city. Then she remembered that Lilith was no longer human, maybe never had been.

Lisa ducked her head under the helicopter's rotor as she waited her turn to enter. The SH-60, which usually carried a crew of three or four, would only carry two this time in order to add a twelfth passenger. They needed all the room they could get and it wasn't feasible to have another helo carry one extra person or split into two groups.

The person in front of her climbed into the machine and Lisa stepped up behind him, then found her place in one of the seats and strapped in. She felt herself getting nauseous again and fought the feeling back with all her concentration. Lisa was not about to let her morning sickness destroy her chance of going on this mission and seeing Hunter again.

She felt relieved as the nausea finally abated.

There were not many windows inside the chopper and everything was painted the usual gun-metal gray. It was somewhat claustrophobic, her elbows touching people on both sides. It reminded her of the inside of the Greyhound they had flown in on and it was just about as noisy. She pulled her straps tight and sat back in her seat. Lisa had never flown in a helicopter before and wondered how it would feel on takeoff.

She soon found out that it was a lot like being on a quickly rising elevator and had to slap a hand over her mouth to keep from retching on the seat in front of her as they headed out over New York.

CHAPTER 73

The beast that was Lilith could smell the scent of human blood all around her as she walked down Park Terrace on all fours. Though she was still primarily bipedal, Lilith found she could move much more quickly on four legs. The sun beat down on her fur-covered skin from above, but Lilith didn't feel it — she was hyper-focused on one thing — Hunter. Even with all the other smells around, Hunter's particular scent was like a beacon calling to her. She could smell that bitch that was with him, as well. It was a good thing she had trusted her instincts about that woman and not let her too deeply into the organization. Gabe had been useful enough, but now she had proven to be a liability, one that needed to be terminated. Lilith would delight in that — her blood would taste especially good.

Lilith gazed up at the helicopters buzzing around like flies and did her best to stay in the shadows to avoid detection. They had thermal imaging sensors, as well, so the beast knew to keep under awnings and trees as much as possible.

Lilith

Lilith figured they had sectioned off this area of the city to keep her contained. If she could still laugh, she would have found that amusing. They could no more contain her than they could a demon from Hell. She would go where she pleased and create whatever havoc she deemed necessary to advance her cause, which was to propagate her race. She could reproduce asexually, but still wanted Hunter for a trophy if nothing else. She knew he would probably find her repulsive, but he would get over that once she found a way to make him into a Lilitu. And she would find a way.

As she advanced toward Isham Park, Lilith thought about the things she had left to do before her children were born and the surprises that were still in store for the assault team that she was sure was on its way to find her.

That was when she saw a helicopter fly low overhead and make a descent over Baker Field. The beast stopped and watched as it slowly disappeared from view over the buildings and trees. Then she changed direction and headed toward Baker Field.

*   *   *

Hunter and Gabe watched from the baseball diamond in Baker Field as the helicopter made its landing, the dirt from the infield swirling through the air and stinging their flesh like needles. Hunter held a hand in front of his eyes, blocking as much dirt as possible. The chopper landed in the grassy outfield, the noise from the rotors making his ears ring. Hunter's hair and clothes flapped in the wind as he waited for the doors to open. He couldn't wait to see Lisa again, eat a decent meal and take a shower.

The first people out were men Hunter didn't recognize, but who he knew were from the Special Ops team. They were mostly dressed in dark civilian clothes and sunglasses and wore rucksacks. They were all armed with formidable-looking weapons, a few of which he could tell were grenade launchers. They got out of the chopper and spread themselves around the area as if they were securing the perimeter. Once that was done, a big man with a scar across his nose, who Hunter figured was the leader, motioned for the other team members to exit the helo.

Lisa was the first one out. She immediately spotted Hunter and once she cleared the spinning blades of the Sea Hawk, sprinted to Hunter's awaiting arms. They kissed as if they had been apart for years instead of days.

After a few seconds, Lisa held her husband at arm's length. "Hunter, I have to tell you something."

Hunter raised his brows. "What?"

"I volunteered to help track down Lilith."

Hunter nodded and said, "Well, I guess that shower can wait a few more hours," then kissed his wife again.

*   *   *

Gabe smiled at the public display of affection between Hunter and Lisa and walked past the couple to meet with the other CIA members.

"Glad to see you made it, Gabe," Jason yelled over the sound of the chopper, slinging the strap of the big MK16 over his shoulder.

Gabe shrugged. "Wouldn't miss it. I see you diggers are armed to the gills. Probably a good idea. She's really big now, and strong. She has claws and teeth and she can move fast. Animal fast."

Jason nodded, then turned and watched as the helicopter rotors picked up speed and the machine rose into the sky above them.

"Well, looks like we're on our own," he said. "You have any trouble getting here?"

"None to speak of. Once I got rid of the parasite it was a simple matter of just filling Hunter in on the situation."

"Must have been hell infiltrating that group. Anything we need to know?"

"I know that most of the group ran off when Lilith started…mutating…and I never saw them again, but…" Gabe trailed off, lost in deep thought. Her intuition was suddenly in high gear.

"But what?" Jason asked.

"Something just doesn't feel right. I'm not sure what it is, but we need to watch our backs."

"Always," Jason said.

Fredrichs turned and made a circular motion above his head, indicating that the team should gather around. Hunter and Lisa were the farthest away from the group and were somewhat slow in getting the message.

"Hey, you two lovebirds mind joining us?" Jason said as the others chuckled.

Before anyone had a chance to react, a white blur shot out from behind the dugout and tackled Sly Johnson, who was standing on the far side of the group with Samson, checking over his rucksack. Samson was knocked back off his feet and Johnson hit the ground with a thud, letting loose a yell of surprise. Weapons were raised but no one shot for fear of hitting the commander. The beast moved so fast it was over in seconds.

Then, it was gone.

Everyone ran toward Johnson, who lay prone on the grass, completely still.

"Oh, shit, shit, shit! Where the hell did that thing come from?" Samson said, picking himself up off the ground and hoisting his weapon.

Gabe was the first to arrive. She knelt and looked the fallen man over. Johnson's eyes were staring, but he wasn't seeing anything—his throat had been ripped out all the way to his spine. She could actually see the vertebrae, ivory-white and slimy with gore.

Gabe thought she was going to be sick and quickly

averted her eyes as the rest of the group warily gathered around.

"Well, I guess we've had our first run-in with Lilith," Jason said.

"She moves so fast you can hardly see her," Mac said. "Johnson never even had a chance."

"Maybe none of us do," Sammy said.

Lisa suddenly screamed and everyone jerked their heads in her direction.

"What is it?" Gabe said, then glanced around and realized she already knew the answer — Hunter was missing.

CHAPTER 74

After the diversion of Lilith's first attack, she doubled back behind the dugout, ran onto the field and grabbed Hunter from behind, backhanding Lisa and knocking her to the ground. The monster dragged Hunter toward the outside of the ball field and beyond the dugout while holding his jaw shut with one hand. She was incredibly strong and Hunter was as helpless as a child, unable to cry out. When she got him outside the field the monster released him and as he stared into her silver animal-eyes, Lilith growled two words.

"Lisa dies."

Hunter understood only too well. Either he went with Lilith willingly, or she would kill Lisa. He had no choice but to go. He would have to think of a way to escape later.

Pushing Hunter ahead of her, Lilith headed out of the field and into Inwood Hill Park.

*   *   *

"Oh, God, she has him again," Lisa said, picking herself up off the ground. She rubbed the left side of her face where Lilith had struck her.

"That bitch. I'll kill her," she growled and began to run out of the park toward the exit, but Gabe caught up to her and grabbed a shoulder. Lisa shrugged it off and turned on her with eyes of fire.

"Ms. Singleton, you're injured," Gabe said, tenderly touching Lisa's bruised jaw. "And you can't chase after them alone. We have to track them with the whole team."

"Why?" Lisa shouted. "The team obviously is no match for her, so what difference does it make?"

Lisa was hyperventilating as if she had just run a seven-minute mile and her heart felt like a carbine set on automatic fire. The rest of the group came up cautiously behind Gabe.

"Lisa, I admit she got the jump on us, but we have a way to track her," Jason said.

Lisa eyed him warily. "You do?" she said.

Jason called over his shoulder to one of his men.

"Harrison, front and center. Show the lady your new toy."

He stepped to the side and the wiry, blonde-headed man filled in the gap, slid off his backpack and reached inside. He pulled out a handheld device that looked to Lisa like a barcode reader used by department store clerks with several metal rods of different lengths protruding from the end. On top was a touch-screen user interface. Harrison switched it on and the screen lit up with small icons like those on a PC.

"What is that?" she asked.

Harrison continued to watch the screen as he spoke. "We figured out that since Lilith had been exposed to radiation on board the Ford, she's probably carrying residual radiation in her body. This machine can track extremely

255

small traces of just about any type of radiation, including gamma and alpha particles, which she probably carries in her blood. Just like a bloodhound can follow the scent of a specific human, we can set this machine to follow a specific radiation pattern."

Lisa frowned. "How does it do that?"

Harrison glanced up at Lisa and smiled. "Sorry, ma'am, that's classified."

Lisa eyed the screen just as it started to show an oscillating sine wave, increasing and decreasing in amplitude.

"I'm definitely getting a radiation reading from over that way," Harrison said, pointing behind Lisa and toward the team dugouts.

"We need to follow it while the trail is still hot," Jason said.

"What about Johnson's body?" Phillips asked. "I don't think we should just leave it here."

Lisa glanced at Samson, who had been assigned as Johnson's partner and saw that a deep frown lined the big man's dark face. Jason slapped a hand on Samson's back.

"Don't beat yourself up, Sam. Nobody saw her coming, including me. Next time we'll be ready."

Samson simply nodded, pulling the carbine tight against his back.

Jason held a hand up to his right ear. "Base, this is Fredrichs. We have a casualty, repeat, we have one casualty, Lieutenant Commander Johnson. Request pick-up in Baker Field at drop-off point. We are moving out and attempting to locate target."

Jason glanced around at the other team members. "We've been here ten minutes and already had one death. Let's not lose anyone else. Everyone keep a sharp eye out and keep your weapons ready. And for God's sake, don't shoot any of the other team members or any civilians. Make sure you know what you are shooting first. Alright, let's do it. Harrison, take the lead."

Lisa couldn't wait to shove her Beretta up Lilith's ass and pull the trigger.

CHAPTER 75

George Saunders and his team at CIA headquarters had been working the last forty-eight hours on sorting through every e-mail, phone conversation and Internet connection made by anyone related to Lilith's EVE organization. They spoke to anyone who had ever known Lilith or her associates and had come up with very little.

But in the last couple of hours they hit the jackpot with Jeremy Kramer, an ex-lover of Lilith's and a disgruntled recent ex-member of EVE who had managed to leave the organization and live to tell about it. After flying Kramer in from New York, the man shut up as tight as a bank vault, refusing to speak until his demands had been met.

Kramer, a throwback to the 1990s Generation X culture complete with long, dirty-blonde hair, ripped blue jeans and Nirvana T-shirt, sat in an office with a wall covered in two-way glass as Saunders sat across the table, sipping coffee and trying to be as non-threatening as possible. The director of the CIA and several operatives watched from the other side of the glass.

"If they find out I've been talking to you, they'll come after me," Kramer said. "Those people are crazy. You have to guarantee my safety before I say anything."

Saunders sat his coffee down on the table and loosened his tie. "Don't worry, Kramer, we've got your back. But remember, just being associated with EVE could mean trouble with the CIA, so I can only guarantee your safety if you give me something useful."

Kramer seemed to think about that as he wiped his nose with the back of an arm. According to the background check, Kramer was educated and extremely intelligent, with a master's degree in biology, but acted more like a hormone-enraged teenager. Saunders figured he probably had some kind of drug problem that made him paranoid and agitated. The commander marveled at the fact that some of the smartest people were often the easiest targets for recruitment into organizations like EVE.

But by the time Kramer was done talking about Lilith and her plans for Manhattan Island, Saunders and everyone in the observation room were scrambling to contact Fredrichs and his team and praying that they weren't already too late.

* * *

Jason's comm unit had been patched in directly to Saunders, who was relaying some rather disheartening information. Lisa and the entire team listened over their own phone links with growing dread.

"Are you sure?" Jason said, grimacing at the news.

"Afraid so," Saunders said. "I see no reason why he would lie. Kramer's crazy, but he's not psychotic. I can't say the same for the rest of Lilith's followers."

"And he has no idea where the device is? It's just somewhere in Manhattan?"

"That's about it. I can't ask you to stay—that's up to

you. But let me know your decision ASAP."

Lisa, along with everyone else in the group, was now staring at Jason with a mix of horror and disbelief as they stood only a few hundred yards outside the exit to Baker Field.

"Well, you heard the man," Jason said. "Lilith's followers are alive and they have planted a backpack nuke somewhere in Manhattan. At about ten kilotons, this bomb will flatten everything within a two-mile radius and make Manhattan uninhabitable for the next century. An ideal situation for Lilith and her brood. Even with much of the city evacuated, there are still a few hundred-thousand people on the island, so there will be an unthinkable number of casualties. Apparently, Gabe, you weren't in the loop on that one."

Gabe shook her head. "Lilith might have suspected something. She must have thought I was useful at the time. I guess I'm lucky she didn't kill me."

"I would say you're probably right. Anyone have any opinions on what we should do?"

Lisa spoke up first. "Personally, I don't think there's a chance in hell of finding that bomb. I say we locate Hunter, kill Lilith and get out of Manhattan before it becomes a wasteland."

"I'll have to agree with Ms. Singleton," Phillips said. "This city is huge and we have no clue where the bomb is. In the meantime, Lilith is about to give birth and on top of that, she has a hostage."

Everyone nodded and murmured in agreement. Lisa thought that Jason actually seemed relieved as he keyed a number into his Android.

"Fredrichs to base, patch me through to Saunders again."

Several seconds of silence.

"Saunders here."

"Commander, we've decided to forego the search for

the nuke. We simply don't have the capability or the time to find the device. We're going to attempt to rescue Hunter Singleton and hopefully capture or destroy Lilith in the process."

"I understand, Jason. I've already informed the mayor and he's having as many people as possible evacuated off the island. Good luck and watch yourself. Keep me informed and let me know if you need any assistance."

Jason clicked off the Android and sighed.

"I'm not going to ask any of you from the Ford to take part in this mission, knowing that bomb could go at any minute. Anyone who wants to go back, let me know now."

No one said a word.

"Then let's do this," Jason said as Harrison once again switched on the radiation detector and the team edged farther into the city.

CHAPTER 76

Lilith screamed with an animal ferocity that made Hunter's blood run cold. She was in some kind of pain, and deep inside, Hunter found that he was not only glad, but he prayed that she would die. It would make things so much easier. His head ached, his stomach was twisted in knots and he had never wanted to take a shower and eat a hot meal so much in his life. This was definitely one of those times when miraculous intervention would be welcome.

She lay only yards away next to a large uprooted elm tree, writhing in pain on the grass of whatever park they were now in, somewhere along the western edge of Manhattan. They had traveled for hours and the sun was already beginning to fade as the day crept to a close. Lilith was evading detection and Hunter realized that her senses were probably highly acute, like that of an animal. She could detect anyone before they even got close. The uprooted trees and garbage that lay strewn everywhere from the storm provided extra cover, as well. He thought about running, but it would be useless. She would only find him again and if he ran for the ship, he would put them all in danger. She would also kill his wife.

He had to think.

Lilith howled, her white coloring reflecting the sun like the fur of a wild arctic polar bear but with musculature that was much more well-defined. Lilith's mouth was a yawning cavern of jagged, razor-edged ivory filling her elongated jaws and her ears had grown to points that rose above her head, offsetting silver eyes full of evil cunning. Lilith's long talons dug into the ground, plowing up the grass and soil into small heaps. She was part bear, part wolf, part lion—a hybrid of several different predatory animals. No animal like this had probably ever existed during the reign of humankind, at least not that Hunter had ever heard of. It was like myth come to life. Some part of him, the newspaper reporter, wanted to document it, grab a camera and get a photo. If only he could.

The other part of him just wanted to kill the beast.

He wondered what could be wrong with her, what could be causing such pain. Was she changing again, growing even larger?

Then like an epiphany from above, it hit him and Hunter suddenly realized what was happening.

Lilith was giving birth.

CHAPTER 77

Hunter sat with his back up against an old park trash can that had been blown over by the hurricane. He couldn't believe what he was seeing. Lilith had begun to give birth and Hunter, who was only a few yards away, could see the shadow of...something...protruding from between her legs as she strained to push it out. But it didn't look as if it was moving and he could hear no sound coming from it. Maybe the thing was dead, stillborn.

He began to wonder for the hundredth time when Lisa, Gabe and the CIA team would find him. He knew they would eventually come, but he was afraid for their safety. Now Lilith had a child or children to protect and she would be twice as dangerous, making it more impera-tive than ever that she be stopped.

Hunter watched across the grass of the park as the miracle...and the horror...of this birth played out. There were groans and disgusting sucking sounds that made his stomach turn as he reached up to plug his ears. What kind of "children" would they be? Would they resemble anything human? He doubted it. Lilith had mutated to the point that she was no longer recognizable as humanoid and he figured her children would be the same. The spawn of Satan. Had the spirit of Lilith herself reincarnated, traveled through time and space and taken over the body of this particular Lilith? Or had the true genetic power of the beast been unlocked? He would probably never know.

Hunter had witnessed some bizarre events in his life, but this was the most terrifying yet. With their astounding rate of growth, there would soon be a whole army of Lilitu and there was nothing he or anyone could do to stop it.

*   *   *

Lisa watched as the waveforms fluctuated on Harrison's radiation detector, increasing in amplitude with each step.

"Jason, the radiation reading is getting stronger," Harrison whispered. "We're definitely closing in. I'd say we're within a hundred yards. It looks like they've been hanging back in the trees so I'd say they're probably still inside the tree line."

Jason held up a closed fist, signaling for the group to stop, then turned to face everyone.

"Alright, we're going to go in quick and silent, grab Hunter and get the hell out of here. If we can, we'll capture Lilith or take her out. I'm only going to take three people with me."

MacIntyre quickly stepped up. "I'd like to go along. She's my sister, so who knows, maybe I can still reason with her somehow."

Jason seemed to consider it.

"I'd like to take you, Commander," he finally said, "but I have to warn you, if she attacks, we'll be shooting first and asking questions later."

Mac nodded. "I understand. I'd still like to be there."

Jason waved him over.

Lisa stepped up also. "Jason, I have a personal stake in this, as well. I'd like to go along. Like I said, I can handle myself in tough situations."

"I believe you can, Ms. Singleton." He waved her over. "Slater, you're with us. The beast can probably smell us a mile away, so the rest of you wait here until we get back. Listen up on the radio and be ready if we call you. Harrison, you're in charge until we return. Keep your eyes and ears open."

Jason turned to Lisa and Mac. "You two ready?"

"As ready as we'll ever be," Lisa said.

The quartet moved forward and disappeared behind a clump of fallen trees.

CHAPTER 78

It was dark and still. Lilith had finished with the painful ordeal of giving birth to monsters and had crept over to where Hunter sat mesmerized with horror and fascination. Lilith stood before him, her hulking form silhouetted by the rising moon, and said only one word.

"Watch."

It came out more like a guttural growl than a spoken word. The voice didn't sound human. It sounded demonic. But Hunter knew what Lilith meant—she wanted him to keep an eye on the...whatever the hell it was. Hunter should have been terrified, but his anger and frustration left no room for fear. Hunter nodded his understanding and she moved off across the park in search of what Hunter assumed was some type of sustenance for her and her offspring. He really didn't want to know what that sustenance might be, and he definitely was not going to be moving any closer to the shadowy mass that lay on the ground, as silent and unmoving as death.

But he knew it wasn't dead.

Lilith

Hunter hadn't moved for hours. His back and his butt were sore as he sat up against the metal trash can, sickened by the sight of Lilith in her birth pangs and thought about things — where he was, why he was there and how he was going to get away. He knew that killing Lilith was out of the question. Even one of those CIA grenade launchers might not stop her.

More than anything, he wanted to see Lisa again, to hold her and never let go. They had been together mere minutes when their world exploded and now here he was, hungry and thirsty and tired. But there was no use feeling sorry for himself. The best thing he could do was think about something positive, try to encourage himself, believe that he would find some way out of this and hopefully destroy Lilith and her spawn in the process.

So Hunter did the only thing he could do.

He prayed.

*　　*　　*

There were slim pickings around Manhattan, especially since the storm had hit. That damned hurricane tore up everything, didn't leave nothin' untouched, the old man thought as he shambled through Morningside Park, pushing his grocery cart as he went, stepping around a fallen tree here, a fallen tree there. The cart contained everything he owned in the world — some ragged clothes, a few magazines and newspapers, a flashlight, an extra pair of shoes — things that he had managed to find on his rounds through the city. Most he found in Central Park and along Broadway. Funny what some people discarded as junk. To someone like him, it was pure gold.

Victor Slocum's clothes hung off of him like rags on a skeleton and a scruffy, gray beard covered his frail jaw. He had to squint to see since he couldn't afford glasses. Born and bred in the Bronx, he was a veteran of the war

268

Toby Tate

in Viet Nam, served as a corporal in the Army in the late sixties, fighting the Commies on the front lines. The heat, the stink, the fear and the death had eventually taken its toll on his mind and when he returned he was told he had post-traumatic stress disorder. To him it was just a fancy word for crazy. Thing was, he knew he was crazy and he didn't care. He didn't want to be cooped up in some VA hospital for the rest of his life and was too mentally unstable to hold down a job. He had no family to speak of and no place to go, so he panhandled. New York was a huge city and people were sympathetic, though not as free with their money as they used to be. Damned economy.

But maybe tonight he would get lucky, find one of those mp3 players with headphones attached, forgotten by a worn-out jogger and left on a park bench. He would love to be able to listen to some old Sinatra or Tony Bennett, maybe.

The soup kitchens and flop houses were closed for now, blown away by the wind or flooded from the rain, so he would have to sleep in a doorway somewhere and try to scrounge up some grub wherever he could.

Victor shuffled up to a trash can that hadn't been toppled by the hurricane and parked his grocery cart next to it, then looked down inside for some fresh leftovers. There weren't any people around, he knew, so it was unlikely he would find anything, but you could never tell.

The moon tonight was bright and full and he could see everything pretty clearly inside the can. Didn't look like there was much in the way of food, just soda bottles, empty fast-food wrappers and newspapers soaked from the rain.

Then the moonlight suddenly disappeared — something was blocking it. The old man lifted his head from the trashcan and stood squinting at a lone figure hidden in the shadows of a giant still-standing sycamore tree. Cataracts had long ago ruined Victor's eyesight, but whoever it was, he was huge and built like a grizzly bear.

Victor had never been mugged—what could you steal from a homeless man? But occasionally street thugs liked to harass him just because they could. He was hoping this dude was just lost.

"Can I help you?" the old man croaked. "You lookin' for somethin'?"

The beast answered with only one word, but it was the way it spoke that made the old man's spine freeze.

"Blood," it growled.

When it lumbered out of the shadows, Victor saw it more clearly and let out a strangled plea for help that no one could have possibly heard. Had a polar bear escaped from the zoo? But this thing was even bigger than a polar bear. He couldn't move—as if his shoes were nailed to the ground. The hulking thing advanced slowly on four over-sized, clawed feet, muscles bunching and rows of long, pointed teeth dripping with saliva inside its opened, cavernous mouth. He could feel his heart pumping, adrenaline flowing through his body like ice water. The thing was actually graceful, catlike in its movements, which seemed to make it all the more terrifying. Its snow-white fur looked silky and beautiful in the moonlight, an irony that made the old man almost want to laugh as it closed in for the kill.

Victor thought the beast's hot breath stank of rotten meat as he stared into the silvery eyes of death. He felt like his neck had suddenly been placed in a hydraulic press when Lilith clamped her huge jaws around his throat and decapitated him in one bite.

CHAPTER 79

Most animal tracking, as Vince Slater knew from growing up in the woodlands of Virginia, was done using what was called "sign tracking," incorporating clues from trails, scat, and anything that indicates animal presence. Many animals tend to spend the most time in "transition" areas between forests and streams, forests and fields or fields and streams because they offered the best hiding places and abundant food sources. Like humans, animals will usually take the path of least resistance through a forest, mountain or swamp.

But what they were tracking had the intelligence of a human combined with the strength and sensory input of an animal. Add to that the evil intent of this particular being, and you would find nothing more lethal and dangerous in the entire world. As highly skilled in his profession as he was, and as much death as he had seen, Slater was still apprehensive.

He was glad he was carrying the MK13.

The tracks they were following were from a "pacer," meaning that it moved its legs on the same side of its body to walk. But like a bear, it could also break into a gallop in-stantly. Also like a bear, it could walk on hind legs. Because the ground was so wet, the prints were fairly clear even in the moonlight. The tracks were as big as the biggest bear tracks Slater had ever seen. The thing obviously weighed a hell of a lot, more than a full-grown Sumatran Rhino judging by the depth of the prints, and just as mean. He almost felt silly following tracks that were so well-defined even a layman could see them.

Paralleling those tracks were the prints from a pair of running shoes, the same ones Hunter had been wearing, according to his wife.

They moved stealthily, weapons drawn, watching in all directions and spaced about ten feet apart. They passed the marble and granite monument of the Grant National Memorial in Riverside Park and crossed over a deserted road, following close behind Slater.

After another hundred yards, he held up a fist and the group stopped. He motioned for Jason, who quickly made his way to Slater's position.

Slater pointed straight ahead. In the distance was the shape of someone leaning up against what looked like an old metal trash can.

It was Hunter.

*   *   *

Lisa knew she needed to stay put even though she could see her husband's silhouette. She would know that shape anywhere, but she wasn't about to jeopardize his safety. Her Beretta was in her hand and ready to fire. She watched as Jason moved up to where Slater was and the two talked. There was no way of knowing if Lilith was anywhere near, but Lisa was getting the feeling that they had been lucky and found Hunter alone. If she was close, she was probably stalking them right now, watching their every move. Lisa glanced around at the uprooted trees and trash strewn about the park—there were a million places to hide here, which is probably why Lilith chose it.

Behind her, Lisa saw that MacIntyre was holding his M4A1 and was decked out in black jeans, black T-shirt and black Keds, making him almost invisible in the darkness. Even the white skin of his face was shaded by a black ball cap like the one she wore. She smiled at him and he smiled back, but Lisa could tell it was forced. She was going through hell, but at least she knew she would probably get Hunter back. Mac had no such future to look forward to—his sister was lost forever. She suddenly felt a pang of empathy for the man.

Slater broke away and moved back to where Jason had been and Lisa heard Jason over the comm link whisper, "Hunter is about one hundred meters ahead and appears to be alone. He may be sleeping. We will slowly edge our way to his position until we know what the situation is. Watch me closely and follow my lead."

Jason gave a nod to the group and then began to advance toward Hunter.

CHAPTER 80

Hunter sat back against the hard metal can, his eyes closed, hoping to catch some much-needed sleep. Instead, he kept seeing Lilith and hearing her unearthly screams. He could envision no way out of this situation—it was testing his faith, severely. He forced his mind into a different avenue of thought as he tried to picture what his unborn child would look like. He imagined holding...her? Him?...at the hospital and handing out cigars to everyone in the waiting room. Lisa's parents would be there and Hunter imagined the looks on the faces of her Chinese father and African-American mother. How those two ever managed to get together was a source of amazement to him. Maybe his own mother and father would make the trip from Oklahoma to meet the newest addition to the Singleton household.

Hunter opened his eyes and gazed at the wet lump laying a few yards away and although he didn't want to go near it, had figured out that it must be some kind of egg. Eventually, it would hatch and creatures more horrible than he could imagine would emerge. They would probably mature in a matter of months and then they, too, would reproduce. In a few short years they would over-run the entire country and eventually the planet.

Hunter decided he didn't want to think about it any-more and closed his eyes once again.

His mind drifted back to happier thoughts of his own human child and nursery room furniture, baby books, diapers, strollers, video cameras, parties, first day of pre-school…when he suddenly felt something on his shoul-der. At first, he thought it was a bug and tried to brush it off. When he touched it, he realized it was a human hand.

He jumped awake and turned quickly around, star-tled. Behind him, over the top of his trash can, he saw the camouflaged face of the leader of the SOG team, a finger to his lips.

"Is she around?" the lips whispered.

Hunter slowly shook his head, still reeling from the shock. "She's hunting," he whispered back.

The team leader nodded toward Lisa and the waiting team members. "Come on, follow me. Quietly."

Hunter didn't think running would do any good, but thought that perhaps with the firepower of the SOG team, he would stand a chance. He rose from the ground and crept silently behind the man, toward a cluster of fallen trees.

Beyond the trees was the most beautiful sight Hunter had ever seen — his wife.

He immediately threw caution to the wind and ran to Lisa's awaiting arms.

"We have to stop meeting like this," he said.

"Shut up and kiss me."

They kissed passionately for several moments, oblivi-ous to the world around them.

"I hate to break this up, folks," Jason said, "but we need to get out of here before the bomb goes off. I'm going to make a command decision and say that finding Lilith will have to wait."

Hunter stood for a moment, absorbing what the team leader had just said.

"Did you say a bomb?" he asked.

Jason nodded somberly, relaying the story told to them by Saunders at CIA headquarters and then stretched out a hand to Hunter.

"By the way, I'm Jason Fredrichs and this is Vince Slater. He's on my SOG team."

Slater nodded a silent greeting at Hunter.

"So you're saying those assholes have planted a nuclear bomb somewhere in Manhattan? How do you know?" Hunter asked.

Jason shook his head. "Look, we don't have time to get into all that. We need to get back to the Ford and weigh anchor before we all become toast along with the rest of the island. There are a lot of people aboard the ship that have been evacuated and if we're not aboard within the next hour, they're going to leave us here."

Hunter couldn't believe what he was hearing. "So you're going to leave the island? Just like that? Without even trying to find the nuke?"

"Hey, believe me, I'd love to try to locate this bomb. But we simply don't have the means at our disposal. Our job is to get you and the other civilians to safety and that's what we're going to do. So let's move out."

Jason began to walk back the way they had come when Hunter stuck out a hand that hit the spook in the middle of his Dragon Skin vest, stopping him short.

Jason went to grab the hand and Hunter struck it away with a lightning-quick upward swipe of his arm. The man was twice Hunter's size and probably did not feel like being challenged, especially in the middle of a possible combat zone. But Hunter had to make him listen.

"Wait, Jason, hear me out. I have an idea."

Hunter knew that the man was feeling the pressure

of responsibility to his SOG team members and the Ford crewmembers that were under his command. There was no way of knowing how much time they had left before Armageddon struck and wiped them off the face of the Earth. For all he knew, they had none. But Hunter gambled that Jason's humanity would win out over his military training, at least temporarily.

"Okay, go ahead. You have two minutes," Fredrichs said.

But instead of speaking, Hunter turned to his wife.

"Dump everything out of your backpack and split it between Vince and Jason."

Lisa hesitated, staring at her husband like he had just escaped from the local asylum.

"It's okay. Do it," he said, giving her a wink.

While Lisa unshouldered her backpack and began dumping the contents, he turned to Jason.

"I assume you have an extra pistol on a shoulder holster. Let me have it."

The big spook didn't move.

Hunter held out a hand. "Please?" he said. "Trust me, Jason. I know Lilith and I know what I'm doing. If I take time to explain, it will be too late."

After a few seconds of hesitation, Jason reached under his shirt, pulled out the Beretta and handed it to Hunter butt first.

"I hope you know what you're doing," he said. "For all our sakes."

"I need all of you to wait here," Hunter said, grabbing the pistol. "I have to do this myself. Understand? Don't come over there until I call you."

He turned and took the empty backpack from Lisa, who looked him in the eyes and whispered, "I trust you. Be careful."

Then, Hunter was gone.

CHAPTER 81

The dead feet of Lilith's victim bounced along the concrete, resembling the carcass of a freshly-killed deer, blood and gore streaking the ground like the trail of an immense slug. Most of the city was still without power, so she was hidden in shadow for nearly the whole route between Riverside and Morningside parks. She held the headless corpse, which had not yet grown stiff from rigor mortis, in her huge maw by one arm, the other arm flopping on the ground like the appendage of a broken doll. It would make a wonderful first meal for her young.

Lilith eyed the buildings that lined both sides of the road as she strode through it, a proud lion returning from the hunt. It looked like a university campus, huge and sprawling. She could see there was no one inside any of the structures and most of the trees had been laid flat, like every other tree in the city, by the storm—*her* storm. A storm that had probably killed hundreds, maybe thousands.

Lilith found that she enjoyed killing. Even shooting that man on board the Navy ship was exhilarating. It was like a drug, addictive and intoxicating. The smell and the taste of blood reached her on the most primeval level, like a shark in a feeding frenzy. And she still had powers yet to explore; powers that would make her a god. There would be no stopping her.

And soon, the bomb would decimate the city with a blinding ball of white-hot fire, turning it into her radioactive playground.

As she pondered these things, her olfactory senses were suddenly bombarded by the smell of several humans. She recognized them as the people she had seen earlier by the helicopter, just before she had killed one of them.

She stopped in her tracks, trying to decide what to do. Would they ambush her? How could they? She had already sensed their presence. Were they really that stupid?

When she remembered she had left Hunter there to guard her egg, Lilith dropped the corpse in the road and took off at a gallop, her paws thumping the ground with the power of a runaway freight train.

*　　*　　*

Hunter sat in the dark against the same sycamore tree where Lilith had given birth and waited. The egg stank like the backside of a camel and it was all he could do to keep from vomiting. He knew that Lilith would probably come from the direction she had gone. He had been praying that his plan would work, that it wasn't some hare-brained scheme that was going to get him and the entire team killed. If he was dead, who would raise his child? He wished he would have gotten one of those wireless Android phones from Jason—he could really use some encouragement right now.

The nine-millimeter Beretta felt good in his hand. He had used one before when he was in the Navy. They were reliable guns that packed a punch, which was exactly what he needed. A grenade launcher would be even better, but that wouldn't serve his particular purpose.

What the hell was taking Lilith so long? Hunter knew there were still thousands of people in the city, most of them in the emergency center at Madison Square Garden. You could never get *everyone* out of a place as big as Manhattan. Most of them had probably decided that the sheer size of its skyscrapers alone would protect much of the island from the wind, so they stayed. The flooding had been bad from the storm surges, but nothing like a tsunami, thank God. People who lived in apartment buildings were probably safe from most of the flooding, and nearly everyone in Manhattan owned or rented an apartment or a townhouse.

As Hunter wondered what he should do next, he felt a presence behind him. He sprang from the ground and turned to find Lilith staring him in the face. A rumbling growl came from deep within her massive chest as she watched his movements with red-rimmed, silver eyes.

Hunter held up a green backpack that bulged with the weight of Lilith's egg and showed her the pistol.

"I think you know what I'm going to do with this, don't you," he said, doing his best to keep his tone confident and fearless, pointing the pistol at the backpack. "You're going to show us where that bomb is, right?"

Lilith was still and silent and Hunter figured she was considering her options. If he harmed the egg, Hunter knew his life would be over with a flash of tooth and claw, but he hoped that she cared more about her offspring than she cared about having the upper hand and wouldn't call his bluff.

When she didn't move after several seconds, Hunter knew he had his answer. He glanced toward the area where Lisa and the others waited and whistled loudly.

"Come on out!" he shouted.

From behind the clump of fallen trees stepped Jason, Lisa, Mac and Slater, guns trained on Lilith. She watched them with catlike calm as they slowly approached and stopped beside Hunter.

"You're going to show us where that bomb is, or your life and the life of your unborn children ends right now. What's it going to be?"

Lilith breathed another growl, this one sounding like a sigh of resignation, and padded off toward the southeast.

Jason pressed a button on his GPS watch and said on his Bluetooth, "Harrison, get a fix on my position and follow behind us."

CHAPTER 82

Their shadows crept along the street like wraiths under the light of the moon as the twelve-member team followed behind the beast that was Lilith. Hunter had figured she must weigh at least a ton by now, and she never seemed to stop growing. When would she be full grown? At two tons? Three tons? It was mind-bending. He couldn't help but wonder how she kept from starving to death.

As they walked quickly along 115th Street, Chin, an Asian man that reminded Hunter of a young Jet Li with somber, intelligent eyes and muscular forearms that looked like they were corded with steel cables, silently indicated he wanted to look in Hunter's backpack. Hunter glanced ahead at Lilith, then shrugged and handed Chin the bag.

Chin grabbed it and unzipped the top, then peered down inside. The man seemed to study it, nodding his head slowly as he did so.

"Amazing," Chin whispered.

A slimy, ovoid-shaped mass, translucent and somewhat malleable, the egg was like a giant gummy worm. It was nearly the size of a bowling ball, but light, probably no more than a couple of pounds. Yet it was almost unbelievable that a being the size of Lilith could come from something that small.

"I'm a bio-chemical engineer," Chin whispered. "I would love to study this thing. I'd be willing to bet no one has ever seen anything like this. There are only five species of monotremes known to exist in the world."

Hunter raised an eyebrow. "Mono-what?"

"Monotremes. Mammals that lay eggs. The only ones known to exist live in Australia and New Guinea. I'll bet we could learn a lot from studying this egg."

Chin zipped the pack and handed it back to Hunter, who slipped a strap over his shoulder.

As they began to make a turn onto Broadway, Hunter thought the only thing they could learn from Lilith and her brood was a quicker way to die.

* * *

The Columbia University main campus came into view on their way down Broadway. Trees lay across its soggy green lawns like broken pencils and windows were shattered in several buildings. The pavement was still wet from the deluge of rain and cars sat in the middle of the street, blown there by the one-hundred and fifty mile-per-hour winds. Everywhere they looked showed signs of damage from Hurricane Alex. After miles of walking, they had seen several emergency vehicles attempting to navigate the impassable streets. The few people they had met along the way quickly turned a different direction once they glimpsed Lilith. Hunter imagined one of them soiling their pants at the sight of her and figured he would probably do the same if he was in their shoes.

Hunter glimpsed Lisa a few feet behind him and she gave him a thumbs-up. He knew she knew that he was worried about her stress level and how it was affecting the baby. If he had his way, Lisa wouldn't even be here, but the woman was stubborn. Just like him.

He scanned the road ahead and wondered how much longer it would be until they arrived at their destination and whether or not it would even do a bit of good. Could they really diffuse a nuclear bomb? If they couldn't, then he hoped the end would be quick.

CHAPTER 83

After hours and miles of walking down Broadway, Lisa's feet felt as if they were on fire. She was so glad she had decided to wear her Nikes today, otherwise she probably wouldn't have made it. When people talked about the length of a city block, she would definitely remember this as a reference, she thought.

They must have been a sight, a dozen people dressed in dark clothing and carrying enough firepower for a small army, following closely behind a snowy-white beast from hell. Lisa almost laughed at the ridiculousness of it, except that it wasn't funny. Manhattan was about to get nuked and them along with it if they weren't fast enough to diffuse this bomb. Lisa had seen plenty of videos of atomic bomb explosions and their effects. The blast would be brighter than the noonday sun and would level everything around it in a perfect circle, blowing a hole in the earth as deep as the Grand Canyon. The mushroom cloud would rise miles into the stratosphere, carrying radioactive particles that would rain down like the plagues of Egypt for years to come. After 9-11, New York certainly didn't need any more tragedies. It was a mind-numbing-ly horrific thought. What the hell was it with Lilith and nuclear fission, anyway? First the Ford and now this. She obviously thrived on radiation and wanted as much of it around as possible. She seemed to have an insatiable appetite for destruction and chaos—she certainly had created enough of it.

As she watched Hunter walk in front of her, Lisa thought about how glad she had been to see him again and how things would hopefully be normal once this horror show was over. They could get back to living their dull, ordinary lives and raise the child they had always wanted. Lisa could think of nothing she would rather do.

In the meantime, they had just passed the Lincoln Center and the Metropolitan Opera House and were coming up on the Trump Tower and Columbus Circle, only blocks from where the carrier was moored. Were they almost there? How much farther could it be?

*   *   *

It was nearly ten p.m. when the team reached Times Square. The scene was desolate—the giant screen overlooking the square had been smashed by debris from the high winds, water stood a foot deep in many places and glass from the shattered windows of hotels and businesses littered the streets like gravel. Signs and pieces of building awnings lay on the tops of cars, pushing them down like crushed aluminum cans. Lisa was sure looters probably had a field day in the once vibrant city. She thought of all the times she had wanted to visit New York, seeing it on TV during the Thanksgiving parades and on New Year's Eve, now just a shadow of its former self. Lisa saw the outline of the famous ball drop tower in the distance and marveled that it had weathered the storm.

They abruptly stopped under a sign that read *Subway*

carved into an angled silver awning with a Quicksilver sign on one side and a Skechers store on the other. The letters were inset with unlit neon tubes that would normally make the letters glow red. She stood close to Hunter and grabbed his hand in hers as they stood staring up at the sign. They were on 42nd Street at the entrance to the subway station. Lisa did not have a good feeling about this.

"SOG team members," Jason said, motioning them forward. "Captain Phillips and Commander Crane, keep an eye on our escort." The SOG team members huddled around their leader as he laid out some sort of plan Lisa couldn't quite make out.

The huddle broke up and Jason said, "SOG team, break out your Nova Tac flashlights and lanyards. Electrical power hasn't been restored to this part of the city yet, so it looks like we're gonna be in the dark for a while."

All six men broke open their backpacks and pulled out long, black flashlights. Lisa glanced at Hunter, who held his Beretta in hand, ready to put several holes in Lilith's egg if she so much as flinched.

"Gabe, Blakely, Anderson and Samson, watch our backs while we're down there," Jason said. "The rest of you, be alert. Maintain the usual spacing and don't lose sight of each other. Keep your phones on and the line clear."

The men hung the flashlight lanyards around their necks and switched on their lights, casting eerie shadows along the floor and walls as they descended into darkness.

CHAPTER 84

The Times Square subway station was huge and the floor still wet from flooding. The air was damp and reeked of mold. Normally the busiest station in New York, it was devoid of people and utterly dark. It was also the perfect place for an ambush. Jason was worried as hell, but didn't let it show. No use in making everyone more nervous than they already were. The flashlights were bright as automobile headlights and would burn for five hours on high power. They also had a strobe effect that would disorient any would-be attackers long enough for his team to get the upper hand.

As for that big lumbering beast they called Lilith, she was completely unpredictable and Jason didn't like that. He didn't trust her at all, which is why he had decided to have an ace in the hole just in case. He had never been in the New York subway and was unfamiliar with the layout, though he had ridden the Metro in D.C. on quite a few occasions. He wanted to assure their chances not only of success but of survival and took some extra precautions without Lilith's knowledge. The less she knew, the better, he figured.

Their footfalls echoed against the walls as they moved through the station. Without the flashlights, it would have been pitch black.

After a few hundred yards, they stopped next to a large, yellow, rectangular trap door. Lilith stared down at the door as if willing it to open. Jason got the idea and he motioned for Samson and Anderson to help him raise it. Jason managed to get a knife blade under it and realized the hatch was made of steel, at least two-hundred pounds. The men wedged their hands beneath the plate until they got a grip on it and flipped it over backwards. It clanged loudly on the concrete floor, revealing a staircase that led down into more blackness.

"Holy shit," Anderson said. "It's a tunnel beneath a tunnel. This must be an old abandoned station. These things run for miles beneath the city, a perfect hiding place for a nuke."

Jason nodded. "Yeah, you can take out Times Square and Rockefeller Plaza all in one blast. That would create a nice big cloud of radioactive debris."

Lilith padded down the stairs as if she had no problem seeing in the dark, which Jason was sure was the case. The team followed close behind, the ground swallowing them up like the open maw of a hungry shark.

*   *   *

Hunter wondered what he had gotten them into. Was Lilith leading them into a trap or to the nuke? They were descending a staircase down to another level of the subway station that had been unused since the 1970s. Hunter had once researched subways years ago to learn about the Metro trains just before taking a trip to D.C. The NYC subway system was one of the largest public transportation systems in the world, with nearly eight-hundred-fifty miles of tracks running both above and below ground. Add to that the unused sections of tracks like this and it was a virtual labyrinth, harboring homeless people, gangs, rats and probably the occasional toxic waste. It was a city unto itself.

When they reached the bottom of the stairs hundreds of feet below, they found themselves on a subway platform. Shining his light in either direction, Hunter saw the subway tracks disappear into blackness. Lisa was standing close and Hunter reached over and squeezed her hand. She looked a little on edge, but Hunter could feel his nerves buzzing, as well. Being led by a wild beast down into a dark, subterranean passage that harbored a ten-kiloton nuclear weapon and possibly a gang of crazed militants was enough to make anyone edgy.

"It's like being in the pit of Hell," Gabe said as she sidled up next to Lisa and Hunter.

Hunter nodded in agreement, his flashlight playing over some colorful graffiti on one wall of the station.

Lilith began to move off in one direction and Jason indicated the group to follow along. They lined up single file to move down the raised concrete walkway beside the tracks. Hunter saw rats down by the rails several times, but when the light hit them they scurried out of sight. There were two sets of tracks in the subway, one going each direction, and between the tracks I-beams were spaced about every six feet from ceiling to floor. In some places there were four-foot by five-foot cinderblock walls between the I-beams. On the far side were more I-beams and another wall behind that, which Hunter figured could be anything from the ground to another subway tunnel. Ancient light bulbs were screwed into light sockets for about the first hundred yards or so. There was probably no electricity down here even when the power was on, Hunter thought. There were beer cans and liquor bottles that looked fairly new scattered in places along the tracks that indicated someone had been here recently. The smell of vomit mixed with urine permeated the air. Why anyone would want to come to this God-forsaken hole was beyond Hunter, but having been homeless himself once, he knew that the cool shelter of the tunnels could look very inviting to someone on a hot, humid night. He was surprised that there hadn't been more flooding, but figured the speed of the storm may have prevented that.

They walked along for another few hundred yards as the darkness closed in like a black hole trying to envelope them. Hunter suddenly felt the hair on the back of his neck stand up just as Jason held up a hand, indicating the group should stop. Everyone stood stock-still and held their breath as Jason gazed over at the far side of the tracks. Lilith stopped as well, eyeing the group from her place at the front of the line.

Automatic fire suddenly rang out from the opposite side of the tunnel, and Hunter, Lisa and the entire team dove off the walkway onto the tracks below.

CHAPTER 85

Jason ordered everyone to douse their flashlights and use the night scopes on the rifles in an attempt to locate where the shots had come from.

"Was anybody hit?" he asked

The Dragon Skin vests had done their jobs — both Harrison and Phillips had taken hits but were only bruised from the impact of the bullets. Jason saw Phillips holding a hand over his chest, trying to get his breath back. He knew from experience that even through a vest, a bullet could knock the breath out of you or sometimes break a rib.

"Sounds like they're using AK's and pistols, Jason," Anderson whispered over the Android phone.

"Yeah, and whoever it is has been trained in military tactics" Jason said. "I don't like this. They got the jump on us and I didn't even see it coming. Hunter, do you still have the egg?"

"Affirmative," Hunter said, breathing rapidly over the headset.

"Good. Keep a hold on that thing. If you lose it we have no leverage and we're up a creek."

Then somebody spoke from the other side of the track.

"Throw down your weapons and nobody gets hurt—we have you covered," a male voice said.

"That ain't gonna happen, my friend," Jason shouted.

No answer.

"Jason, I saw one of them poke their head up over a concrete barrier," Mac whispered. "I have an idea. Be ready to hit the strobes on your flashlights when I give the signal. Cover me."

Although uncertain of exactly what Mac had in mind, Jason raised his MK16 and sighted back and forth with the carbine along the concrete barriers. He could see a couple of heads poking over the top like ducks in a shooting gallery, but decided to shoot over their heads instead of *at* them. The rounds did the trick and they fell back behind the barrier. He figured whoever these people were, they didn't have night vision scopes or they would have been firing by now.

Luckily, the team had managed to crowd in behind one of the cinderblock walls. They were safe for now. He swept to the right and saw Mac in his scope register yellow against a blue background. Mac was moving toward the concrete barrier as if he had no problem seeing in the dark without the aid of night vision goggles.

Jason's jaw dropped when he saw Mac reach down over the barrier, grab one of the men and fling him out onto the track like a sack of dirty laundry. The man yelped and thudded to the ground with a grunt as Mac grabbed the next man and did the same, continuing quickly down the row until five men lay on the tracks.

"Now!" Mac yelled, and all of the SOG team members flicked on their flashlights in the strobe position. The ensuing flashes of light were so bright it made Mac shield his eyes. Most of the men hadn't even picked themselves up off the tracks before Jason, Harrison, Anderson, Blakely and Gabe had jumped over and disarmed all five, locking their wrists in flexi cuffs behind their backs. The flashlights dangled on their lanyards as they were switched to fifty percent power to conserve battery energy.

The five men were hauled to their feet just as Lilith appeared from nowhere, and with a howl of fury, leapt at her brother.

*   *   *

Mac couldn't believe his little sister was inside the body of this mammoth white beast that now had him pinned to the ground. Her hot breath smelled like rotten carrion, and her jagged teeth dripped with saliva, ready to rip his throat out. Even with his great strength he didn't know how long he could hold her back. The silver eyes inside her massive, fur covered head almost seemed to burn though him. Her paws were as big as dinner plates and the long, curved claws could disembowel him with one swipe. A low rumbling growl came from deep inside her. Rather than fear, all Mac felt was rage.

"Go ahead and kill me, Lilith. It's what you've always wanted to do, isn't it?" he said, the great weight of the beast causing him to gasp for breath.

Hunter suddenly ran toward the two, holding up his backpack and waving it like a prize. "Hey, Snow White! Come and get it!"

"Hunter, what are you doing?" Lisa screamed.

Lilith turned and leapt through the air, launching herself toward Hunter and her young like a two-thousand-pound projectile.

Before she had even gotten halfway, Mac saw Jason set the sights of his MK16's night vision scope on Lilith's massive chest and fire, sending a grenade through her and out the other side, then into the roof of the subway tunnel, where it exploded on impact. Covering his ears against the deafening explosion, MacIntyre scrambled away, barely avoiding the concrete and debris raining down around him.

Lilith lay in a heap in the middle of the subway tracks, her breathing labored, blood pooling beneath her like a dark, red lake. A hole the size of a watermelon gaped from her back, the fur around it was matted with gore.

Mac walked back down the tracks toward the group, eyeing Lilith as she lay sprawled on the ground. He knelt down, stroked her head, then exchanged sorrowful glances with Hunter and Jason.

"I'm sorry," Hunter said softly.

Nodding, Mac turned his attention back to what remained of his sister. "Me too."

CHAPTER 86

The prisoners were men ranging in ages from early-twenties to mid-fifties, and all of them wore urban camouflage. They looked like a team of commandos and probably wouldn't be easy to crack. Jason knew they were running out of time, though, so he'd have to make one of them talk, and soon. He gave the men a once-over as they sat in the dirt next to the tracks and decided which man he was going to break from the group—the one that looked like the easiest to interrogate. They all stared back at him with steely-eyed defiance, except for a young man with frightened eyes and sandy blonde hair who looked like he was in over his head. The second Jason looked at him, the man averted his eyes.

"Grab that one," he said to Harrison.

Harrison stepped over to the young militant and hauled him up on his feet. The young man didn't make a sound or ask any questions, but the guy next to him, an older man with a weathered face and a deep scowl, said, "Don't tell these fuckers nothin', you got me?"

"Shut-up, asshole," Harrison said. "You're next."

The young man remained silent, eyes forward and face expressionless as Harrison and Jason dragged him off into the darkness.

*   *   *

Lilith was barely breathing and losing blood by the gallons, but Hunter was helpless to do anything. Not that he really cared, but Mac was not taking it well.

Suddenly, from somewhere beyond their line of sight, the young prisoner screamed like a victim in a medieval torture chamber. It reverberated through the subway tunnel and finally subsided.

Hunter's blood froze as he made a move in that direction, but Blakely grabbed him by the collar and shook his head no. Hunter understood as he stared back out at the darkness.

CHAPTER 87

After what seemed like hours, but was actually only minutes, Jason came strolling into view with Harrison, who was helping the prisoner walk. The young man looked like hell, stumbling along as he went.

As they got closer, Hunter noticed a red smear on one leg of Harrison's pants. It looked as if he'd wiped blood from the blade of a knife on them. He glanced at the hand that was draped over Harrison's shoulder and noticed that the forefinger was wrapped in a blood-soaked piece of torn fabric. But Hunter didn't ask any questions.

Jason waved everyone over.

"These assholes are mercenaries. Mostly ex-military looking to make a few extra dollars, or from what little Davey here told us, a whole lot of extra dollars. The bad part is they were hired by somebody in the government. If what that kid told me is true, this shit reaches all the way to the top, or at least close to it. But our concern right now is finding that nuke and keeping it from going boom. The kid said they just finished setting it up when we got here, so we still have some time, but not much. It just so happens that he's also the one who set up the nuke and knows the code to disarm it. I suggest we get moving as soon as possible."

*   *   *

The two men had seen the entire firefight and subsequent capture of their comrades from behind a wall in an adjoining access tunnel. Luckily, they had missed being shot themselves, but just barely. There were rust holes and now bullet holes spaced periodically along the wall that allowed them to view everything without being seen. They couldn't risk turning on their own flashlights, but could make out what was happening in the other tunnel fairly well.

Minutes later, they heard Dave Jenkins screaming in pain and knew he was being interrogated and would probably talk. Now they watched as the SOG team leader spoke to his group. Though they couldn't quite make out what he was saying, they knew that disarming the nuke would be their next move. They had to act soon or the whole mission would be totally screwed and they could kiss half a million dollars goodbye.

The commander of the assault team turned to his subordinate and whispered, "We've got to get them out of there. Wait until the team moves off down the tunnel. I'm pretty sure they're going to leave our guys behind with maybe one guard. We should be able to take him. Then we'll set our guys free and go after Dave. If we have to, we'll take him out."

The other man nodded grimly and the pair turned and moved off down the passageway in the opposite direction.

CHAPTER 88

They walked for miles under the streets of New York, a billion tons of concrete and steel pressing down on them. The darkness was an all-encompassing force that even the ultra-bright flashlights barely penetrated. Lisa felt as if she was being smothered. There was also the nuke. But if she thought about it too much she would panic, and she really didn't need that right now, especially for the sake of the others in the group. Hunter and Gabe gave her the strength she needed to go on.

Gabe and Hunter had been alone together for quite a while and Lisa had thought about that. But she knew Hunter was a one-woman man, so she was never worried. In fact, she had been more worried about Lilith than she had been about Gabe. She still seethed with rage when she thought about Lilith. Lisa wished she could have had the chance to put a bullet in her, but Jason had done it for her. At least someone had done it, she thought. But Lisa realized that hate was not a healthy thing and knew she would have to rid herself of it.

Eventually.

Lisa saw there was an opening up ahead and the space suddenly grew wider. They were in another subway station, not quite as big as the one at Times Square, but big nonetheless. An old, rusted sign on one of the walls said 34th Street. They were below Penn Station and Madison Square Garden.

Was this where the nuke was?

Wasn't Madison Square Garden one of the designated emergency shelters for Manhattan during Hurricane Alex? The capacity of that place was about eighty-thousand people.

Lisa suddenly felt ill as she realized Lilith had calculated exactly where to plant the bomb to cause the maximum number of casualties.

*   *   *

The two mercenaries found the opening in the wall that they were looking for and turned into it. They would have to walk the tracks in darkness much of the way to avoid detection.

"When we get to where our guys are, disarm that CIA spook first, then we'll get our team and go after Dave," he said. "Once we catch up to him, we'll assess the situation and see whether we'll have to take Dave out or not. It may be the only option."

As the two men made their way along the tracks, the leader thought he heard movement from behind and quickly turned off his flashlight and stopped. The other man stopped, as well. The two stood frozen on the tracks, listening.

Nothing.

"Must have been rats," the commander said, switching his light back on and continuing to walk.

After a few hundred yards, they heard voices and once again switched off the light.

"That's them," the commander whispered. "Alright, nice and easy."

He motioned for the other man to move forward and raised his AK47 in the firing position. They walked along the rails until they saw the light from the SOG team member's flashlight. As they drew closer, they could hear one of their own men speaking and saw a large, black man in dark civilian clothes holding an M4A1 and pacing slowly back and forth. They stopped and waited.

The black man stopped pacing and was facing away from them, down the other end of the tunnel, as if looking for someone, probably his own team. That's when the two mercenaries made their move. They walked quickly, avoiding running since it might alert the man to their presence.

They were within fifty yards when Samson turned and saw them, but it was too late. They both had their AK47s trained on him and he knew he would be dead before he raised his own carbine.

"Drop the weapon," the man in charge said.

"No, you drop *your* weapon, asshole," a voice from behind said.

The two men slowly turned their heads around and saw two grenade launchers pointed at their backs. It was Slater and Chin, Jason's ace in the hole.

"Thanks, guys," Samson said. "I'm glad you showed up when you did. But we have another problem."

"What's that?" Slater said as Chin took the weapons from the two mercenaries.

Samson pointed to a pool of drying blood inside the pile of debris near the subway tracks.

"Lilith is gone."

CHAPTER 89

Hunter could see that the young mercenary, who they were calling Dave, was in pain, holding his right hand tightly with his left. Hunter wasn't big on torture, but he didn't have a lot of sympathy for a man who would trade innocent lives for money.

As the group was moving through the abandoned station Hunter spotted several rats, lots of graffiti on the walls and cheap wine bottles scattered around the floor. The stench of urine and feces mixed with stale air was making him a little nauseous. Where did these people come from? There must have been a million places to slip into the underbelly of New York and maybe never come out again.

They came to a room that looked like a utility closet, but was actually an elevator shaft. The doors were open but the elevator itself was gone, along with all the pumps and motors that drive the elevator. Dave jumped down inside the shaft. Jason turned to the group.

"Everyone wait here. Harrison, come with me," he said.

The two men slid off their weapons and backpacks then followed Dave down into the shaft.

There in the middle of the floor of the elevator shaft, Hunter could see a large, green backpack that looked like something someone would take on a camping trip. Harrison pushed the elevator cables aside and carefully unzipped the backpack as the other two men and everyone outside the shaft watched. Hunter realized he was holding his breath and slowly exhaled as the backpack fell open to reveal a large, polished metal cylinder, a couple of smaller cylinders, a battery and a digital timer all connected with a dozen wires. It looked simple enough, but it was unnerving to think that much destructive power could be transported so easily.

Harrison knelt and looked the device over. "Looks similar to the old MK54 SADM backpack nuke, but a lot more compact and a lot more powerful. Someone had to have some serious connections to get hold of this."

"Can we disarm it?" Jason asked.

Harrison shrugged. "The timer was set to give these bastards enough time to get off the island, but we've already spent most of that trying to find it."

Jason gave the young mercenary, who was busy nursing a severed fingertip, a kick in the shin.

"Alright, dipshit, shut this thing down or we'll cut something else off," he said.

Jenkins' black-rimmed eyes were hollow and vacant from pain and terror, like someone who had just escaped a serial killer.

"I can't remember the exact code," he said.

Jason looked dumb-struck. "What do you mean you can't remember the exact code?"

Jenkins shrank away, as if he was trying to crawl into the cinderblock wall of the elevator shaft.

"I mean the timer doesn't allow for any mistakes. If you put in the wrong number, it goes off automatically."

Jason put a hand on top of his head. "Okay, so you're telling me you're not sure what the code is?"

Jenkins simply nodded, whimpering like a frightened animal in a cage.

Jason stood for a moment, as if considering his options. He looked down at the timer—if it was right, Hunter could see they had less than two minutes to clear out and get back to the ship. They wouldn't even make it a block in that amount of time. He knew Jenkins was probably yanking their chain, thinking they would leave and take him along. But that wasn't going to happen, either.

Hunter had an idea.

"Why don't we just leave him here and get the hell out while we can?"

Jason shot him a look and Hunter could see the gears turning in the operative's head. He seemed to get the message.

"Hey, give me the cuffs out of my assault pack, will you?" Jason said to Anderson. "The steel ones."

Anderson reached into Jason's backpack and produced a small, black case with a pair of Smith & Wesson black steel handcuffs.

"What are you gonna do with those?" Jenkins asked, his voice wavering.

"I'll show you," Jason said, pulling the cuffs out and dropping the bag to the floor. Before the young man could move, Jason grabbed his right arm, snapped a cuff around his wrist, then yanked it over to the steel cable of the elevator and snapped the other cuff around the cable.

Jason grinned sardonically. "Since you can't seem to remember the code, I figured this might help jar your memory a little bit. Just think, Jenkins, this close to the blast your bones will be ashes before you even have a chance to scream. It'll be quick, trust me."

Jason climbed up out of the shaft, followed by Harrison.

"Let's move out while we still have time to get back to the ship," he said.

The group picked up their gear, switched on their flashlights and started making their way out of the station, when Jenkins yelled, "Wait! Don't leave me down here, man. I swear I don't know the code!"

Jason stopped walking and glanced back at Jenkins.

"Sounds like a personal problem to me," he said.

"Okay, okay, wait! I think I might remember it," Jenkins said, his voice hoarse and ragged. Hunter could tell that between the blood loss and the fear, the young man might be going into shock. He just hoped Jenkins could put in the right code, otherwise it was about to get very hot very quickly.

CHAPTER 90

Scientists say that in a split second a one-megaton nuclear explosion creates a flash of ultraviolet light and a fireball tens of millions of degrees, scorching everything within the blast radius for half of a mile. Just to look at the flash would cause retinal injury and blindness. Metal, concrete, wood, glass and living matter all fuse together into one mass in the incredible heat.

Hunter couldn't imagine what it would be like to be this close when it went off. Would it be like standing inside a microwave oven with your guts being roasted, or would it simply peel the flesh off your bones like paper mache in a blast furnace?

Hunter watched with trepidation as the drama played out before him. He held onto the backpack with Lilith's egg in it, looking back through the dark at the young mercenary alone in the elevator shaft with nervous sweat dripping off his brow. Lisa was holding his other hand, squeezing it with anticipation. If the bomb went off, he prayed that they would all be spared a slow death. He wanted it to be quick, especially for Lisa's sake and for his child's sake. He couldn't stand the thought of her suffering the pain of being burned alive, not even for a microsecond.

He watched as Jenkins knelt next to the backpack and carefully turned it towards him. Hunter could feel a cold breeze blowing from somewhere in the station and wondered if they were near an exit. He wished they could find that exit right now and get the hell out of there, but he knew they couldn't run far enough to escape the reach of the bomb even if they wanted to. There wasn't even time for a helicopter to swoop in and pick them up. And what about all those people on the Ford? They would be doomed along with whoever was still on the island of Manhattan. He guessed there were at least a few hundred thousand, maybe a couple million or more. The island would be a complete wasteland, as barren as Hiroshima or Nagasaki was after World War II and just like those cities, uninhabitable for years to come.

Dave glanced up at the group, his eyes wide with apprehension. Everyone had spread out to watch the proceedings, keeping their distance as if it would somehow protect them from the blast.

"Just concentrate, Jenkins," Jason said. "Don't worry about anything else but putting in that code. That's all you need to think about right now."

That seemed to reassure the young man somewhat and he cast his eyes back down on the small, shiny metal cylinder that could potentially unleash the wrath of God.

Hunter only prayed that Jenkins didn't have a death wish.

Jenkins' good hand disappeared inside the backpack and Hunter heard the first beep of a button being pushed, followed by another, then another.

Jenkins was moving painfully slow, concentrating his effort on entering the correct code. No one in the group dared to breathe for fear that even that might cause Jenkins to punch in a wrong number.

Another beep.

Then another. That was five. How many numbers were there?

Dave looked back up at them. "Last one," he said.

He reached down to punch in the last number.

Suddenly a blur of white shot past the group directly toward the elevator shaft and they heard Dave scream in terror as Lilith dove in on top of him.

*   *   *

"Lilith, no!" MacIntyre screamed as everyone raised their guns to shoot. But they knew Jenkins was already dead.

Hunter grabbed the pistol out of his waistband then raised it toward Lilith. He knew there were only seconds left on the timer and the clock was ticking.

Jason laid a hand on top of Hunter's arm.

"Don't, he's gone," Jason said. "The bullet might ricochet."

"I know. I just want to get her attention."

Jason nodded in understanding and yelled, "Lilith, we have something of yours. Do you want it?"

The beast glanced through the door of the shaft and Hunter could see her maw dripping with bits of shredded flesh and cloth and suddenly felt sick. He swallowed hard and held up the bag containing the egg.

Slowly Lilith squeezed through the door of the shaft and moved stealthily toward them. Everyone in the group began to back up except for Hunter and Jason. All of them had their guns trained on the beast. Hunter noticed that the wound from where she had been shot with the grenade launcher was nearly healed. Great, he thought—on top of everything else, she can regenerate healthy tissue at lightning speed.

"Hunter, be careful," Lisa whispered from behind him. Hunter pointed the gun at the backpack.

"Well, it looks like we're back where we started," he said, knowing there were only seconds left and hoping that was enough. "Think about your situation here, Lilith. You're not getting out of here with your egg, and if we stay here, we all get incinerated. So, you have a choice. You can enter that last number in the code, which I suspect you know, or we can all say our goodbyes. What's it going to be?"

Lilith loomed ever closer to them, her shoulders as high as a man. Her ears stuck straight up off of her huge head like the ears of a wolf and her sharp claws clicked ominously along the concrete floor as she walked on all fours. Her white fur was course and matted with dirt and blood and her breathing was still somewhat labored, but strong. The rumbling from deep within her chest reminded Hunter of the idling diesel engine of a tanker truck, but he was mesmerized by the sight of two silver eyes and two jaws full of fangs so long he wondered whether she could even close her mouth completely.

There was no sign of humanity left in Lilith whatsoever.

She stopped in front of them, sniffing with her fleshy snout, eyeing them like a lion stalking a herd of gazelles.

Everyone jumped when the bomb started beeping.

"Shit, the final countdown started," Harrison said. "If we don't disarm that thing in the next few seconds, we're all going to get the worst sunburn of our lives."

Hunter jiggled the backpack, letting the egg bounce from side to side, then jabbed it with the pistol to emphasize his intention.

"What's it going to be, Lilith?"

Beep.

The beast furrowed its brow and stopped in its tracks. Hunter wondered if Lilith was thinking, or if she could even think at all. Maybe she was nothing more than impulse, an animal driven by instinct. The instinct to kill.

Beep.

Three beeps so far, if Hunter was counting correctly. How many more would there be before they were consumed in the world's biggest blast furnace? Ten? Or five? Or maybe none.

Beep.

Lilith stood her ground, completely silent and still, waiting. Was she waiting for the nuke to go off? Or was she considering her options? She really didn't have any, Hunter thought. It was either disarm the nuke or die.

Beep.

Hunter wiped sweat from his brow. It was getting much too close for his comfort and he braced for the inevitable.

Beep.

As Hunter was about to give up hope, Lilith abruptly turned and padded back toward the elevator shaft and reached down inside with a massive paw. Then Hunter heard a sound as sweet as anything he had ever heard in his life.

Nothing.

CHAPTER 91

Lilith had entered the final number into the timer and disarmed the nuke with no time to spare, Hunter was sure. Was there still some humanity left in her after all? There was no way to be sure. But she *was* a killer. Now every gun was trained on the beast in a standoff as she once again began advancing toward the team. She wasn't finished with them yet. Jason shrugged off his backpack and pulled an M9 Beretta out of a side pocket. He dropped the pack, chambered a round in the pistol, took a shooting stance and pointed it at Lilith.

"What the hell are you doing?" Hunter asked. "That gun's not going to do anything."

"Don't worry, I'm not trying to kill her. It's a little something Chin made up for me."

Before he could fire, Lisa stepped up between the two men and said in Jason's ear, "Let me."

Jason glanced at Lisa, and without taking his eyes or his aim off Lilith, slid the gun into Lisa's hand.

She squeezed the trigger once, the tranquilizer dart striking Lilith in her thick neck just under her muzzle.

She roared in pain and advanced toward the team, huffing and puffing like an angry bull ready to charge. Lisa chambered another round and fired, hitting her in a spot just under the other dart. Lilith was striding forward with the fury of a locomotive and was almost on them when her front legs gave out and she slid to a stop a few short feet from Hunter and Lisa.

Lisa slowly lowered the pistol.

"Go to sleep, bitch," she said.

Lilith tried to stand, got her feet under her, then toppled over sideways like a drunken horse and lay still.

*   *   *

Getting the team, the prisoners and the nuke out of an abandoned subway tunnel in the middle of the night was no easy task, but compared to hauling up Lilith's huge carcass, it was a Sunday morning stroll. Hunter reminded himself to stop volunteering for crazy stuff, but he wanted to see the Lilith beast one last time. It must have been the reporter in him—he wanted to remember every detail. She actually looked peaceful lying there on the concrete floor of the tunnel, snowy white and sedated. He tried to remember her as a human and decided that he actually liked her better as an animal. At least he could have a little sympathy for an animal. For Lilith the human, he only felt contempt.

The CIA had managed to find another way down from 34th Street so they didn't have far to take her, but to say she was heavy was an understatement, Hunter thought as they fastened a harness around her and began to pull her along the floor. Once they got her to the stairwell, the winches took over and she rose into the air as if she were being levitated by a magician.

Lisa had stayed with Hunter and they made their way up to 34th Street while the rest of the group met up with Samson, Chin and Slater farther down the tunnel. The prisoners were taken by helicopter to some unknown location and Hunter never really got to say thanks to Jason Fredrichs and his team or to Gabe, the woman who had saved him. But that's how it was—the heroes always seemed to have the thankless jobs as they disappeared into the night like the Lone Ranger and moved on to the next assignment. Maybe they would meet again.

As they rode in the Sea Hawk back to the Ford, Blakely informed Hunter and Lisa that they would have to be debriefed when they got to the ship. Hunter nodded in understanding and glanced at his wife as she sat next to him. He reached down and squeezed her hand and thought about how fortunate he was to have the love of such a strong, beautiful woman.

And soon they would be parents.

That thought made Hunter smile as he gazed into Lisa's dark, Asian eyes.

"What do you think we should name our baby?" he asked, yelling over the sound of the helicopter engine.

Lisa laughed; a beautiful sound to his ears.

"To tell you the truth I haven't thought about it much in the last few days. I've been a little busy," she said.

"Yeah, I guess you have."

"What do you think we should name her?"

"Her? How do you know it's a her?"

"Oh, I don't know, just a feeling."

Hunter didn't care one way or the other, he would be fine with a boy or a girl—as long as they were together, he was happy.

They had managed to actually get a seat by the only window this time and Hunter looked out over Manhattan, going over the last few days in his mind. Had all of it really happened? It seemed like a dream now, something that took place long ago in a faraway land. It was like a fairy tale and a nightmare rolled into one. He considered possibly even getting therapy after this ordeal just to make sure there were no lasting effects from the parasite that had controlled him for those few days.

Then, he glanced back over at Lisa and she smiled at him and rubbed her still-flat belly.

On second thought, Hunter decided she was all the therapy he needed.

CHAPTER 92

After days of research, interviews and a few searches and seizures, George Saunders had finally amassed the evidence he needed to make the bust, and he wanted to be there personally when it happened. As he rode in the back of a black SUV on its way to D.C., he opened his laptop and started going over files, re-reading e-mails, getting all the facts straight not only to reassure himself that they had an airtight case, but to convince himself of the truth of the whole thing. He was disillusioned, heartbroken and on the verge of depression. How could he have not seen it? How could he have been so blind?

But Saunders knew that was the nature of deception—it always turned out to be the ones you thought were your friends, the ones you least suspected.

To be honest, for someone that was good at uncovering secrets, it wasn't all that hard to find evidence, but it still left a sour taste in his mouth. For a person as high up in the chain of command as this man was to so willfully lie, cheat and steal, and even partake in mass murder, made Saunders' blood boil. It was this type of thing that made him wonder who the hell he could trust. The answer always came back the same: trust no one. Blind trust had almost cost him the entire city of New York and possibly more—much more. Thank God he had followed his gut instinct. It had never steered him wrong.

Saunders closed his laptop, not wanting to see more, and leaned back in his seat. Outside his window, moonlit pine trees and wooden fences soon gave way to ranch-style houses and then office buildings. After a few minutes, he drifted off to sleep.

*   *   *

Senator James Clayburn, Chairman of the Armed Services Committee, sat in his office on Constitution Avenue in Washington D.C., wondering how everything could have gone so wrong. Why had he ever agreed to this fiasco in the first place? His entire career, his entire life now lay in ruins with no hope of repair, a web of deceit unraveled by his own friend, George Saunders. He was an old man, but still young enough to retire and enjoy some time with his grandchildren. Now there was no chance of that. It was all a nightmare, a hell of his own creation.

He thought about his options. He could claim insanity, but who would believe that? It was all too carefully conceived and meticulously planned to have been organized by a madman and even so, was it any better being locked up in an asylum than it was in jail? Somehow, he doubted it.

He could claim blackmail, which was closer to the truth. Lilith had him by the balls—literally. She had first seduced him when she was twenty-two and just out of college. Since her mother had died, Clayburn was living all alone in that sprawling house in Virginia. His other kids were grown and married with kids of their own and Lilith's brother from her mother's first marriage was a commander on the very ship that Clayburn had gotten her access to. She had come to him the night of her first day back from college graduation, dressed in a blood-red teddy that still made him break out in a cold sweat when he thought about it, and slipped silently into his bed. Without a word, she had leaned over and kissed him, her lustrous blonde hair brushing against the sides of his face, and then ever so slowly worked her way down.

That had been five years ago and he still couldn't put it out of his mind.

Then she started asking for favors in return for sex. He knew what she was, knew that she had powers, but she didn't want to control him that way. She wanted him to do it of his own free will, and he did.

As an ex-Navy captain and intelligence officer, Clayburn had knowledge of many of the military's most guarded secrets and as a powerful U.S. senator he was able to use that knowledge to the utmost advantage. He helped Lilith change her identity to Julia Lambert, helped her recruit the mercenaries for her "project" and had even helped her get aboard the Ford as part of the media group. It was difficult throwing the CIA off her trail, but not impossible.

The hardest part was getting access to the nuke. Those weren't easy to come by, even with the chaotic state of current world affairs. But he had managed to find a backpack nuke from some shadowy individuals, and an American-made one, at that. The senator had recruited a few greedy, unscrupulous arms dealers, convincing them that the Lilitu could be an invaluable asset on the battlefield if they could be brought under control. He had proven her cunning by releasing her in a populated area.

They saw dollar signs and most of them detested Manhattan and New York, anyway. They would let Lilith do her thing, let her repopulate Manhattan, quarantine the island, then go in and get all the Lilitu they wanted.

Train them for battle, sell them for millions as the perfect destroyers.

Basically, Clayburn had been playing both sides of the street, as it were.

But the big-mouthed bastard, Kramer, one of Lilith's many boyfriends, had been recruited into her little "club" and then decided at the last minute to cut and run when he discovered he didn't have the stomach. Unfortunately, Clayburn didn't move fast enough to eliminate that problem.

The senator was not proud of what he had done, but you had to hand it to him—he had almost pulled off quite a feat. If he had to do it all over again, he would probably choose a different path and not slept with Lilith. But how could any man resist such a temptation? Clayburn had watched boys and men become weak in the knees from looking at Lilith ever since she was a teenager. It was animal passion, an insatiable desire she induced that simply could not be denied.

Clayburn recalled the time several boys from the high school football team had made unwanted advances on Lilith when she was just sixteen. She had been on the cheerleading squad and somehow they had cornered her after a game. She was the only girl left in the girl's locker room—there was no chance of escape. They boxed her in like a pack of wild dogs surrounding a lone fox.

Every single boy had ended up in the hospital with multiple fractures and internal injuries. Clayburn had received angry calls from several parents and even the school about that particular incident, but in that case, he felt she had been justified. So had her brother, John, who had congratulated her on a job well done. He had hated jocks and enjoyed hearing they had gotten their asses kicked by a girl.

Then Lilith had begun searching for herself, looking for meaning in her life, her powers. She found it in the extremist environmental movement. She detested human kind, even her own humanity, and decided that her powers could best be used in advocating for the rights of animals.

But soon, peaceful protests evolved into violent brawls and attempted assassinations. It continued over the years, with Clayburn doing everything he could to keep Lilith out of the government's crosshairs, throwing them a bone now and then in the form of a "crazy loner" who could be set up to take the fall for Lilith and her impulsive actions.

Then her own brother had turned her in. Clayburn had to do some fast thinking. He decided to play along as the concerned father, pretending to help the CIA in their investigation of her.

But like a house of sticks, lie was built upon lie and eventually those sticks would buckle under the pressure and come tumbling down. Call it karma, call it bad luck, call it whatever you wanted—this time there was no one to take the fall, only James Clayburn. But he had always been aware this day may come and he was prepared.

The senator opened the top drawer of his desk and pulled out a document, laid it flat on his desk, smoothed it with his hand and looked it over.

Satisfied, he reached inside his suit coat, grabbed a black Glock 19 out of its holster, stuck the barrel in his mouth and squeezed the trigger.

CHAPTER 93

Plum Island Animal Disease Center, Plum Island, Connecticut
One week later

Lilith was enclosed in a steel-barred cage guarded by several men in dark clothing with MK16s strapped to their backs, arms crossed in front of them like military interrogators.

But the real interrogators were the ones with the white masks and the scalpels, and the questions they had could only be answered by slicing, probing and inspecting under a microscope. They would get their answers, but it would take time — lots of time.

Not far away was an incubation chamber illuminated by a heat lamp. Inside the chamber was a bowling-ball-sized egg, slimy and gelatinous. A small, shadowy mass could be seen through the egg's translucent, outer membrane as it pulsated with life. Soon, the egg would hatch and creatures never before seen by science would emerge. The creatures could answer a million questions about evolution, about creation, about life itself and perhaps offer man a true glimpse into the Earth's past. It was more than a living fossil—it was a living myth.

Inside the cage, Lilith was sprawled out and secured to a huge, stainless steel table while the scientists did their work, cutting open her tough, resilient flesh and peering in at her internal organs. Plastic tubes ran to various parts of her body, keeping her sedated, feeding her the necessary nutrients and oxygen to keep her alive and removing the waste products. Machines beeped and hummed outside the cage, taking readings on her bodily functions, alerting the team of any abnormalities or fluctuations.

None of the scientists on the team noticed when a single, perfect tear formed in the corner of Lilith's right eye, trickled down the side of her enormous head and fell soundlessly to the floor.

EPILOGUE

River City, North Carolina

Hunter had his ear to Lisa's belly as she sat on the couch in their family room, listening intently, trying to detect even the faintest sound.

"I think I heard something," he whispered.

"What do you hear?" Lisa asked, squealing like a schoolgirl.

"Hang on, hang on," Hunter said, holding up a palm. "It's tapping."

"Tapping?"

"Yeah. It sounds like Morse Code." Hunter started spelling out the letters. "H-E-L-P M-E, I-T-S D-A-R-K I-N H-E-R-E."

Lisa slapped Hunter on top of the head in mock disgust.

"Oh, you think you're so funny," she said.

Hunter stood up, rubbing his head. "Hey, don't damage the brain cells, baby."

"They're already damaged."

Hunter plopped down next to her. "What did the doctor say?" he asked.

"It's too early to tell the sex, but it looks healthy. We should know in a few weeks if it's a boy or a girl."

"Have you still been feeling sick?"

"No, that's pretty much past. Now I just feel bloated."

Hunter's eyes wandered down her trim, athletic body. "Well, you still look great. They say sex with a pregnant woman is the best sex."

Lisa smiled demurely, gazing into Hunter's dark eyes. "Oh, is that what they say?"

Hunter nodded and felt himself starting to get warm under the collar. They shared a passionate kiss and he thought that nothing in his whole life had ever felt this good. When they finally came up for air he took a few minutes to catch his breath, leaned back and closed his eyes in satisfaction.

"Well, so much for your story, huh?" Lisa said.

"The real story anyway. Hell, even the mayor of New York doesn't know the whole story. Sometimes I feel like Baron Munchausen, just a guy with a bunch of fairytales nobody's ever going to believe."

"I believe you," Lisa said.

"That's reassuring."

"Well, how do you know I wasn't just part of your dream?"

"Honey, you are my dream."

"You always know what to say, don't you?"

There was a long silence as they sat on the sofa holding each other and Hunter thought about how to bring up the phone call he had received last night. He figured being straightforward was the best tactic.

"By the way, I have some news," he said.

Lisa furrowed her brow and stared up at Hunter.

"Good or bad?"

"I guess you would call it good, depending."

"Depending on what?"

"On whether I accept the job or not."

Lisa sprang up, nearly smacking Hunter on the chin with her head.

"You got a job offer? From who? You haven't applied for any jobs."

"Looks like winning all those awards at the newspaper for the past five years have paid off. The American Wire Service called last night and wanted to know if I was interested in trying out as a full-time correspondent. No cubicle, no commute—just work from home. There would be travel involved, but it would probably mean a substantial raise, too. There's a ninety-day trial period, but I'm pretty confident that I could get through that."

"Hunter that's amazing! Are you going to accept?"

"Well, I like to keep my options open. Of course, I could be persuaded to take the job if a certain someone were to offer sexual favors."

Lisa reached down, grabbed Hunter by the hand and led him into the bedroom.

* * *

Sitting in a neighborhood bar in Boston, a man stared into his drink and thought about the last week and his own death and subsequent resurrection. In fact, there was no doubt in his mind that he had been dead, though there was no bright light, at least not that he could remember. No long-deceased relatives coming to greet him at the pearly gates. He doubted very much that he would ever see any pearly gates, anyway. It just wasn't in the cards. Not for him. His allegiances lie elsewhere.

He remembered swimming into Manhattan, dragging himself up onto shore, then trekking through the streets and marveling at the utter destruction caused by Hurricane Alex. Driven by rage to his ultimate destination, he slept next to fallen trees or on park benches for the next couple of days, watching as emergency vehicles sped past on their way to hopefully save someone. He had been amazed that anyone was still alive.

Then, he had been killed. Actually, slaughtered would be more descriptive.

Yet here he was.

The man took a drink of the Seagram's Seven and Seven, the alcohol burning his throat like it was sterilizing his esophagus on the way down. It felt warm in his stomach and his head was feeling light, as if he could fly. Maybe he could. There was no telling what he was capable of with these newly acquired powers. It must have been the uranium that had done it, he figured. Had to be.

But he needed to be smart. He had to be shrewd and use his powers cleverly, instead of ripping people's heads off and demanding obeisance, though he would enjoy that, he would have to lay low for a while.

It seemed he had also discovered a new purpose in life, a new directive, given to him in a dream. Several dreams, actually. Dreams that he knew were not dreams at all, but messages, directions laid out in detail. It wasn't just about him anymore. It was about something bigger... much bigger. It would mean liquidating his considerable assets, but it could be done. He was sure his business partners would squabble about it, but what could they do? He owned fifty-one percent of the company, which made him essentially the boss. He would sell off his stocks and his holdings, put it together with the millions in his offshore accounts and begin his rather formidable task. The task given to him by *them*. It would probably take a few weeks to put everything together and then it would only be a matter of months before construction was completed. By the time anyone figured out what was going on, it would be too late.

He took another swig, set the glass down.

He thought about Hunter Singleton, the smug bastard. Something would have to be done about that asshole. Killing him would be satisfying, but much too easy. No, he needed to suffer, to pay for his arrogance. Hunter needed to feel the pain of loss, the torture of knowing that something you love has been ripped away from you. Like it had been from him.

But there was time. He would plan it all out well in advance, get the proper funds together, the right people. He could make it work. He had the brainpower and the physical power, the best of both worlds. He was still human, but also much more. He was a vessel; a vessel with a purpose. He was going to unleash powers upon the earth that had not been witnessed since the dawn of time. He was the key to a lock that would soon be unlocked. What waited behind the door was a reality that was both beyond imagination and beyond terrifying.

That made the man smile as he downed the last of the Seven and Seven. The whole thing sounded like arrogant boasting and maybe a little cliché, but it was all true. All of it.

Now it was time to go.

He turned and slowly scanned the bar. Poor, pathetic creatures, partying and living it up while a darkness they couldn't possibly comprehend was about to close in around them. They had no idea what would soon happen to their world. Enjoy your puny, worthless lives while you can, he thought, then turned back to the table and pulled out a fifty dollar bill, threw it down. His head was reeling with the alcohol and he knew he probably shouldn't be driving. But what the hell, he was a god, right? Who needs a car? He could snap his fingers and teleport himself instantly if he wanted. But he didn't.

He took one last look around, scoping out some of the women, sunglasses hiding his silver eyes. The human females were looking pretty good tonight, but he just wasn't

Lilith

feeling in the mood. His libido would have to wait. Right now, there were more important things to do. Climbing out from behind the booth, Lawrence Hendricks aimed himself toward the front door of the bar and headed out into the world.

ABOUT THE AUTHOR

Toby Tate has been a writer since about the age of 12, when he first began writing short stories and publishing his own movie monster magazine. Lilith is his second novel.

An Air Force brat who never lived in one place more than five years, Toby joined the Navy soon after high school and ended up on the east coast of the U.S. Toby has since worked as a cab driver, a pizza delivery man, a phone solicitor, a shipyard technician, a government contractor, a retail music salesman, a bookseller, a cell phone salesman, a recording studio engineer, a graphic designer and a newspaper reporter. Toby is also a songwriter and musician. He currently lives with his family near the Dismal Swamp in northeastern North Carolina.

Find out more about Toby and his other books, as well as his music, on the web at www.tobytatestories.com and on Facebook, Twitter and MySpace.

CPSIA information can be obtained at www.ICGtesting.com
Printed in the USA
LVOW101454180213

320616LV00016B/846/P

9 781937 771515